UNHINGED

BARBRA LESLIE

A DANNY CLEARY NOVEL

UNHINGED

TITAN BOOKS

Unhinged
Print edition ISBN: 9781783297023
Electronic edition ISBN: 9781783297030

Published by Titan Books
A division of Titan Publishing Group Ltd
144 Southwark Street, London SE1 0UP

First edition: November 2017
2 4 6 8 10 9 7 5 3 1

A CIP catalogue record for this title is available from the British Library.

Printed and bound in the United States.

What did you think of this book? We love to hear from our readers. Please email us at: readerfeedback@titanemail.com, or write to us at the above address.

To receive advance information, news, competitions, and exclusive offers online, please sign up for the Titan newsletter on our website:
www.titanbooks.com

Dedicated to the memory of my sister
Pamela Vail (Leslie) Lowes
who died on August 1 2017

I can't find the words to express how much she is missed

UNHINGED

PROLOGUE

New York City

I'd had enough of hospitals to last me a lifetime. But this time, I wasn't the patient.

Most of the time – when we were walking down the street, or in bed – I forgot how slight Dave really was. I remembered my first impression of him, when he was posing undercover as a slacker pawn shop clerk without two brain cells to rub together. Dave was good at what he did, and when he was in character, his walk was different, his speech, even the way he wore his clothes. Later, when I got to know him, when his true self emerged as some kind of vigilante superhero security expert, I thought he was untouchable.

I'd thought that about my late husband Jack, too.

Dave wasn't unconscious, he was just sleeping. The nurse swore to me he was just sleeping. But I'd been there for four hours since getting the call, and he hadn't stirred. I watched him, observed the measured movements of his chest. He'd been shot. He'd been on an easy job, a job I was supposed to be helping on, protecting a wealthy elderly couple from their estranged son. The son had skipped bail on a manslaughter charge and apparently blamed his parents for everything that had gone wrong in his miserable life. There were mental health issues there, but the old couple didn't like to talk about that. Dave knew the family from a job he had done six or seven years ago, and he was fond of the couple. Less so of their wayward son. Who, as it turned out, was the one who had shot Dave in his upper right arm.

It's not like on TV, being shot. I'd had a bullet graze my bicep once, and at the time the doctors had told me all the horrific things that can happen when a person is shot in the arm – the subclavian artery being severed, bleeding out immediately, or nerve death, amputation. Dave, the nurse had told me, was lucky. The shooter had used a .22 caliber firearm – more suited to hunting rabbits than humans – and the hospital had operated and removed the slug. He would live, and he would probably – probably – regain full use of his right arm, with enough physical therapy and dumb luck.

I watched him, and waited. Waited for the monitors to start beeping loudly and a legion of doctors and nurses to come in and hustle me out of the way, then tell me how sorry they were, but they'd lost him. If I waited long enough, I was sure it was inevitable. I had this effect on men.

I closed my eyes and prayed wordlessly. I replayed the nurse's assurances in my head: *he will be fine.* But there were other things in my head, other voices screaming at me, telling me that this was wrong, and it was my fault; it was my hubris – thinking I could be whole again – that put Dave in this hospital bed. Even Dave's strength was no match against the evil that followed me around like a bad smell. The cautious happiness I'd been relaxing into had made way for the return of the mantle of pain and dread I'd worn for the last two years. Enough. It was enough.

I got up and leaned over Dave, kissed his forehead, and walked out of the room to the elevators. Dave's buddy and colleague Ned was getting off one, and I hopped in. "He's going to be fine," I said brightly. "I'm just going to grab something to eat. I'll be back."

Ned smiled and tilted an imaginary cap at me, and looked like he was going to say something. I kept my face bright and cheerful through some miracle of will. The elevator doors shut before Ned could speak.

I got a cab back to the bolthole that Dave kept in Manhattan, a third floor walk up in Hell's Kitchen that was rented in a fake name and paid for a year in advance with cash. Neither Dave nor I were what you could call tidy, and the place was in desperate need of some TLC. I wished I could clean it for him, at least, before I left. But there was no time. I threw what clothes of mine I could see into the small suitcase I'd brought, and spent twenty frustrating, sweaty minutes searching for my passport. After grabbing a few things from the bathroom and the nightstand, I left, closing the door behind me softly. I'd been happy in this dump. The thought made me feel sick, lightheaded. On my way down the stairs I realized I hadn't left a note, but it wouldn't matter. And really, what could I say?

The smells on the street assaulted me when I left the building. I hadn't noticed them before, but I was fighting a growing nausea. I walked until I could hail a cab on 11th Avenue.

"The Sansevoort," I said. I didn't look at the driver. I was just glad his cab was clean.

"The hotel, miss?" the driver asked. He was looking at me in the rearview so I just nodded. It was in the Meatpacking District, not far away, and I'd walked past it before. The Dutch name somehow stayed in my brain, and Dave had mentioned that Ned stayed there sometimes when he wanted to push the boat out, because it had smoking rooms. In this culture of the vilification of smokers, I'd filed that fact away. And while I wasn't exactly a full-time smoker – I picked it up and put it down as the mood struck me – my fingers itched to hold one.

I spent a couple of minutes considering trying to score some crack somewhere, but found that I didn't want it. I didn't want to spend the time and energy looking for it, and once I got started there might be no stopping.

I would be checking into the hotel. I was going to order up a glass of wine. Or probably a bottle, and of something I wouldn't normally waste money on, even though I could afford to now. I would write a couple of notes: one to my brothers, and one to my nephews. And when I was done with all that, I would put a note on the door for the maids to tell them not to enter, take the gun out of my bag, and this would all, finally, be over.

I'd cheated death before. This time, no one was taking my life from me. I would be in control of my own end.

I would be with Jack and Ginger. I knew for certain that there was something beyond this world; Ginger had been with me too many times, and I knew the difference between my imagination and her presence. She had been my twin. We were tied, we had always been tied, by something beyond science and a split egg in our mother's womb.

I would finally draw a black curtain over the memories that haunted me: of Jack bleeding out under my hands, of Ginger being raped and killed, of Darren lying in the snow with an arrow in his chest. The violence that gravitated to me and the people who loved me would end, and the man who was hunting me would most likely be placated by my death. If he wasn't, if he still wanted to target the Clearys, I had three very capable and competent brothers who could steer the ship. Not to mention Dave's crew, who wouldn't see my family hurt if they could help it. We'd formed a bond, all of us, and it went beyond my relationship with Dave.

A sense of serenity washed over me, and I felt a peace I hadn't experienced in years. A wave of calm and love made tears roll down my cheeks.

"You're okay, miss?" the driver said. We were in front of the hotel.

"Thank you, yes," I said. I gave him a fifty and told him to keep the change. "I'm better than I've been in a long time, sir. Thank you for asking."

Ginger, and Jack. I was going to see Ginger and Jack. My dead twin, and my dead husband.

An hour later, I was sitting cross-legged on the king-size bed, flipping through channels on TV and waiting for room service: a bottle of Prosecco and ridiculously overpriced macaroni and cheese. While waiting, I'd fixed myself a gin and tonic from the mini-bar, and was eating a small bag of potato chips that would probably cost me ten bucks. I would drink the wine and eat, and write my notes, including one for housekeeping telling them not to enter and to call the police. Although I was sure I wasn't the first person to check into a hotel to die, I hated the idea of some poor maid having to find me. That's why the bathroom was best, and easier to clean up, too.

I felt calm, and actually quite cheerful. All thoughts of Dave had very effectively been shunted to some corner of my brain. I was looking forward to my meal, and debating ordering a movie from cable to have on in the background while I wrote. The notes would be short, in any event. My brothers knew what I'd been through, and they knew how much I loved them. I doubted they'd even be surprised.

The note to Matthew and Luke would be more difficult, but that's what I was hoping the Prosecco would help with.

A short tap at the door, and I bounded off the bed, grabbing a twenty-dollar bill I'd set on the credenza to tip the room-service waiter.

I began to open the door, but someone pushed it hard, so that it hit me square in the face. In the nose, in fact.

I'd broken people's noses before, but even in my fighting days I'd managed to avoid being struck there. Like this, at least. The pain was instantly blinding, and there was blood in my mouth and on my face. A man came in and locked the door behind him. I held my hand to my face and tried to will the pain away enough to assess the situation.

Definitely not room service. Or if it was, this hotel had to do some serious customer service training.

I started laughing. I had blood streaming from my nose, a strange man had burst into my room who did not seem to have any Prosecco on his person, and I couldn't stop laughing.

The man just looked at me. This was not, obviously, the reaction he had been expecting.

"You're not room service," I said, through the blood. Which made me laugh even harder, bent over at the waist. A touch of the old hysteria. Happens to me sometimes, in moments of physical or emotional pain.

"I followed you," he said. I thought he sounded a bit slow, but I also knew not to trust my instincts in that moment. "From Dave's place. I followed you up the street and got in a cab after you did. I followed you here. I followed you right up to your floor." He sounded proud of himself, and almost incredulous at how easy it had been.

The mention of Dave snapped me out of my hysteria. My adrenaline shot up, and I could almost feel the blood rushing away from the pain in my face, to my brain and my limbs. But I pretended to still be incapacitated.

This was the man who had shot Dave. This was that elderly couple's son, the couple Dave was supposed to be protecting. That *we* were supposed to be protecting, but I had swanned off on my own errands. This man had shot Dave. He was mentally ill, I knew that, and I had more compassion and understanding than your average person when it came to the mentally ill.

But he had shot Dave. And right now, while I didn't see a gun, he could have one in his pocket.

I took my hand away from my bloody nose. "Do you mind if I get a towel, please?" I said calmly. I nodded in the direction of the bathroom. "I don't want to get blood all over the carpet. It's not fair to the cleaning staff."

The man, whose name I suddenly remembered was Nicholas, looked at me oddly. He'd probably been expecting a fight, or for me to beg for my life. I may have been planning on dying in this room, but I'd be damned if I was going to let anybody else have the pleasure of taking my life.

He waited a beat, and it occurred to me that he was on something. I didn't know if he was on his medication now, lithium maybe, or on some street drug. But his reactions were definitely off.

Except when he'd burst into the room, I thought. Yup, his reaction time then had been spot-on.

He nodded, and started heading towards the bathroom. *Shit.* My gun – well, Dave's gun – was sitting on the vanity, under a hand towel. I'd put it there for later, and put the towel over it in case the room service person caught a glimpse of it. It was the first towel Nicholas would see when he walked into the room, if he was planning on grabbing one for me. Besides, he was a big man, somewhere north of six-two or -three, and well over two hundred and fifty pounds, I estimated. I wasn't looking forward to hand-to-hand combat against someone with that much of an advantage.

As we both walked into the room, I pushed him out of the way before he could do anything.

"Sorry," I said. "I'm going to puke."

I brushed past him and retched blood into the toilet. It wasn't hard to do.

Nicholas moved out of my way politely, as I thought he would, and turned to look the other way. Men can't handle watching other people vomit. Especially women. I had three brothers. This, I knew.

I straightened up, blood and mucous still streaming from my mouth, and grabbed the gun, kicking Nicholas as hard as I could in the back of the knee before he had time to turn around.

I was relieved I hadn't taken my combat boots off. The old adage "die with your boots on" had stuck with me, and while I was no soldier, the idea of committing suicide in bare feet seemed somehow obscene.

I didn't kick Nicholas as hard as I'd wanted – he'd moved too far away, into the hallway – but his knee still gave way. Without pausing, I swung the gun in a wide arc, hitting the side of his head with the butt of it while he was down on one knee.

I heard a crack, a very ominous crack, as he hit his head on the opposite wall. He was absolutely still.

I stood still for a minute. "Shit," I said. I hoped he wasn't dead. He'd shot Dave, and who knows what he had planned for me, but he was ill. I didn't want to kill him.

I looked around, grabbed the hotel's hairdryer – thankful I'd sprung for a nice hotel in which to kill myself; the hairdryer wasn't mounted to the wall – pulled his arms behind his back, and tied his wrists together. The cord wasn't long enough to be very effective, so I ripped a lamp out of the wall, wrenched the cord from it, and used that as well. Better safe than sorry, and all that.

I felt around his neck for his pulse. It was there.

I sat back on my haunches and surveyed the scene. Between the profuse, unchecked nosebleed and my retching blood for effect, the bathroom looked like a crime scene. Which I supposed it actually was. I felt my nose, gingerly. I didn't think it was broken after all, but I couldn't be sure. Wearily, I picked up the towel that had gone flying when I'd grabbed the gun, and put it to my face.

"Room service," a voice said from the other side of the door, and then a knock.

I stood slowly, my muscles stiffening now that the adrenaline had abated, and opened the door with the towel to my nose. I was covered in blood, and behind me a large man was unconscious and tied up with electrical cords. But this was New York, and the young man with the cart tried very hard not to look surprised. As far as he was concerned, I supposed, this could be nothing more than some extremely kinky play.

I took the towel away from my face and smiled, which, considering the fact that my teeth were probably coated in blood, seemed to scare the poor kid more than anything. I reached for the bottle of Prosecco on the cart and started to peel the foil off the cork.

"You'll want to call the police, I think," I said. I sounded nasal. "This man," I nodded behind me, "burst into my room."

"Is he…?" The young man had gone white.

"He's fine," I said. "Just unconscious." I popped the cork, and took a swig of Prosecco from the bottle. It tasted like blood. Bubbly blood. I took another one. Better.

"Are you?" He was staring at the blood on my shirt. He'd backed up a couple of steps, and he pulled a phone from his pocket.

"Yes, thank you," I said. I was calm, but it's hard to sound in control when your nose is possibly broken. "I'll just wait here for the police, shall I? Tell them to send an ambulance as well. For him," I added. The kid nodded. He was starting to enjoy himself a bit, I could tell. He was going to have a story to tell.

I looked at the cart. I couldn't wheel it in past the large unconscious man on the floor outside my bathroom, only feet from the door, but I was starving, suddenly. I pulled the cart over so it propped the door open, put the bottle I was holding back into the bucket and carried it into the room, stepping over Nicholas, and set it on the credenza. Then I carefully picked up the plate and the cutlery, and set it down as well.

"We're fine," I said. "I'm very hungry, and it's paid for, right?" I smiled at the kid again, who looked like he wished I hadn't. "Oh!" I said, and stepped over the body on the floor and picked up the twenty I'd had in my hand for his tip, before I'd been doored in the face. "Here," I said, and handed it to him. "Thanks. Just tell the police we'll wait for them." I pushed the cart back toward him, unblocking the door, and stepped back into the room, waving.

Then I opened the door again, and the kid was still standing there, his phone in his hand. "Forgot this," I said. I grabbed one of the two wine glasses on the cart. "Should really be flutes for Prosecco," I said. "Just so you know for next time. But this will do." The kid nodded, staring at me.

I settled in, sitting cross-legged on the bed and eating twenty-four-dollar macaroni and cheese and guzzling Prosecco. When I heard the police in the hallway, I sighed. This was going to take hours, and I doubted they'd let me bring the Prosecco to the police station.

Just my luck. I couldn't even enjoy my own suicide without someone trying to kill me.

ONE

Toronto
Present, four months later

I lay still and waited for the man's breathing to change.

The room smelled like cigarette smoke and sweat, with a layer of something rotting underneath. A bag of forgotten takeout under the bed, perhaps. That was the best-case scenario.

A lamp was still on in the corner: a blessing and a curse. I would be able to find my clothes on the floor, and not have to make sure my jacket was zipped up all the way because I couldn't find my shirt. But I would also be forced to look at the squalor I lay in.

That I had chosen to lay in. Chosen. A clean and sober choice, even.

At least he wasn't a cuddler. He was curled up on his side of the bed with his back to me, and a good foot and a half of mattress lay between us.

He wasn't sleeping yet, but I couldn't wait any longer. No longer attempting quiet, I got up and pulled my jeans on, slipping my underwear off the floor and into my back pocket. I pulled on my t-shirt and then my socks and boots, as quickly as I could. Behind me, I heard the man turn over, and seconds later the flick of his Zippo as he lit a cigarette. I didn't turn around.

"You want some eggs or something?" he said. I looked at my phone. It was two a.m. I didn't answer, but rifled through my bag to make sure nothing had slipped out, that no wallet or keys had made their way under the bed, and that I wouldn't have to come back here again. I could walk out the door and pretend this had never happened.

"Not much of a talker, are you," the man said.

At the bedroom door, I saw his wallet where he'd dropped it when he took off his jeans. I picked it up and flipped through it.

"What the fuck do you think you're doing?" he said. "You think you're going to rip me off?" He was sitting up now.

"No, your five bucks are safe." I looked at his driver's license. "Jeffrey Duncan." I chucked the wallet at him. He misjudged the catch, and it hit him in the forehead.

He was calling me some very unpleasant names as I walked out. I doubted I would be invited back.

When I got outside I pulled my shoulder bag across my body and started running toward home. I was far uptown. I never went out on the prowl anywhere near home. I'd started thinking of myself as a hunter, like a serial killer in search of victims. I knew my shrink, Dr. Singh, would have a field day with that. When she got back from holiday and we started our Skype sessions again, I would probably tell her. I trusted her. She knew more about me than anyone did. More than I did, probably. I'd been a bit lost these last few weeks, while she went wherever she went on vacation. She was so careful, Dr. Singh; she never told me anything personal about herself. She kept our boundaries tight.

I'd started to refer to this as the Summer of the Prowl. I never hurt anybody, of course. They got what they presumably wanted

– although I didn't really care what they wanted – and I got what I needed. Drug-free oblivion, and a new batch of self-loathing to run off, to cleanse myself of, so I could rest.

The air was August humid but somehow cool at the same time, and I could feel my muscles loosening into the run. I thought about keeping my footfall light in my combat boots, each strike of my foot potentially hitting the landmine that would blow me away. Instead of crying, I sweated. Weeks ago I had started visualizing my sweat as the tears I could no longer shed, coming out of my pores. By the time I reached home, my body would be soaked, and alive, and I would feel cleansed. I would shower for a long time, the longest showers of my life.

As I ran, I counted things. Dr. Singh had advised this, back in rehab in Nova Scotia. She called it counting my blessings. It had changed for me, now. I counted the number of days since my twin sister was murdered. The number of days since my husband was murdered. The number of people I had killed. The number of people I had to protect.

Sometimes, I would count the number of months until Matthew and Luke, my nephews, would be safely launched into the world. Happy in their lives. They were in training, now, to be able to protect themselves against almost anything. The older they got, the smarter they would get, and stronger, and eventually they wouldn't need me anymore. Eventually, I would be able to slip out of my life, out of this life, and go back. Go back to crack, maybe. Go back to when Jack was with me, and Ginger. Live with them in my head, or die and live with them someplace else. Though I knew enough not to tell Dr. Singh any of this. She could have me institutionalized if she suspected I was suicidal.

But, no. I would never leave the boys now. I was working very hard, with Darren and Fred, to build a place and a life for my sister's twins, and give them safety and security and fun. I faked it. Faked it every day, being the Fun Aunt. Faked being relatively carefree, when my mind was filled with worry and revenge.

I knew that I was being hunted. That *we* were being hunted. And I was going to make damn sure that if we were found, we'd be ready. All of us.

When I got to the last traffic light before home, I picked up the pace and sprinted. I ran like the devil himself was chasing me.

TWO

On a November evening, some twenty-one months earlier, I had a phone call that would change my life forever.

My twin sister Ginger was dead. A man named Michael Vernon Smith – who at that time was living under the alias Chandler York, and was my brother-in-law's lawyer – was responsible. He was the head of a cult-like group that he referred to as his Family. Some of them had been his former foster children, and he had inculcated them into targeting wealthy, vulnerable people, getting inside their lives and tearing their worlds apart piece by piece. The only way to stop them was to sign over ninety percent of your assets to whatever offshore tax havens or phony charities Smith had set up. If you didn't, Smith promised that the lives of everyone you loved would be ruined, and ruined in very imaginative ways. It was a psychological master play; there was no way out. Even those who didn't value their own lives usually had people they wanted to protect.

The Clearys were high on The Family's hit list. My late husband Jack had been one of Smith's foster kids, and he had bought himself a new identity to escape. In the course of targeting my sister and her husband, The Family had stumbled upon their long-lost brother, my estranged husband. And in the ensuing melee, I had killed three of them, Jack had been killed, and Michael Vernon Smith had lost his eye. But he'd escaped. And before he had, he'd promised that my nephews would be next on The Family's list.

I hoped I would personally get a chance to end Smith's life, mostly because I had more blood on my hands and my soul than anyone in my family ever would, and I wanted to keep it that way.

When my marriage to Jack had broken down, I'd drifted into being a regular at my local bar. I wasn't a big drinker, but it seemed essential to avoid being home alone in my head. Soon enough, I'd found my way to the cocaine that half the staff and many of the regulars seemed to be slipping into the washrooms for. I'd finally found my drug. It took surprisingly little time for my habit to slide into an impressive crack addiction. I took to avoiding my phone, even when it was my twin sister Ginger calling. For the first time in our lives, Ginger didn't understand me. Like anyone in the throes of a full-blown addiction, I was selfish, and didn't think about how my actions would affect the people who loved me. Especially my twin. She jumped down the rabbit hole herself, to understand me. To save me. And in doing so, she helped Michael Vernon Smith and his Family take her life.

As long as my family stayed safe, I'd be happy if Smith simply keeled over from a fatal heart attack, or preferably contracted Ebola somewhere far away and died in agony, bleeding through his eyes. As long as he was dead and we could be sure none of his followers kept after us, it didn't matter much to me how it happened.

* * *

Now I was back from my rehab stint in Nova Scotia – well, to be more accurate, being chained to piers while the tide was coming in, or chasing around a serial killer who liked to remove body parts. Darren and our brother Skipper had found what they thought was the perfect solution to our housing issues. They were at the airport, all of them, Matty and Luke as well, to welcome me, and drive me to what they excitedly referred to as our new home.

The boys were so excited, they blindfolded me for the drive. And I actually allowed it.

I was nervous, on that drive. And a little carsick. But the boys were practically ricocheting off the seats, they were so excited, and I knew that whatever it was, whatever building I was being driven to, I was going to make it work. Matty and Luke had lost their mother the day I got that horrible phone call, and had been packed up and moved to another country. If they were excited about something – and if Darren was too, and he knew the challenges any living space we took would have to face – there was no way I was going to be the voice of doom.

I could tell by the traffic, and by the angle of the sun warming my face behind the blindfold, that we were driving east from the airport. I was relieved that we were driving into the city. Darren, Fred, and I had been exchanging email photos of huge country properties north of the city, where we could live in quiet, and get a relatively good deal on a large property. Room for everyone, and all that. And I tried to get excited about it. I loved the country. But after what I'd just gone through in Nova Scotia, I wanted concrete under my feet, and a cop at every corner.

When the car finally stopped and Luke whipped the

blindfold off my head, I was stunned.

"You wily fuckers," I said, and slapped my hand over my mouth. I was trying to reign in my potty mouth, or at least I had vowed to try. Darren raised his eyebrows, but the boys hooted.

We were in front of what looked like an abandoned factory of some kind. And from the sound of the streetcars in the middle distance, we were downtown. It wasn't an area of town I knew well – I could tell we were east of the city's core – but if I had my bearings right, we were in a not-quite gentrified area, not terribly far from Lake Ontario.

"It was a bakery!" Luke said. "You can still smell bread in there! Almost!"

The brickwork was so dark it looked sooty, like something from Dickensian London. From what I could see, more windows than not were broken or boarded over, and there was some very interesting graffiti repeated along the exterior of the second floor involving multiple depictions of the male anatomy.

It was huge, it was dilapidated, and it was an eyesore.

"It's absolutely perfect," I said. Darren nodded, looking pleased behind his sunglasses.

"Sold?" Matty asked me, his arm slung over my shoulders. He was nearly my height.

"Hmm…" I said. "What do you think, Fred?"

"It's going to cost more than we probably have to make it livable," he said, gazing up at the third floor, which looked like it had been hit by a small airplane. "I don't know."

"You're right," I said. "D?"

"The asking price is ridiculous," Darren said. "I mean, I'm sure we can bargain them down, but we'd probably have to tear the whole thing down and start fresh." He was keeping his face neutral, unable to look at me, kicking at the ground.

But I knew my brother.

"Good point," I said. I looked at Luke, and I looked at Matty.

"Auntie," Luke started to say, serious and man-like, about to start in, I could tell, on the merits of the place. But I'd heard enough.

"This building," I said seriously, "is ugly as hell." The boys were quiet.

"And, I love it," I said. "If everybody agrees, I think I'll buy it."

Even Fred was smiling as the boys tried to hoist me onto their shoulders. I twisted my bad ankle when they dropped me, of course, but it was still a good day.

If you're pretty sure someone wants you and yours dead – or worse – it's handy to have bushels of money. Because I am here to tell you: state-of-the-art security does not come cheap.

Even when one of your best friends is a security expert. Maybe especially when one of your best friends is a security expert – whatever you think might be good enough can, in the right hands and with enough ready cash, be improved upon. The bullet-proof glass that's good enough for the pope is not quite up to snuff, apparently. Not when there are new polymers on the market that could stop anything up to a direct missile hit.

You get the idea.

My brother Darren and I had been bickering about how we were going to find a place – a very, very safe place – for all of us to live together in Toronto. All of us meaning our nephews Matthew and Luke – who each seemed to grow an inch a month

– and their father Fred, along with plenty of room for whichever other family might want or need to stay. Oh, and of course the staff that Matty and Luke had grown up with in southern California, who had watched over the boys since they were born and needed remarkably little convincing to up sticks and move to Canada. Rosen was the former Israeli commando whom Fred had hired back in the day when he started to make real money, and get the attendant threats, and Marta had been their cook-slash-housekeeper. Rosen had no family ties – at least that we knew of, and if he did, he didn't want to bring them to Toronto – but Marta came with a teenage son and her aged, cranky mother, whose English was as nonexistent as the chance of seeing a smile cross the woman's face.

In exchange for the procurement and sometimes installation of our security systems, I'd agreed to house Dave and his jolly band of mercenaries whenever they needed a safe house in town. Or, of course, if they just wanted to visit. After our adventures together, Dave et al had begun to seem like a distant branch of the Cleary clan. Not surprisingly, they fit right in. We all had a screw or ten loose, and we had all seen a lot of death and pain – and had, to greater or lesser extents, gallows humor about it. Our respective quirks seemed to gel pretty well. Especially since we all had one major common goal: protect ourselves, and particularly the twins, from Michael Vernon Smith, and whatever followers he might still have wandering around.

Or better yet, as far as I was concerned: find him before he found us. Find him, and kill him. No courts and no prison, no chance to influence people from behind bars. I hoped I would be the one who could do it, could be the one who got to end the life of the man who had brought about my sister's ruin and death, and left my nephews to grow up without a mother. I had been so close once, and Smith had gotten away.

That would not happen again.

From the outside, the changes we made to the old factory were mostly cosmetic. We left the brickwork as it was, and had the windows replaced. The interior – at least the top three floors – we gutted. Marta and her family had the second floor, and Darren and I had the top level, the fourth floor. The boys and Fred took the floor between us. It made us all feel safer, to have them sandwiched on a floor between us. No one would get to Matty and Luke without going through Rosen, who took a small apartment of rooms at the back of the ground floor, or Marta's fiercely loyal family.

The rest of the main floor was a gym. The gym was going to be both our front – a way to get around the zoning by-laws – and a sort of ad hoc Boys & Girls Club, a place for kids to come after school or on weekends to get in shape and, hopefully, learn some of what Rosen liked to call "the honor code".

For a while, at least, it was everything I could have hoped for.

Until that summer weekend, that is.

THREE

"Another run of shame? This is getting old," Darren said. I'd bounded up the stairs pretending I still had something like energy left, and found my brother lying on the floor of the living room we shared. His feet were on the couch, and he was holding an *Archie* comic at an awkward angle over his head.

"Pfft," I said. I grabbed the beer on the floor next to him, felt it was still cold, and took a long swig. "If I were you, I don't think I'd be throwing that word around so randomly. You're looking at comics with reading glasses on," I pointed out. "At three-thirty in the morning."

"Can I get away with calling *Archie* a graphic novel?" he said. He stuck his hand up and snapped his fingers at me. He wanted his beer back. I handed it to him and went to the kitchen.

"Go to bed already," I said over my shoulder. "The boys start back to school in a few weeks. We've got to get on some kind of sleep schedule."

"*You* go to bed," he said. I returned from the kitchen and handed him another cold beer, after taking a sip, and opened a bottle of water. Darren looked at me. "Oh, wait. You've just been in bed. I forgot."

"I'm a grown-ass woman. I'm a sober grown-ass woman. Who I choose to…" I couldn't think of the word I wanted to use. I liked to reserve "fuck" for simple but effective swearing, and besides, it seemed weird to use it in a sexual way around my little brother. Even if we didn't have anything like a normal sibling relationship.

"Enjoy conjugal relations with?" he said. He peered over his reading glasses, and I caught our dad's face for a second. I smiled.

"Isn't that just in reference to married, uh, relations?" I said.

"Huh," he said. He closed his "graphic novel". "Good point, sir. But I presume you did do some conjugating this evening."

"Jesus," I said. "I am not going to dignify that remark, young man." I downed my water while Darren watched me. He seemed to be waiting for me to say more. "When and with whom I… conjugate, is none of your concern," I said. I looked at Darren, who was still flat on his back with his legs on the couch. He looked very comfortable. "Besides, it's hard to take you seriously when you're reading comics upside down." He opened his mouth, and I put my hand up. "Graphic novels. Pardon me."

"Thank you." He swung his legs down and pivoted, sitting up. "Marta and I were changing the boys' bedding. This was between Luke's mattress and box spring." He waved the comic. "He was hiding it like it was a girlie magazine. I felt it behooved me, as his uncle, to take a gander and make sure it was suitable. Or that it wasn't some kind of postmodern Riverdale porn."

I couldn't wipe the smile off my face. "And?" I said.

"Nada. Innocent as your evening was not," he said. I threw my empty water bottle at him.

"Bizarre. Why would he hide it?" I said. I was lowering my voice, though the boys wouldn't be able to hear me from their rooms downstairs. "Did you ask him?"

"I did," Darren said. He did a spot-on impression of both boys, which drove them both absolutely crazy. "'If you tell Matt I had that, Darren, he will torture me until my life won't be worth living.'" I laughed. If every moment of my life was like this, I could be a different person.

"Were we ever that innocent?" I said. "Seriously."

"You weren't," Darren said. "You were born with that supersized flight-or-fight gene."

"You've been watching *Dr. Phil* again," I said. I sat on the floor and stretched my lower back. Seemed I wasn't getting any younger, and my nighttime escapades – not to mention the long runs after – were taking their toll.

"Besides, I wouldn't call those two kids innocent," Darren said. "Not after... everything."

"No." No. Not after their mother was murdered. Not after their nanny impersonated me and kidnapped them. Not after they – well, Matty – watched their Uncle Jack choke on his own blood. Not after their nanny held guns and knives to them, and drugged them. They would never be innocent again. And while I wished, with everything I had, that the last year hadn't happened, now that it had, I was constantly torn between wanting to preserve whatever innocence and joy they could have left and making sure they were always ready. We couldn't be sure they were safe twenty-four seven unless we wrapped them in bubble wrap and continued to homeschool them. They were caught up with the curriculum here before starting school in Toronto. I was tempted to continue that way – I had money now; we could hire the best private tutors in the city to teach them more algebra and world history than they'd ever learn at school. But their father and uncles seemed to think that socialization was important, living a "normal life".

I was seriously thinking about getting a helipad on the roof, and the boys had weapons and fighting lessons four times a week. As far as I was concerned, we'd pulled out of Normal Station a long time ago. But the boys wanted to go to school, and I was the lone hold-out who thought the risk was too great. But even I could see that my nephews deserved to have a life outside of what we'd never stopped referring to as "the bakery". Or sometimes, "the compound".

Matthew and Luke were the twin sons of my dead twin sister. At least partly because of me, they had lost their mother. I was going to make sure they were safe and protected and, as much as possible at their age, capable of protecting themselves should the need arise. I had made sure that they were surrounded by people who loved them. There was some consistency with Marta and Rosen around, and they worshipped their uncle Darren. I played video games with them, taught them how to properly pop popcorn – none of that microwave stuff – and made sure they saw good movies, ones that had come out before they were born.

My instinct may have been to wrap myself around them, to blanket them with my body to shield them from harm, but I couldn't. There was a part of me that felt that my touch was a curse, that I was a curse. That the best I could do was make sure they knew there was a community, of sorts, in our home, and that they would never be alone unless they wanted to be.

I was in a state of hyper-vigilance and found myself, more often than not, falling asleep during the early hours of the morning on the floor outside the boys' room. Particularly on nights when I'd gone out on my own and picked up the sort of man I'd never want to see in the daylight.

The best mornings were when I woke up on the floor outside their room and one of them would have put a blanket over me while I slept. And sometimes a can of Diet Pepsi next to me. A couple of times I woke to find them both sitting cross-legged on the floor, quietly playing on their phones while I slept. On those mornings, I felt Ginger there with us, and I think the boys did too. They understood better than anyone the twin bond, and were getting to an age when they could see past their own pain to realize how devastating it must have been for me to lose her.

So they weren't having a normal life, but we were all doing our best to make it a good one. And it was working. Sometimes, when I was busy with the gym, or playing *World of Warcraft* with the boys, I actually felt like I could breathe freely.

"Fred home?" I asked Darren. Now that my breathing had returned to normal after my long run, I was starting to notice that I was a little whiffy. Sex with a stranger in a humid room, followed by a five-mile run in combat boots, will do that to a girl. A cool shower and perhaps sleep in my own bed were in order.

Darren was about to answer when we heard someone on the stairs. "Knock, knock," Fred said quietly when he reached the top.

"Just talking about you," Darren said. He stood up and headed to the kitchen. "Beer, Frederick? Water?"

Then Fred appeared in the living-room doorway, and I think I must have actually gasped. Darren turned around.

He had blood around one side of his mouth – his very

swollen mouth; for a minute I worried his jaw had been broken – and it was apparent that he was going to have a very impressive black eye tomorrow. As I got closer to him, I saw red around his neck. Fingerprints, by the look of them.

"I don't want the boys to see me like this," he said. He lowered himself gingerly onto the couch. It wasn't only his face that had taken a beating, then. "I thought maybe you guys could patch me up a bit before I go down to bed." He tried to smile, and winced. "And help me come up with a story for them."

"Darren, get an ice pack. Make that two." Darren gave me a look over Fred's head, a *what now* kind of look, before he went to the kitchen.

"I'm going to have a look at you, but you need to tell us what happened."

"Yes," he said. "It's time, I think." His voice was slow and careful. Not too nasal, though. I didn't think his nose was broken.

"Past time," Darren said. He had two gel packs from the freezer, wrapped in clean tea towels, and something amber-colored in a small glass. He handed me the gel packs and gave the glass to Fred. "Brandy," he said. "For shock. Drink it." Fred wasn't much of a drinker, but he threw the brandy back like a longshoreman. He spoiled the effect by coughing and going even redder in the face, but still.

"Get me one too, would you," I said to Darren. "And the first-aid stuff. It's…"

"Under the sink, I know," he said. "Honestly, I'm nothing but a skivvy." I blew him a kiss and he gave me the finger. I love my family.

I sat looking at Fred, waiting to touch him until Darren

came back with the kit and the nitrile gloves. "Did you get kicked? Kidney, ass… what?" He looked at me. "You couldn't sit properly," I said. "That's not from this." I gestured to his damaged face and neck. Fred's face turned even more red.

"Oh. Yeah. They gave me a couple of good punts in my lower back."

"Do you mean your butt? Because if it's that, you're probably fine. If you got kicked hard enough in your kidneys, in your lower back, we might want to take you to Emerg."

"Danny, we are not going to the hospital," Fred said. I just stared at him with a stern look on my face, and he sighed. "Fine. A couple of kicks landed on my ass, and maybe one or two on my lower back."

"You're probably fine unless you start peeing blood," Darren said from behind him. He moved a small table next to where I had moved a chair in front of Fred, and put the first-aid kit down. He moved a lamp closer to shine on Fred's face. Darren and I looked at Fred together, then at each other.

"I'll just get that brandy," my brother said.

"Now I know why you like wearing those Docs," Fred said. He shifted a bit, and winced.

"Yup," I said. "Any kind of combat boots can be a weapon." I looked down at Fred's Vans and shook my head. "We need to take you shopping, bud."

My heartbeat was strong and steady, and I was keeping my breathing deep and even. After years of being an amateur fighter, this kind of first aid was right up my alley. Not to mention my late husband Jack had insisted I get my first-aid certification.

But my adrenaline was also pumping, and I was trying to use

the mindfulness techniques Dr. Singh had taught me to curtail it. No one was in immediate danger. Fred was home now, and safe. The boys were asleep in their beds. But someone had gone after my family. Someone had given my brother-in-law a pretty decent beating. Fred and I still had a way to go before we could stop blaming each other, deep down, for Ginger's death. But we'd been in each other's lives since I was sixteen. He was the father of the two people who mattered the most in the world to me. Like it or not, he was family.

Darren came back carrying a bottle of brandy and two glasses. He splashed a bit more in Fred's, and a heftier measure for both himself and me. I took a cautious sip, then shot the rest. I managed not to cough, but just barely. It would have killed my street cred.

"So, Fred," I said, pulling on a pair of nitrile gloves, "want to tell us where you've been disappearing to from the boys' bedtimes until, what, four in the morning for the last – how long has it been, Darren?"

"June," Darren said. "Around the time school let out for the summer." Darren had put on a pair of gloves himself, presumably to be my assistant, and he moved the lamp even closer to Fred's face. Not only did it make my job easier, but Fred probably felt like he was being interrogated by boozy amateur first-aiders. Which, of course, he was.

"Water, D?" I looked at Darren. "And a bowl. The big stainless steel one."

Darren sighed heavily and went to the kitchen. Fred tried to smile at me. It looked horrendous.

"I guess I married into the right family," he said. "You know, who better to go to than the Clearys if you've been beaten up? Your dad probably had you putting raw steak on his shiners when you were toddlers." He shut his eyes, which looked painful. I was glad. Shamefully. It was moments like this, when Fred made little cracks about our family, that I remembered how he had an affair with the twins' nanny. A woman who wound up being instrumental in destroying nearly everything I held dear.

"Don't be an asshole, Fred," I said. I tried to sound light. I doubt I succeeded. "I may have to give you stitches if you're so against going to the hospital."

Fred sighed, and looked at me. He touched my hand. "I'm sorry, Danny. I am so sorry." I knew he wasn't just talking about the Cleary thing. Once in a while, Fred's contrition got the better of him. It had taken him a long time to come to terms with Ginger's death, months before he spoke much. Darren had picked up the slack, being both uncle and father to the boys.

"I know, Fred. Let's leave it." I put one of the ice packs in his hand and brought it up to his eye. "I'm going to take a look at your mouth first." I took two Tylenol from the first-aid kit and handed them to him. He chased them with the last of his brandy and then nodded and opened his mouth. Darren handed me the flashlight from our kit.

"Thank you, nurse," I said. Darren snorted. "You haven't lost any teeth. Does it feel like any are loose?" I squirted some distilled water into his mouth and had him swish it around, then spit into the bowl Darren had brought. Fred shook his head no. "The bleeding is from the inside of your cheek being cut on your teeth." I opened a moist sterile wipe and had Fred hold it in place. "You might not want anything acidic or salty for a few days, but you'll be fine." I felt calm. I felt good. Being useful was good. Patching someone up instead of beating them up was good. I motioned for Darren to pour me some more brandy.

"And more for him," I said, nodding at Fred's glass.

"I thought alcohol was supposed to thin the blood," Darren said. "Is this wise, doctor?"

"Bitch, please. He's not suffering from hypothermia. He's got a few little cuts and bruises. This is good hooch. It'll help clean the wound."

"I see you've brushed up on your Civil War field medicine," Darren said. "What a relief, eh, Fred?" Fred tried something like a smile, with his fingers in his mouth. It was not a good look.

"I probably should have had you put gloves on," I said to Fred. I pulled his hand out of his mouth, and the wipe. "My bad." I handed him more brandy. "Swish this around in your mouth, especially on the sore side," I said. "Don't just shoot it." He took the glass from me and cautiously moved it around, wincing. He spit it into the bowl. I put on fresh gloves and stuck a wad of sterile gauze into his cheek. "There. Done. We'll change that in a bit."

Darren pulled up an ottoman and grabbed his glass of brandy. "Now, Fred, while Dr. Strangelove here sees to the rest of your face, why don't you tell us how you got yourself into this sorry state."

Fred nodded, and put the ice pack back to his face.

"It's humiliating," Fred said.

I was torn between sympathy and the urge to tell him to

grow a pair. Darren cleared his throat, and I could tell just by the sound of it that he was feeling something similar. "It's after four in the morning, Fred," Darren said. "Just spit it out."

So I began cleaning the small cuts and abrasions on Fred's face, and he told us about Zuzi.

FOUR

"I haven't been unfaithful," Fred said, the gauze in his cheek making him sound faintly ridiculous.

"Oh, for fuck's sake. You're a widower," Darren said. He stood up and looked down on Fred on the couch. "When Ginger was alive was the time to worry about being unfaithful."

I vaguely wanted to cheer, but I also wanted Fred to be able to get the story out. "Enough, Darren. Fred, continue."

"Yes. Well, you know I started walking a lot in the evenings. I find it hard, sometimes, being here. So many people." He was twirling his glass in his hands. As a natural loner, I could, to a small degree, sympathize. But as the whole place had been designed to provide a safe, secure, and fun home for his children, it was hard to hear this coming from Fred. I had no doubt he loved his sons, but a hands-on dad he was not. "Anyway, once in a while I would stop at Starbucks, or a diner, and sit and read the paper. Watch people."

"So, this girl is a barista?" Darren said.

"Zuzi is her name," Fred said. "And no." He cleared his throat and looked around. I passed him the brandy. "I went into Helen of Troy one night. You've heard of it?"

"The strip club?" My voice was at least an octave higher than usual. "You?" It was an east end institution, Helen of Troy, a huge down-market strip club not far from our place; i.e. in a distinctly non-gentrified area of town.

Fred nodded. "I know. I just… I was walking. It was open. They had a sign outside about their burgers." Darren snorted. "No, really. I mean, I knew it was a strip club type place, but I figured what the hell, never done this before. I'll get a burger, watch the people, walk home."

"Let me guess," I said. "Zuzi is a stripper."

"With a heart of gold," Darren said.

"That's hookers," I said to my brother.

"I stand corrected." I looked at Darren, who had stopped pacing and plopped himself back down on the ottoman. I could tell he didn't know whether to laugh or be angry.

"I saw her dance, but I didn't really pay attention. I mean, I didn't pay attention to the stage much at all. I was actually mortified." I believed him. Fred, whose hair was the kind of red you imagined Anne of Green Gables had, was blushing just thinking about those strippers.

"But just as I was finishing my burger and playing with my phone, pretending to be engrossed in something or other, there she was at my table." I nodded. I'd known strippers, back when I was working as a personal trainer. They were – at least the ones I'd known – in amazing shape. Calf muscles to kill for. Though I was told that there were girls in some of the lower-end clubs who could barely make it across the stage, they were so skinny and strung-out. But working the club selling lap dances was their bread and butter. "She was trying to talk to me, but I just wanted to pay and get the hell out of there."

"I believe you," I said. "Thousands wouldn't." I was cleaning a particularly painful-looking abrasion near Fred's eye with an alcohol-soaked cotton swab, and I may have done it a tad more roughly than the job required. I wasn't sure why I was so irritated. Fred was a grown man, with a perfect right to go to a strip club if he wanted to. And my sister was, after all, dead.

And what with me being in the midst of my Summer of the Prowl, I was not in a position to judge the sex lives of others.

I think it was his naivety that got to me. After all we'd been through, after what Ginger had gone through at the hands of the woman he'd had a fling with, for him to be such a rube was supremely irritating. I put the cold pack back on his eye. "That's good enough for now," I said. "Continue."

"I did clue in," Fred said. "I do know what a lap dance is, Danny. I'm not a total idiot."

Cue Darren snorting. Check. I kept my face straight, somehow.

"There was something about her, though," Fred said.

"There always is," Darren said, and Fred and I both looked at him. "Or so I've heard."

"I never got her to dance for me. I never got a lap dance." Fred leaned back into the couch.

"Lie down there," I said. "Take the weight off your butt." I helped him down and stuck a couple of cushions under his head.

"She made me laugh," Fred said. "Look, it's nothing sexual. It's not even romantic. We're just friends. She's a kid, for God's sake."

"Do you give her money for all this non-lap-dancing time you spend with her?" Darren wanted to know.

44

"Sometimes," Fred said. "She's at work. She has to make some money. And she hates what she does so much, and I hate to see her having to do it."

"I don't blame her," I said. I had never forgotten some of the stories I'd heard from my stripper clients when I was a trainer. "But presumably no one has a gun to her head, right? I mean, if she hates it, can't she go back to school, or find another job, or…?"

"That's what I said." Fred put his hand to his lower back. "We've been spending a lot of time together, in the evenings."

"At Helen of Troy," I said.

"That's quite a name for a strip joint, by the way," Darren said.

"High-minded owners, obviously," I said. I took a deep breath. "It really is late. I need a shower."

"Yes, you do," Darren and Fred both said. They smiled at each other, and Fred put his hand to his face.

"You guys are hilarious." I stood up and stretched. I did need a shower. Aside from any olfactory issues, my muscles were starting to seize up a bit. "So you and Zuzi have become friends, and she hates her job. Lots of people do. So why did you get a beating?"

"That's just it," Fred said. "It's the management of the place. She said it was sold about eight or nine months ago and the new owner brought in new floor staff and so on. They're pressuring the girls to do things outside of work hours. Illegal things," he added.

Darren sighed. "Sex with customers kind of things?"

Fred nodded. "They're basically turning the girls – well, some of the girls, the younger ones – into escorts. Or trying to."

"So you got on your white horse and tried to have a chat with the management?" I was kind of proud of Fred, if so. He looked about as threatening as a hobbit. But then again, I'd seen him take a man's eye out with a corkscrew, so I knew he had reserves of rage in there somewhere.

"More like they decided to have a chat with me. The manager took me aside after Zuzi left my table tonight and asked if I'd like to take her home. Said they were offering this 'service', as he called it, to loyal clientele."

"Fuck," I said. I actually was feeling more sorry for this girl now. I'd never heard of anything quite so sleazy happening in the clubs of the dancers I knew.

"Yeah." Darren went and got some water for all of us. The sky was actually lightening a little bit, and brandy at dawn was starting to feel a bit too *Days of Wine and Roses*.

"I said that, aside from the legality of their offer, shouldn't it be up to the girls to decide whether or not they wanted to see a customer outside of the club."

"I assume they didn't take kindly to you reminding them about the law," Darren said as he sat back down on the ottoman.

"Gutsy move, Fred, but it might have been wiser to just kindly decline. Say something about a wife at home or whatever." It wasn't like he had been drinking, so neither his judgment nor his mouth could have been impaired.

"The guy didn't say much of anything. He was very polite, apologized for any misunderstanding. Then when I left, there were two very big gentlemen waiting outside. They frogmarched me into the alley and did this to me."

Now I was angry. I was supremely irritated at Fred for the falling-for-a-stripper thing – as much as he might deny it, I had a hard time believing he didn't have the hots for this girl – but the idea of these people dragging my brother-in-law into an alley and beating him up, especially over something so awful, made me want to kick someone in the head. At the very least.

"So maybe you should take a break from the place for a while, Fred," Darren said. He looked exhausted, Darren did, and I remembered that he had taken the boys to The Ex earlier that day – well, the day before. The Canadian National Exhibition: an orgy of fairground rides, games, and deep-fried dough. Heaven, in other words.

"Oh, I'd love to. But I do need to get Zuzi out of there," Fred said. "She's on her own – parents both dead and she has no siblings. She's smart and funny, but she feels a bit... damaged."

No parents. No siblings. He knew how to get us. I looked at Darren, and Darren looked at me. He nodded. "For God's sake," I said.

"I know," Darren said.

"We're idiots," I said.

"I know."

I looked at Fred. "We'll take care of it," I said to Fred. "But we're not kidnapping her. Can you just call her and tell her what happened tonight? Tell her not to go in tomorrow night? She must have some sense of self-preservation."

"I actually don't have her number," Fred said.

"So you're great friends, then," I said. "Jesus, Fred."

"We should also call Paul," Darren said. Paul Belliveau: a sergeant with the Toronto Police, and my savior when a crazy drugged-out cop from California came to Toronto and tried to kill me. He and his wife were like godparents to me, whether they wanted to be or not, and the Clearys had adopted them both.

"We can't," Fred said. He closed his eyes. "There's one more thing."

"Of fucking course there is," I said.

"When they were doing this to me," Fred said, gesturing to his face, "they said something about going home to my boys and not coming back there."

"Your boys?" Darren said. He stood up.

"You're just telling us this part now? Are you crazy?" I could barely see, I was so angry. Fred seemed more worried about this stripper's safety than his own sons'.

"Well, I told Zuzi about the boys, of course," Fred said, "and us all living together and everything. She knows about my life. Well, some of it."

"Did you, by any chance, tell her where we live? You fucking moron?" I was clenching my hands together so tightly that I could feel one of my nails break the skin on the back of my hand. It was that or finish the job the men in the alley had started on Fred.

"Not the address, Danny, but she knows I live close by, and she knows we live in a disused industrial bakery." He looked even more pale, if that was possible. "She wouldn't tell them anything like that. And besides, why would they want to come here? I've said no, they beat me up. End of story."

"They know you have sons. The fact that they mentioned it at all is an implied threat," I said. I couldn't believe how calm my voice sounded. Though it was perhaps a tad loud. "And they could really only have gotten that from this Zuzi. She knows pretty much everything else about you, probably. And, they know that you know about their highly illegal slave trade."

Fred looked sick. Good. I left him with Darren and went

running downstairs to the floor Fred shared with the boys.

I stood outside their room and tried to calm my heart. I could cheerfully have wrung Fred's neck – really, I would have been glad, at that moment, to chuck him headfirst down the fire escape but he had been my sister's husband, and he was the boys' father. I was going to have to learn to deal with this.

Upstairs, I could hear Darren yelling at Fred, which made me feel a bit better. I wasn't overreacting. Maybe Darren could talk some sense into Fred, make him understand how stupid he'd been.

I hesitated outside Matty and Luke's door. I hated invading their privacy, but I had to make sure they were okay. I had to watch them breathing for a minute. Then, perhaps, I could calm down.

I turned the door knob as quietly as I could and stuck my head round the door. I could hear the deep breathing of sleep, and the room felt close and too still. While we had two bedrooms for the boys, with a bathroom joining them, the boys had opted to stay together in the bigger of the two rooms. I knew that one would eventually move to the other room, but I think we all liked it this way. I didn't want either of them to be alone.

I crept forward. In the bed next to the wall to my far left I could make out Luke's lighter hair, as my eyes adjusted to the dark. I made my way over to him and squatted next to the bed, hoping he didn't choose that moment to open his eyes. We'd both get the scare of our lives, and he'd probably be in therapy over it for the rest of his life. But I had never realized how deeply kids sleep at this age. Ginger would have known, and I was sure Marta did. I moved Luke's hair off his forehead and kissed the top of his head very lightly. He stirred and murmured something that sounded like a language with no vowels. I turned and started creeping the ten feet to the other bed.

Trying to move silently in the room of two teenagers is futile. I kicked what sounded like a bowl with cutlery in it and nearly slid to the floor on a magazine. Or, perhaps, a graphic novel.

I got to Matty's bed, and my eyes had adjusted enough to the dark to see that he wasn't there. His bedding was all over the place. I looked at my watch. Four fifty-five a.m.

Just as I was about to sound the alarm, press the panic button (literally – I had them installed in all the bedrooms; they acted like an internal fire alarm, waking everybody in the building), Matthew came out of the bathroom, rubbing his eyes.

"Hey, Auntie," he said. "Everything okay?" He was in pajama bottoms and a Joy Division t-shirt that I recognized as Darren's. He was tall, gangly, and skinny, and without his brother's easy grace – yet. Matty had sat with me watching my husband die, choking on his own blood. Matty and I had been in hospital together afterward, after he had been kidnapped and his twin brother had been taken from him, and his mom had been dead for a week. Matty slept in my hospital bed that night, and I'd wrapped myself around him and vowed that nothing and no one would ever hurt him again. Stupid promise, but I made it to myself. I knew better than to make it out loud.

Something in me changed that night. I would never have my own children – not just because my husband was dead; we'd split before that. But I owed it to Ginger to put her boys first. I had to see them to adulthood, leave them everything I could in terms of love and life lessons and even whatever money I had left.

I thought it was pretty likely that I wasn't going to live very far into their young adulthood. I had to give them every single thing I had, until that day.

Once my heart started beating again, I tucked Matty in. "Everything's fine, little man," I said quietly. It was a running joke, since the boys were both nearly as tall as I was now. "Just had to check on you." *And your father's an idiot who spilled his guts to the first stripper who turned his head, potentially putting your lives in danger*, I wanted to say. *Otherwise, everything's just peachy.*

"Cool," he said. "Love you."

My heart lurched. Luke was the more affectionate twin. But Matthew was half-asleep, and his defenses were down.

"I love you double," I said, and kissed his forehead. I started to back away, but Matty grunted and slapped his hand on something.

"Text came for you," he said. He held his arm in the air. "Night."

"Thanks, buddy." I took the phone from his hand gently and he flopped his arm back down. He seemed asleep before it hit the bed.

I stuck the phone in my back pocket and returned to the hallway. I could hear Darren and Fred upstairs, again, but the voices weren't raised now. I was exhausted by my anger at Fred, the deadening effect of the brandy, and the long run home, not to mention having been up for twenty-something hours. I trudged back up the stairs, deciding to tell Fred and Darren I was calling it a night. We'd deal with Fred's fuck-up tomorrow.

I was in the living room I shared with Darren when Matty's phone vibrated in my back pocket. In the space of thirty seconds, I'd forgotten about it.

In one of our many talks about planning and safety for the

boys, Darren, Fred, and I had decided that while we wanted to give the twins as much fun and freedom as possible – and not make them feel like they were living in some kind of very odd witness protection program – they had to tell the three of us their passwords for everything, and let us know immediately if they changed them. It wouldn't be forever, we promised them.

The latest text, the one that had just vibrated, read:

> Whoops, sorry dude! It's mid afternoon where I am. Hope your phone is off. My bad.

The text was from Dave. And there was another one, from probably half an hour earlier.

> Found that book I was telling you about. Sent it. Oh, and tell your auntie to call me, okay? Her # accidentally got deleted from my phone.

Then he used the nerd emoticon, with the cross-eyed guy with glasses.

Accidentally, my ass. And I didn't blame him, after the mess I'd made with him. I went back downstairs to put Matty's phone on the table outside their bedroom, went back upstairs with my level of exhaustion somehow, if possible, doubled in the last couple of minutes.

Another ridiculous stranger's bed, another long run home, and then Fred arriving in my living room looking like he'd just been trapped in the Octagon for two minutes with Georges St-Pierre. Not to mention the story of Zuzi the Stripper, and possibly a nice case of human trafficking he'd dragged us all into.

"Boys are fine. I'm having a shower, and then I'm sleeping for about fourteen hours. Don't wake me unless there's a solar flare or something." Fred opened his mouth to speak, and I stopped him. "We'll deal with everything tomorrow, Fred. Keep Tylenol by your bed, and water, and take some as soon as you wake up." He nodded, and Darren nodded, and then I nodded. Good. Nods all around. For once, from my family, no talk. I liked it. I especially appreciated it at nearly dawn, when I'd been up for twenty-two hours.

Ten minutes later, after a quick, blissful shower, I was crawling under my duvet, and as I was falling asleep, for a moment I felt a burst of something like happiness.

I would talk to Dave tomorrow.

When I woke, I could tell by the angle of the light that it was late morning. Other than ravenous hunger that hit me about two minutes after I opened my eyes, I felt good. Even the hunger felt good. Healthy. Whoever invented sleep knew what she was doing, I'll tell you that for free. It may only have been four or five hours, but I felt restored.

Just as I was considering hauling ass out of bed, Darren's knock – a sort of two-knuckle slide across the door – preceded his entrance.

"Fuck, Darren," I said. "I have been awake for about thirty seconds."

"I just talked to Dave," Darren said. He sat on my bed, his phone in his hand.

"You did?" I said. Or rather, I squeaked. I cleared my throat.

"He just got confirmation from a friend – well, he couldn't go into how he got it, you know what he's like, and I think he's somewhere in Asia, but he didn't say."

"Yes?"

"Michael Vernon Smith. He's in Toronto, Danny. He crossed the border about thirty-six hours ago, or at least Dave's pretty sure it's him. Obviously with a different passport."

"Obviously," I said. I was sitting up. I couldn't remember sitting up. "Of course, as far as we knew, he could always have been in Toronto." I pushed Darren off my bed with my feet and got up. "Now we know. Now we have information." I was awake. I was fully fucking awake. Outside of being under the influence of cocaine, I didn't think I'd ever felt as awake. "Information is power."

"He sent Rosen the CCTV," Darren said.

We all had the same high-security Internet connection, but Rosen was a tech wizard, and could talk geek with Dave's people.

"I'll meet you down there in five," I said. Darren nodded. On his way out the door, I stopped him. "Darren," I said. "We are going to get him."

He tried to smile. "Unless he gets us first, right?"

"Not gonna happen, my brother. Not going to happen."

In the bathroom, I brushed my teeth so hard I made my gums bleed. Terror and exhilaration: my favorite combo.

FIVE

"It's him," I said. We had watched the footage three times: Michael Vernon Smith, in an unseasonal tweed cap, thick black-framed glasses, and a full beard, collecting his baggage from a luggage carousel at Pearson International Airport.

"How can you tell?" Darren said. His nose was nearly at the screen, and Rosen gently moved his shoulder out of the way. "That could be Michael Caine, for all I know."

"The facial recognition software Dave's team uses caught him." Fred pointed at the image we were looking at, freeze-framed. "The algorithms analyze the spatial geometry of a human face. Facial hair and glasses may make the result a bit less accurate, but what most people think of as disguises don't cut it. It's really the area between the brow and the chin that the software is analyzing, the pupillary distance, and the space between nose and mouth." I looked at Fred, whose own nose and mouth were both looking quite a bit worse for wear today. "The best way to fool the software is a very large pair of sunglasses, and they tend to frown on those when a person's in the security area of an airport."

"Big Brother strikes again," Darren said. He handed me his coffee.

"He has his uses, that Big Brother," I said. I stared at the image in front of me. I was calm. We knew that Michael Vernon Smith had flown into Toronto, but nobody had been tracking him in real time. He could be anywhere now. He could have driven up north to Thunder Bay, or he could be standing on the sidewalk outside by now. I felt lightheaded for a moment, somewhere between euphoric and deflated.

"I didn't spend much time with the man, unlike you and Fred," Darren said. "I wouldn't know him if he was standing in the room with us, other than the pictures I've seen." He clapped me on the shoulder. "I'll get the boys moving."

"If you could wait a minute please, Darren," Rosen said. He was unfailingly polite and courteous, despite the fact that we had drilled it into him that he wasn't a servant. "There's one last bit Dave flagged for us all to see." He opened a new video file, one of Smith wheeling his suitcase out of the arrivals hall. At the door, Smith took off his cap and looked directly up at the camera, and smiled. He held the pose for a couple of seconds, put the cap back on, and left the building.

"Play it again," I said. Rosen played the short video again.

"Did he just wink?" Darren said.

"Yes," Rosen said. He said it slowly, like he said most things. "I think so."

"Motherfucker," I said.

"Do you think it was for law enforcement?" Fred said.

"No, Fred," I said. My heartbeat had finally gone up. My spidey senses were definitely tingling. "That was for me."

We were silent for a minute, all of us staring at the screen. Then, from upstairs, we heard a glass break. I was moving before the sound had even registered in my brain. After a second, Marta's mother started yelling in Spanish, and the sound of Marta placating her filtered through the ceiling. Darren laughed first, and then we all did.

"I can't believe we didn't think about better soundproofing," I said, for the tenth time since we'd moved in.

"It's good security," Rosen said, as he did every time I complained about how everybody on the main floor, the gym floor where Rosen lived, could hear Marta's mother's tirades.

"She's better than a guard dog, that lady," Fred said. The tension in the room had eased a notch. "So what do we do now?" he said.

"I make coffee, and call Dave," I said. I could see Rosen and Darren give each other a meaningful look. I blushed and hated myself for it. None of the men in my life could understand why Dave and I hadn't paired off already, formed some kind of romantic vigilante duo, fighting evil and making babies, or something. Only Darren had some idea of what had happened between Dave and me. What a coward I'd been. What a coward I was.

"I'll go see what's eating Mama Estela," Darren said. He was the only one who could get her to smile. "And then maybe Marta and I will see about getting space ready for the crew." He was heading for the stairs.

The atmosphere was odd, almost manic. Since that day back in Maine when Fred and I had faced down Michael Vernon Smith and one of his followers, we had all been waiting for confirmation that Smith had made it out of the Maine woods alive, one of his eyes destroyed by the corkscrew that Fred had stabbed him with, and that he was coming after us.

Knowing he was here, in our city, after all this time, was almost a relief. Almost.

"You said they're in Asia," I called to his back. "There's nothing they can do here. We've got things covered, Darren."

"I'd say we need all the help we can get, Danny," Fred said. He pointed at his own face. "I'm no help to you. And these are our boys."

"Mr. Lindquist is right, Danny," Rosen said. He stood up, and put his hand gently on my shoulder. "This is not a time to put personal grievances ahead of the mission." His nostrils were flaring a bit, which in Rosen-land meant that he thought he was being funny.

He may not have been a Cleary, but he had joined the ranks of men in my family who seemed to find making fun of me irresistible.

"Stop calling him Mr. Lindquist. Call him Fred," I said automatically, for the hundredth time. "And this isn't funny, Mr. Rosen." I called him that when I was peeved. He hated it almost as much as he hated when we called him "James".

"No, it's not," Rosen said. No nostrils flaring now. He was looking me straight in the eyes. "We are all here – all of us are here – to make sure that those boys upstairs have a good life. In our different ways, we all failed them. And we are going to do everything we can, use all of our individual strengths, whatever we have at our disposal, to keep them safe and happy."

I nodded, chastened. I did forget, sometimes, that I wasn't the only person under this roof who felt responsible for what had happened to Ginger, and to the boys after that. Rosen had watched them grow up from toddlers, and when they had been kidnapped from school, part of his role in my sister's household had been to keep an eye on the boys' welfare.

"Wellll, strictly speaking, Marta didn't fail anybody," Darren said from behind me. He hadn't gone upstairs yet. "That woman is blameless. I'm thinking of marrying her." Rosen smiled, a rare enough thing.

"You're an ass," I said to my brother. "And don't let Mama Estela hear you. She'll have the priest here, and there will be no backing out of it."

"I could do worse!" Darren yelled over his shoulder.

"You have," Fred and I both replied, and we grinned at each other idiotically.

"It's raining," Rosen said, nodding at the window above his computer desk. "We'll keep the boys inside today. Some sparring, movies." He shrugged. He had just described his favorite day, though he would never admit it. Rosen was a fan of 1980s American teenage films, and from what I could gather, he and the twins were currently working their way through John Hughes' oeuvre. As I loathe both romantic comedies and movies about teenagers, I generally opted out.

"Let me know when you get to Cameron Crowe," I said. "*Say Anything...* is the only film of that genre I will watch."

"It just came in on Blu-ray," Rosen said, trying not to seem excited. "We can change the schedule. You should join us."

He's here, my brain kept repeating. *I am standing here talking about eighties films and Michael Vernon Smith is somewhere close by.*

"Maybe I will," I said. "Let's see where we are later." I wanted coffee and breakfast before calling Dave. Oh, and maybe a bump of coke. Ha, ha. "See you at Marta's, if not before. We'll tell everyone about this," I nodded at his computer, "and talk about safety."

"Again," Rosen said.

"Again," I agreed.

We had a routine throughout the summer since school had let out for the boys, though none of us had day jobs, per se, other than the gym. Each floor was self-contained with its own kitchen, and for the most part we all came and went as our individual schedules dictated. But one of us, usually Fred or Darren, would make sure the boys were up and dressed by ten-thirty or eleven in the summer. No one with the Cleary gene is a morning person.

At five p.m., whoever was home would congregate in Marta's kitchen for food. It was the only meal we always ate together, unless we were out, and it often lasted the entire evening, with some of us draped onto the fire escape out back to catch some early evening sun. Marta would sometimes set up a grill on the makeshift patio she'd created outside, and she might have chicken or shrimp going, leaving one of the boys to tend to it while she stood in the kitchen, slowly sipping her one *cerveza* of the day while she chopped and stirred and chided and cooked. Darren could often be persuaded to go grab a guitar, and the boys would, less often, grab theirs. Darren had been teaching them to play, though neither had picked up the music gene. Fred would sit with Marta's son Eddie to practice his Spanish, and I was trying to learn how to cook. Well, I was trying to learn to chop things.

There had been some memorable nights this summer, nights I hoped the boys would keep with them always. When

Laurence came to visit at the end of July for a week, and he and Darren had played guitars and sang Celtic folk songs very late into the night, until finally Mama Estela started trying to teach them some Mexican ones. The boys and I had laughed so hard that night, my abs were sore the next day. Or the night Rosen and Fred had engaged in an epic Scrabble tournament – just the two of them; none of us could possibly compete with either – and the boys had fallen asleep on either side of me on the couch Marta kept in her kitchen, Luke's head on a pillow on my lap and Matty's on my shoulder. I'd stayed there until dawn, long after everyone else had gone to bed, tears streaming down my face.

We were making a life for them, the best life we could. Darren had left his band, which I railed against. Certainly the boys did; they were proud of their uncle, the rock star. He shrugged it off, saying he'd start another one someday; that he was going to write and record his own stuff; it was no big sacrifice. But I knew better. Darren had never had a life away from the road, not really. He'd certainly never had any passions other than his music. But I knew that being shot in his lung back in Maine by one of Michael Vernon Smith's people had also affected his ability to sing. Or at least, to get up on stage and sing all evening the way he used to. He didn't have the stamina anymore. He quite literally didn't have the lungs for it.

Michael Vernon Smith had a lot to answer for.

And now he was here. He was in Canada. He was in Toronto. As I walked slowly back up to the third floor, I could feel the desire to get to him, to hurt him, to make him suffer as he had made my family suffer – I could feel it down to my fingertips. My skin was nearly on fire with the desire to kill him. And I was happy.

This was what I'd needed. He was here. I would find him. I would do what needed to be done. And, by God, I would enjoy it.

SIX

"**D**anny," Dave said. He sounded very far away. He *was* very far away. I was sitting on my bed with the door shut. "I take it you got the message."

"And the video," I said.

"You saw the wink?"

"I saw it." There was a pause. "Where are you?"

"East," he said. He sounded like he was outside. I heard car horns, traffic. A city, then. "Very east." Bangkok, maybe? Shanghai?

"Okay," I said. No more questions about that, then. "Dave," I started, and he stopped me.

"Don't, Danny. Please," he said. "We'll talk about it another time. Okay?" He sounded tired. He had just finished doing God knows what in God knows where, and did not sound like he wanted to have The Talk. Which, of course, suited me down to the ground.

"Good. Well – good." That's me, the scintillating conversationalist.

There was a pause. "Listen, it's stupid o'clock here," Dave said. "Well, midnight or something, but I've been up for two days."

"Right, sorry, I didn't think."

"I'm flying into Toronto in a few days," Dave said.

"That's what I wanted to talk to you about," I said. I realized I was pacing in front of my open window, and I jerked the blinds shut. "Next steps. What we do now, that kind of thing."

"We'll hash it out when I get there," Dave said. "But, Danny, there isn't much we can do, for the time being."

"What do you mean?" I said. "He's here. Smith is here."

"Probably. But unless he checks into a hotel under his own name, or the name he used to get into the country, it's unlikely we'll find him." He said something loudly in a language that could have been Thai, could have been Indonesian... hell, it could have been Greek, for all I knew. "Someone's waiting for me. But for the time being, the only thing you can do is wait."

"Wait," I said. "Wait for him to come after us. After the boys. Because I've always been known for my patience."

"It's not ideal, Danny, but it's what you've been preparing for. Just turn the alert level from orange to red, and sit tight." A car horn beeped, loud and tinny, very near him. He yelled something and it sounded like he was running in a rainstorm. "I've got to go. Two or three days and we'll be there. Be vigilant, and call me if anything happens."

"Like what," I said, but he'd hung up.

Fan-fucking-tastic. I had somehow missed this possibility, in my mind: the torture of knowing that Michael Vernon Smith was close by but being unable to find him. I almost wished we didn't know he was here, because, effectively, nothing had changed. My only comfort was the knowledge that when Dave got here, things would probably move along.

I was surrounded by people I loved, and people I was very

fond of – even Mama Estela had grown on me. But their safety was my responsibility. Rosen was smart, dedicated to the boys, handy with weapons, and certainly a fighter. I'd studied Krav Maga with him, and had the bruises to show for it. But he was also a paid employee as well as being a member of our tribe, and I could and would never expect him to put his life on the line for us. Darren was a good shot and in decent shape for a man in his thirties with one lung, but he was more of a nurturer than a warrior. Fred – well, Fred was Fred. Though after watching the speed at which he'd gone after Smith with the corkscrew back in Maine, he shouldn't be totally discounted. It showed he had more courage than I would ever have given him credit for, and I knew he would do whatever he needed to do to protect the boys. His careless chat with Zuzi the Stripper notwithstanding.

As for Marta and her family, they were here to help make this place feel like home for the boys, and for all of us. But as far as I could tell, Marta's greatest weapon was her ability to produce copious amounts of very moving tears. Her son was younger even than the twins. Regarding Mama Estela – well, there had been much late-night chatter about her on my floor. Darren claimed to have seen her passport at one stage, and said she was in her late eighties. I thought she could be anywhere from sixty-five to a hundred. When she wasn't holding her back and claiming – according to Marta, who had to translate – to be close to her deathbed, I didn't doubt that she had the heart of a warrior in her five-foot frame.

We were a motley crew, alright.

Within the confines of the law – well, mostly; I've said it before and I'll say it again, I'd rather face a weapons charge than face Michael Vernon Smith without a gun in my hand – we were as prepared as we could be with the time we'd had.

In a few weeks, school would be back in session for the fall. The plan was that the boys would be taking the subway to school like most other kids their age did, but not now. Now, they would be driven there every morning and picked up again by one of us. We had gone over all of this the last time Dave and his crew had been in town, all the security procedures we should employ to keep us safe. Some things had slackened a bit – we'd let the boys ride their bikes to the beach in the summer. It seemed cruel, on some of the hot, idyllic summer days we'd had, to have them chaperoned by one of us twenty-four seven.

I paced around the room, feeling like a caged animal. Waiting for something to happen? Not my strong suit. Feeling powerless? Even less so. I wanted this to be over. I wanted Michael Vernon Smith to crash through my window that very minute, so I could have done with it. With him.

Instead, I changed into old jeans and a t-shirt and went down the hall to make coffee. As it was brewing I began cleaning out the fridge, tossing yogurt that was probably fine and what looked like Chinese takeaway that Darren had probably only ordered last night. I had to do something. My brain was awash with thoughts of revenge, mixed with shame and confusion about my feelings for Dave, and what I'd done, leaving him alone in the hospital without so much as a note. I would get through the afternoon, and at dinner we'd all have a pow-wow and tell the boys what we'd learned. I hated that they had to worry about these things, that they even had to know about them.

Ginger, where are you? I thought. She used to be with me. I used to feel her with me. The times I sensed her presence had grown fewer and fewer, and now she seemed nearly gone. She'd given me strength when I needed it, when I didn't think I could do what needed to be done, or when I was fantasizing too much about retreating into a life of crack cocaine and solitude. She'd kept me in the world, and I needed her now.

"What'd you throw that out for?" Darren said from behind me, and I nearly jumped out of my skin. "It's, like, two days old." He was looking at the Chinese takeout cartons at the top of the trash can, which I had taken from underneath the sink and put on the floor behind me where I could dump the contents of the fridge into it more easily. "Everybody knows that leftover Chinese lasts a month. I believe there have been studies to prove it. Something about the MSG interacting with the takeout containers. Very scientific."

"Take it out," I said. "It's at the top." The coffee was ready and I poured some for both of us.

"Danny, I am not eating from the garbage," he said. "I know I'm unemployed, but there are lows to which I will not sink." He proceeded to pluck the carton from the trash, open it, and stick it in the microwave.

"You know you're a moron, right?" I said.

"Yes, but don't use that word."

"You're intellectually challenged, then." We drank our coffee, leaning against the counter, and grinned at each other.

"So, what's the plan then?" Darren said. "You talked to your boyfriend?"

"Don't be an asshole," I said. "He'll be here in two or three days."

"In the meantime?"

"In the meantime, nothing. We keep an eye out."

"Fuck," Darren said. He slapped the back of his neck a couple of times, a trait from childhood. I'd noticed he'd picked it up again, in times of stress.

"Fuck," I agreed. "We'll talk about it tonight, with everybody. Rosen's going to keep the boys today. Working out and movies."

"And you?" he said. He took the Chinese from the microwave and stirred it, stuck it back in. "What are you going to do until then?"

"I'm going to the strip club," I said. It came out of my mouth before I thought about it. Yes. I would go and check things out at Helen of Troy and see if this Zuzi chick was working. I could get an idea of whether she was telling the truth. Fred was probably blinded by some kind of hero complex thing. Or something else that I didn't want to think about, when it came to my dead sister's husband.

"A fine plan," Darren said. He rubbed his hands together. "A rainy afternoon at a peeler bar. I think I'll come with you."

"No. You stay here with the boys."

"Danny, I can't handle any more eighties movies."

I didn't want Darren to come. An idea had come into my head, in the past minute or two, that a strip club might be just the kind of place where a girl could score a little coke. Just a gram. Not to cook it, not to make crack and zone out. Just a few lines to get the synapses firing. I needed my spark back, my creativity. Even Dave knew that; he'd scored some for me back in Nova Scotia when we badly needed to brainstorm. I'd only used it that one night. But that night was... well, the last time I really felt alive. And as soon as I thought that, I knew it was true. I was going through the motions of life, trying to keep us all together, but I wasn't sure how much longer I could keep going. Once Michael Vernon Smith was dead, his threat to the boys and the rest of my family gone, I wanted to be gone too.

Darren was eating his food from the carton and looking at me. "Danny?"

"I'm thinking," I said. My voice came out funny, and I had tears in my eyes. I felt tired. I felt so tired, all of a sudden. Jack was gone, Ginger was gone, and I'd royally screwed things up with Dave, because I wasn't capable of loving anybody again. I knew it, and now Dave did too. And I had one last fight on my hands, a fight I would have to wait for. I wanted nothing more than to get a hotel room and a big bag of crack, and watch stupid TV. I wanted to turn my brain off and crawl into a hole. In that moment, I knew I wasn't capable of being that woman, day in and day out, the woman who kept spinning her wheels, running miles in combat boots and lifting weights and fighting. The woman who was constantly going over every possible permutation of worst-case scenarios, waiting for the day when evil came back into our lives.

I needed someone else to do it. I needed Jack. I needed Dave.

"Oh, kitten," Darren was saying. He put his food down and pulled me in for a hug.

"Kitten?" I said. I rested my head on his shoulder for a minute. "Where the fuck did that come from?"

"No idea," he said, "but I kinda like it." He was patting my back and swaying a little, holding me as though I was a kid. "No strip clubs for you today, sister," he said quietly. "You need a long nap."

"Yeah," I said. I did. Sleep had never been easy for me, and lately it was as elusive as smoke. I'd felt fantastic when I woke up, but as deeply as I'd managed to sleep, it had only been for a few hours, not nearly enough to make up for the deficit I was running on.

"I do too, actually." Darren let me go. He grabbed both of our mugs and poured the coffee down the drain. "Go to bed for a while. I'll call Skip and Laurence, tell them the news, and I'll crash for a while too. I'll set an alarm, wake you up before dinner."

"What about Fred and his stripper?" I said.

"The stripper can wait until tomorrow," Darren said. "Not priority one just now. You feel me?"

"I feel you." I headed down the hall to my room. Darren could keep the plane in the air for a few hours. Thank God for him.

"Danny?" I turned around at Darren's voice. "It's going to be okay."

"I highly doubt it," I said, "but I love you for saying so." *Nothing is going to be okay ever again*, I wanted to say. I smiled at my brother, and went to my room.

After I locked my bedroom door behind me – I had ensured that all doors in the building had good locks installed, though none of us tended to use them – I got to my knees beside my nightstand and reached for the pistol I had duct-taped underneath. It was illegal to store firearms that way in this country, but my peace of mind trumped that law any day. I checked that the cartridge was loaded, and sat on the floor with it in my lap for a long time.

I tried to meditate to help relax my mind for sleep, something Dr. Singh had recommended. I doubted she would approve of meditating with a loaded gun in your hand, but what she didn't know, et cetera.

I did fall asleep, curled up on the floor next to my bed with a loaded gun at my side. Whether it was the meditation or the loaded weapon that calmed me, I couldn't tell you.

SEVEN

Marta and Mama Estela had obviously been arguing for much of the afternoon. Marta was in a rare bad mood, and her mother – who seemed to cheer up a bit when she'd had a good screaming argument – was nearly smiling. Dinner was less elaborate than usual; Marta had all the fixings for fajitas laid out on the table. There were platters of chicken and beef strips, along with roasted red peppers, onions both fried and raw, two kinds of lettuce, her homemade *pico de gallo*, refried beans, a couple of bowls of shredded cheese, and what looked suspiciously like store-bought tortillas. I could see Darren eyeing them with his eyebrow raised, and Luke elbowed him.

"Don't mention it," he said under his breath, plopping a tortilla on his place and ladling sour cream a quarter of an inch thick over the entire surface. Ah, the appetite of the twelve-year-old boy. "She already got an earful." Luke swung his eyes at Mama Estela, who was chugging a beer at the counter and managing to mutter to herself at the same time.

"Yes, I threw out all the flour," Marta said. She didn't miss a trick. "The man on the news, he said that you should throw all your flour away." Mama Estela rolled her eyes, looking so much like a Cleary that I nearly did a double-take. "It's poisoned," Marta was saying. She looked like she wanted to cry.

"There were concerns of listeria in some processing plants," Rosen explained to us. He was carefully picking out protein and vegetables and arranging them beautifully on his plate. I had never seen him eat a processed carbohydrate, which I told him repeatedly was a very obnoxious trait. "It was on the news. Certain brands, with specific expiry dates, were recalled."

Darren and I both nodded, and busied ourselves with assembling our fajitas. We knew better than to get in between Marta and her mother. I almost wished I hadn't taped my gun back under my nightstand before coming down.

It wasn't the flour, of course, that had everyone on edge. Every person in that house, including Marta's son Eddie, had moved here with their eyes wide open to the potential risks. None of it had been easy – Rosen and Marta had upped sticks and moved countries so they could stay with the boys. In Fred's more obnoxious moments he pointed out to Darren and me that the fact that we were paying them more than double the going rate would have had some influence on their decisions. I liked to point out that they agreed to come to Canada before any talk of salaries was mentioned. I doubt they would have accepted so easily if Darren hadn't been part of the package. While they showed Fred respect, it was apparent to anyone with a scintilla of emotional intelligence that there was no love lost there. They had witnessed the tension and fallout in Ginger's house when her husband Fred had fucked the boys' nanny, who just happened to be an evil bitch of the Smith Family, and instrumental in getting Ginger killed.

That kind of mistake sticks in the craw. Sometimes I pitied Fred for the guilt he'd always carry, and sometimes I hated him for his role in the whole debacle. But he felt the same about me, so we were even-steven on that score.

Everybody at Marta's seemed slightly jangly. Darren and Rosen talked to the kids about what Dave's crew had uncovered, and that while we knew Michael Vernon Smith had flown into Toronto, we couldn't be sure he was still here. And so on. I was only half listening. I slipped upstairs right after I finished eating. Darren and Rosen were handling everything, and I couldn't sit still. I had to move. I had to do something useful.

I had to see about getting some coke.

I jumped into the shower for five minutes, then changed into one of my basic bar uniforms: jeans, combat boots, and a well-cut black shirt. I slicked my dark hair off my face – it was short now, very short, which every male in the house had made clear was not their favorite look. My hair is naturally blonde, like Darren's, but I felt almost like an imposter as a blonde. I didn't have the personality for it. Ginger did. Ginger glowed. I glowered.

I spent about three minutes putting on eyeliner, mascara, and some red lipstick. Darren had told me that with my new shorter hair, I looked a bit like the chick from *The Matrix* movies. And apparently I smiled about as much as she did, as well. But that actress, Carrie-Anne Moss, had a lean, shapely body, whereas with all the running I'd been doing my naturally thin body was starting to look gaunt again. Not like when I'd lost thirty pounds on the Crack Diet. I didn't think I looked unhealthy. But the angles of my face were becoming more severe, and of course I was firmly into my mid-thirties, when a face loses the softness of its twenties. I tried to look at myself objectively, which isn't something I did with any regularity.

I didn't look like somebody a stranger would mess with, I didn't think. "Lesbian dominatrix on her night off" was the phrase Darren and Fred had come up with, when they'd had the chance to see me when I was on my way out to prowl. They seemed to think it was a teasing sort of insult, but I liked it.

I started to leave, but slipped back into my room and rooted through the shoebox I kept random bits of jewelry in.

I slid heavy rings on each hand. The better to hit you with, my dear. I definitely wasn't on the prowl tonight; there was no way in hell I was picking up any man who was leering at exotic dancers in Helen of Troy. But I was a woman alone going to a strip club in the evening, a strip club where my brother-in-law had been badly beaten the night before. I was on a fact-finding mission, a foray into enemy territory. But if someone was going to get hurt, I was damn sure it wasn't going to be me.

I debated slipping a gun into my boot, but it was possible the bar had a metal detector at the door. Some clubs did, nowadays. Even a very thorough bouncer might have found that I was carrying. I didn't particularly mind going down for shooting Michael Vernon Smith, but I wasn't keen on the idea of facing charges for carrying a loaded firearm into a strip club. However, in my bag I carried my honeycomb brush – an innocent-looking round hairbrush that concealed a very lethal-looking stiletto dagger in its handle. It had been a gift from Dave, months back. I was as thrilled with it as some women would be with diamonds.

Always be prepared, that's my motto. The Boy Scouts stole it.

My plan had been to slip out undetected, but it was earlier

than I would usually head out, and with today's news, it wouldn't be fair for me to just disappear. So with great trepidation, I made my way back down to Marta's kitchen to let everyone know I was going out for a couple of hours.

I walked in on an unusual quiet moment. Everybody was eating and/or checking their phones. Even Mama Estela had the news on. My boots weren't silent, so my entrance was impossible to downplay.

"Oh," Darren said. He looked at me, expressionless, over his reading glasses. "Kitten with a whip, I see."

"This is how I always look," I said. Defensive? Me?

"I have seen you wear makeup about five times in the last year," he said. "Now you look like you're trying to be an evil Kardashian sister."

"Bitch, please. I do not have their… assets."

"You could be their skinny German cousin," Rosen piped up.

The boys were laughing like a pair of six-year-olds. Mama Estela looked me up and down with her eyebrows raised up to her hairline, and muttered something in Spanish to Marta, who blushed and continued scrubbing the table. I wondered if I had overdone it a bit with the lipstick.

"Now that you've all had your fun," I said, "I'm going out for a few hours to meet a friend. I will not be late." I looked at Darren when I said that, so he knew that I wasn't out doing the nasty, two nights on the trot. "Where's Fred?"

"Gone out," Darren said, looking at me meaningfully.

"Oh?" I didn't want to say anything incriminating in front of the boys. "And one of you gentlemen didn't want to join him?"

"He didn't tell us he was going."

"He texted us to say we should wait up. He wants to watch a movie with us," Luke said. He was eyeing the leftovers on the table as though deciding whether or not to go back into battle.

"Well, good," I said. "Maybe I'll watch one, too, as long as it's not something that will make me want to rip my eyes out of my head. And remember, this is the last night of staying up late. School soon."

"*Say Anything...*?" Rosen said. He looked at the boys. "It's your auntie's favorite film." I was going to correct him, but the three of them started jabbering about downloading soundtracks.

"I really won't be long," I said to Darren quietly. "Maybe I'll run into Fred."

"Jesus," he said. He rubbed his eyes. "Text every fifteen minutes, please."

"Every thirty, and don't worry," I said. "Strictly getting the lay of the land."

"I've heard that before," Darren said. He glanced at the boys and lowered his voice further. "We have enough on our plates, Danny. This isn't our fight."

"Just making sure," I said. I turned and clomped out of the kitchen, a little put out that nobody had at least told me I looked, I don't know, good. It's disconcerting for a girl to have a room full of the males in her life bust a gut when she changes her look a little.

Good thing I'm not much of a girl.

Helen of Troy was about a twenty-minute walk from the bakery, and the rain had just stopped. It was good to be outside, to feel like the dingy streets in our part of town had been washed clean.

I thought I could smell the beach, Lake Ontario being only a quarter of a mile away, but it was probably the rain and wishful thinking. The oppressive mugginess in the air had been flushed away, but it was still a warm enough evening. I felt rested after my long nap, and energized. I had to be doing something, and this was all I could think to do tonight that might be of any use. Besides, if Fred was there, he was going to need backup. He must have it bad for this girl, I figured, if he was going back a second night, after getting the stuffing beaten out of him less than twenty-four hours ago.

I walked with purpose, and with even more awareness than usual. The street was quiet; most people were probably inside eating dinner. Besides, it wasn't a part of town with a lot of foot traffic. I kept thinking of Fred wandering back into that place, and sighed heavily as I walked. As if I didn't have enough to worry about, without him falling in love with a stripper in peril and wanting to play white knight. But it made me pick up my pace. And think of a strategy for when I walked in – I wanted to keep a low profile. And if Fred had somehow managed to make it past the bouncer at the door, I didn't want him to see me right away. Or more to the point, I didn't want to be seen with him. I wanted to talk to Zuzi by myself, woman to woman. Fighter to stripper, as it were.

Helen of Troy was trying to be an up-market strip club in a down-market neighborhood. The sign was in neon red cursive, smaller than you might expect, and the brickwork looked like it had recently been painted, a creamy white that would have to be repainted every few months to keep it looking good. But it did look good.

I felt happy. I always felt oddly happy when I was about to walk into a bar. Not because of the alcohol – I enjoyed wine, but it didn't rule my life like crack had. No, it was the theater of it, the becoming a different person depending on what I wanted to achieve. If I went on the prowl in an upscale suit bar, I dressed and spoke differently to when I targeted a basic pub. In Helen of Troy, the stakes were even higher, and the buzz I was getting as I approached the door made me smile. I paused for a second to wipe the smile off my face, though. I was going to be cool when I made my entrance, polite but unsmiling, until I got a sense of the place.

Voices to my right made me turn my head.

Fred, getting into a black town car with what looked like tinted windows. He was climbing into the backseat, of his own volition. Nobody was with him, no stripper or bouncer.

But inside the car, through the open door as Fred got in, I caught a glimpse of a man. My view lasted for perhaps three seconds, but I knew who that man was.

Fred had just gotten into a car with Michael Vernon Smith. And that car had pulled into traffic, turned left and away.

EIGHT

My hands weren't even shaking. I noticed, somehow, how calm I felt.

I called Fred's number first. It went directly to voicemail. I didn't leave a message.

I dialed Darren, and when he answered I quickly told him what I'd seen.

"Okay," he said, and I knew my brother's trying-to-sound-calm voice. The boys must be close by. "Are you going to make the calls?"

"Yes, I'll make the calls. You take care of things there." I could hear Matty's gurgling laugh in the background, and Eddie's high-pitched, uncontrollable giggle. "Take care of the boys."

"On it," he said. "Call me back when you've talked to everybody."

I stood on the sidewalk, lost in inaction for a moment. If only I had grabbed a cab the second they'd pulled out, I could have followed them. But it was early evening, and while there might be cabs around here at closing time, I didn't see any now. And it was too late.

I phoned Dave and got his voicemail. It was early morning wherever he was – Tokyo? – and he could be on a plane, or sleeping. Then I phoned Paul Belliveau. Handy having a cop friend on speed dial.

"Hey, Danny. You should have brought the boys up to the cottage this weekend," he said when he answered the phone. He sounded relaxed and happy, as though he was on his third beer.

"I should have," I said. I wished we had. I couldn't remember the reason Darren and I had decided not to go up north to the Belliveaus' holiday cottage when they'd invited us. The boys loved it there, and so did we.

I told him what I'd just seen and the events of the last twenty-four hours, quickly. I was hoping he'd volunteer to make the calls for me: to the FBI, RCMP, and whatever other law enforcement agencies were looking for Smith. I didn't like to interrupt his weekend, but I wanted him to take care of this for me so much that my fingers were actually crossed. I have nothing against law enforcement, but there was a quality to some of them that brought out teenage snarkiness in me. Especially after what I'd been through with the RCMP in Nova Scotia. Not to mention Harry Miller, the Orange County cop who'd been one of Smith's acolytes.

"I hate to do this," I said. "Tell Joanne I'm sorry. But I'm standing on the side of the road right now. You can use shorthand when you talk to these people. I just seem to piss them all off."

"I wonder why," he said. "I'll make the calls." He sounded very serious, and very sober. "But I want you to get yourself back to The Fortress, and I mean now." Belliveau had had a good look at our place, at our security, and since then liked to call our home The Fortress. *Ha bloody ha.* Still, I liked it. "I'm coming back down. Oh shit, I can't drive right now. I'll eat something and leave in an hour."

"Beer?" I asked.

"Beer," he said. "Two or three. Danny, how sure are you? Really? You said you only saw him for a few seconds? It's possible you saw him because you know he flew into town."

"I know," I said. "And I wouldn't say I'm a hundred percent." I was pacing up and down the sidewalk, and a car slowed beside me. I looked in the window, and the male driver made a gesture that indicated that he thought I was on the game. I gave him the finger and he drove off. "Maybe eighty? Probably more. Besides, Paul, what else could it be? Why would Fred be getting into the back of a town car?"

"Well, why would he get into Smith's town car?" Belliveau said. Good question.

"The boys," I said quickly. "It must have been something about the boys."

"But they're safe," he said quickly. "You talked to Darren."

"Yes. And I heard them in the background. Everything was fine."

"I'm sending a patrol car to pick you up and take you home," Paul said. "Call me again when you get there safely."

"Don't bother," I said. "I'll get there faster on foot."

"It's not just about speed, Danny, it's about—" he started to say, but I just told him I'd call him when I got inside, and hung up.

I pulled out my stiletto-hairbrush, adjusted the strap of the bag across my body, and started running toward home.

Zuzi the Stripper could wait. But if she had anything to do

with bringing Fuckface Smith back into our lives, I'd tear her into little pieces. With a smile on my face.

I'd done so many runs of shame throughout the summer that it only took me six or seven minutes to get back to the bakery. Every light was on, it seemed.

Both of the ground-floor entrances to the bakery had been installed with biometric iris scanners as well as smart locks, which unlocked the main deadbolts with the push of a remote button, which we all carried on keychains. But because we didn't want to call attention to ourselves, to our home, by having such sophisticated equipment in a neighborhood like ours, we had built a false entrance into the front door, the one off the sidewalk. So anyone wanting to gain entry had to go through the front door – a push-button coded security door; not as obvious and certainly not as expensive as a biometric scanner – and then stand inside an entranceway about five feet long to access the iris scanner.

A pain in the ass. A welcome and necessary one, as far as the adults were concerned, but a pain in the ass nonetheless.

Rosen was waiting inside for me, a shotgun held at his side. I nodded at him, and tried to smile. He just said, "Tell me what you want me to do."

If there's anything better than a loyal and armed ex-commando guarding you and your family when you don't know when the boogeymen might try to attack, I don't know what it is.

I hugged him, a rare thing. His body was like coiled wire. He didn't relax into the hug, but he patted me on the back. "Where is everybody?" I said.

"The boys are on the thing," he said. The Xbox, he meant. He hated it so much he refused to even name it. It usually drove me around the bend the number of hours the boys could waste on that thing, but I've never been so glad for their distraction.

"Good," I said. "Good." I stood for a minute. After the shock of seeing Fred get into the town car, and seeing Smith inside it, and then the sprint home, the peace felt almost anti-climactic. I was ready now. I was ready to take on all comers, to attack anyone who tried to get inside.

"You'd better put that away," I said, nodding at the gun. "I called Belliveau. We'll have cops here any minute."

"Lock it up?" he said. He looked perturbed. He didn't want to relinquish his watch.

"Lock it up, but stay close to the gun safe." The last thing we needed was for some enthusiastic cop to do a full search and take any of us in for careless storage of firearms.

"Why are you holding a hairbrush?" Rosen said. "Emergency grooming?"

"Funny." He had definitely spent too much time with the Clearys. I showed him the stiletto.

He shrugged. "Better than nothing," he said. He walked into the back, where he kept the main gun lock-up.

He was a hard man to impress.

Darren was on his way down the stairs. "I haven't told the boys anything yet," he said.

"Well, we're going to have to think of something quick," I said. I told him about talking to Belliveau. I threw my brush back into my bag, and pulled out a bottle of water. I felt sweaty and flustered. I wasn't looking forward to a police visit, and the boys would know who was at the door as soon as the bell rang. We had monitors with a live feed of the entrances in every room.

What can I say? Security and privacy don't always go hand in hand.

"The truth," Rosen said, from around the corner. "Tell them the truth."

I looked at Darren. "He's right. I'll meet you up there in five." Darren nodded and took the stairs two at a time. I poured water into my mouth and called Paul Belliveau. I'd almost forgotten, which would have meant that he'd probably have helicopters and, who knew, a SWAT team coming.

"I'm in the car," Belliveau said by way of greeting.

"I'm home. Safe as houses." I watched Rosen doing push-ups. The man was a machine. And, like me, seemingly unable to stay still when he was waiting for trouble. "Darren and I are about to tell the boys. Any chance we could avoid a whole gang of cops showing up at my door?"

"I'll be there in three hours," he said. "I called in a couple of favors. You're not in my division but I'll take your statement myself." He swore, and I heard his car horn. "I'm getting off the phone, Danny. Call me again if you hear from Fred, or if you hear… anything."

I assured him I would, and trudged up the stairs to talk to the boys. It was not a conversation I was looking forward to.

Matty, Luke, and Eddie were all sprawled on the floor of the third-floor family room, the boys' sanctuary, and where we tended to congregate for movies. They paused the game when I came in. I sat on the floor, cross-legged. Darren, who was sitting on the couch opposite me, looked nervous. He did not have a poker face.

"What's going on?" Matty said. "Did something happen to Fred?" The boys didn't call Fred "Dad", and I'd never had the heart to ask any of them if that was a new thing since Ginger had died, or if they never had. I couldn't remember them calling him anything when I'd gone to California to visit them all, years ago.

"He's fine," Darren said. Eddie stood up as if to leave, but I motioned for him to stay.

"It's okay, Eduardo," I said. "No secrets, remember?" It was something we'd drilled into the kids. We tried to be honest with them, even with things kids their age shouldn't have to hear. But they'd had an unconventional upbringing, and to keep them safe we had to live a different way. They understood that. I hoped they understood that.

"I went to meet Fred after dinner," I said. "He was at a pub down the road." Honesty is one thing, but telling the boys that their father had been hanging out at a strip club night after night was not, in my view, necessary.

"But you're all dressed up," Luke said.

"Luke, I'm wearing lipstick," I said, and laughed. "Honest to God, you guys drive me crazy sometimes. Can't a girl put on lipstick in this house?"

"Not if that girl is you, apparently," Darren said. "You scared us." He pretended to shiver in horror, and the boys laughed. I threw a cushion at him.

"So what's the problem? Did you and Fred get into a fight? Argument, I mean." Matt was trying not to use the words "fight"

86

and "argument" interchangeably, at Rosen's urging.

"No. What happened was, just as I arrived, I saw your dad getting into a car and driving away. And his phone's off." I cleared my throat. "It was a big car, sort of like a small limousine. A town car. And Fred got into the backseat."

Luke and Matty looked at each other. I had no idea what they were communicating to each other, but the way they did it reminded me so much of Ginger and me that I nearly welled up. I shook my head and willed it away.

"Now, here's the sort of scary part," I said. "There was a man already in the backseat when Fred got in, and I think – I think, I'm not a hundred percent sure – that it was Michael Vernon Smith."

Eddie stood up, then. He'd been trained and schooled like everybody else under this roof, and he knew that name. He knew that Michael Vernon Smith was the reason why we lived with so much security, and he knew that Smith was responsible for his friends' mother's death. "I'm ready," he said. "I'll kill that man if he does anything bad." Eddie was ten, and small for his age. But I'd seen him training with Rosen, and the kid was fearless. His fists were clenched, and he looked fierce.

"Come here, Eddie," I said, and patted the floor next to me. "Sit with me." I kept my eyes on the twins. Eddie hesitated but did what I said. I put my arm around him and kissed his temple. "I feel safer knowing you guys have been working with Rosen. And I trust you with my life. With all our lives." I grabbed his chin and looked him in the eye. "But you are not going to have to kill him. Okay? You're safe. We're all safe here," I said, and looked at the boys.

"Fred's not," Luke said.

"Danny isn't even totally sure it was Smith, guys," Darren said gently.

"No," I said. "And Paul is on his way here right now to talk to me, and take a statement." They loved Paul, especially Matty. He remembered Paul from the hospital, on the horrible night when I'd sat powerless over my husband's body as he bled out. Jack and I had gone to rescue the twins from their kidnappers, and it had gone very wrong. At the hospital, Paul Belliveau was the only person in authority who insisted that a traumatized Matty be allowed to stay with me, when the nurses wanted us in separate rooms. "Remember, every law enforcement agency in the country – and in the States, and everywhere – is looking for this man. If it was him, they'll find him."

"*You'll* find him," Matty said. He looked me dead in the eye. His were so much like mine, deeply set and intense. "You'll find him, Auntie, and you'll kill him." I held Matty's stare, and nodded, a micro-nod that only he would notice.

"We have to find Fred though," Luke said. "Why aren't you guys out looking for Fred?" He had tears on his face, and my heart broke, right there in my chest. If Matty was like me, Luke was the image of his mother, and there were times it was almost painful for me to look at him. Of the two boys, most people would think that Luke was the sunny, stable one. But he had been away from his family – kidnapped – for longer than Matt had, and after that it was months before he said much of anything, to anyone except his twin. Darren and I had spent many hours late at night quietly talking about, and worrying about, Luke.

"Luke, if we had any idea where to look, we would," Darren said. "But the police are looking, and they're looking hard. And remember, we're not even sure…"

Luke got up and left the room, and a second later his bedroom door slammed. Darren started to go after him, but Matt was already halfway across the room, and stopped him. "He'll be okay," he said. He looked at me. "Just find them." And he followed his brother down the hall.

I gave Eddie a squeeze, then stood up. "Darren, maybe you should take Eddie down and have a chat with Marta and Mama E. Put them in the picture."

"I can do that," Eddie said.

"Yup, you can," Darren said, "but I'm going with you. I didn't get enough to eat at dinner. I want to raid your fridge." He grabbed the kid by the shoulders and marched him out, and as they left the room I heard Eddie advising Darren not to tell his mother, Marta, that he hadn't gotten enough dinner. She'd never forgive herself. She wouldn't stop until she got him fat.

I paced back and forth. I tried Fred's cell again, leaving a third message. I looked at the time. Paul Belliveau wouldn't be here for at least two and a half hours.

Waiting. I can't do waiting.

I wanted crack so badly I thought I was going to lose my mind.

I thought of Matty's eyes, the look he'd given me. I thought of Luke, and all he'd been through, and how much he was like Ginger. I thought of everything both boys had endured: losing their mother violently, and being kidnapped, torn away from their home, from their home country, even. I couldn't let them lose their father too. He might not have been the most hands-on parent, and my feelings about Fred were at best complicated, but Luke was right: I couldn't sit here while Fred was out there with that man.

And even if I was wrong, even if that wasn't Smith in the back of the town car, who was it? Why was Fred's phone off? He never turned his phone off. He was addicted to technology, refused to even put it on "Do Not Disturb" when he slept.

No. Luke was right. I couldn't stay inside the safety of this fortress while a member of my family was in danger. Darren and Rosen were here, and Belliveau was on his way.

I took the stairs two at a time down to the main level and grabbed my bag where I usually left it. I peeked around the corner and saw that the light was on in Rosen's bathroom. I went around to the door at the back, through the gym, and to my car, a basic Honda, but with bullet-proof windows that Dave had had installed for me. He "knew a guy". Dave knew guys everywhere.

I should have done our safety checks before I peeled out, but I wanted to be off the property before Rosen came after me. A block away, I pulled over and sent a text to Rosen and Darren, saying:

> Back soon. Everything's fine. Stay there.

We had GPS on all our vehicles, so if they wanted to know where I was they could find me. That old trade-off of privacy versus security, and we had opted for security.

I chucked my phone back into my bag, and pulled into traffic.

I felt better. I was not one for inaction. Unless, of course, crack cocaine was involved, in which case I could happily stay rooted to the same spot for days. Or at least, the old me could.

A few minutes later, I was pulling into the parking lot behind Helen of Troy.

This was where Fred had been beaten up. This was where he

had told his new stripper friend all about his life. And this was where Fred had gotten into a car with the man who'd killed his wife.

Someone in this building knew where Fred had been taken. And I was going to start with the stripper.

NINE

After the adrenaline flow of the last couple of hours, I somehow thought that walking into Helen of Troy would be dramatic, that the music would scratch to an abrupt stop and every head would turn in my direction in a moment of dramatic silence when a female customer entered alone.

In fact, if it hadn't been for the stripper stage, it could almost pass for a regular bar. The décor was a bit dated, despite the promising exterior, and the servers were slightly more buxom than in your average bar. Unless Hooters was your average bar. Their skirts were ridiculously short, but I'd seen female wait staff in outfits nearly as revealing in my Summer of the Prowl. The bouncer at the door barely glanced at me, engrossed as he was in his sudoku. As I paused inside the doorway, surveying the room – and clocking washrooms and exits – a waitress balancing a tray of four pints of beer cheerfully told me to sit wherever I liked. The place appeared to seat maybe two hundred people, and was about half full. People at maybe half of those tables seemed to be eating food. From a glance, the cheerful stripper onstage really did look like she could be working herself through college, and the music wasn't overly loud.

All in all, I'd been in pseudo-English chain pubs here in town that had more atmosphere of danger or sleaze. This was the place where the girls were being forced to turn tricks against their will? True, it was still early, but I could only see three or four dancers working the tables to sell lap dances. At first blush, I couldn't even spot any private rooms, or VIP rooms, where the girls could take their high-rolling customers for more effective wallet-bilking.

There were two business types chatting quietly at the bar, sharing a plate of calamari. I took a stool at the other end of the bar, and wished like hell I could smoke in here. What's the world coming to when you can't smoke in a strip club?

Other than the bouncer, the bartender was the only male staff member I could see. He approached with a smile, wiping down the bar in front of me and putting down a coaster. "What can I get you, miss?" he said, which made me happy. I hated ma'am.

"Vodka and lemonade, please," I said. I smiled, but in a distant way. I was pretty sure he was going to try to chat – which was a good thing; I could get info from him – but I did not want to encourage him to flirt. Then I told myself to get a grip. This guy was surrounded by beautiful dancers all night, girls with a lot more youth and… assets to offer than I did. It made me relax a bit.

When he put my drink down, he asked if I wanted to run a tab.

"Uh, no," I said. That would mean giving him a credit card, and in case Michael Vernon Smith did, in fact, have anything to do with this place, there was no point in advertising myself. I pulled a fifty from my wallet and laid it down. He nodded and made change, and when he laid what looked like thirty-eight bucks back on the bar – twelve bucks for a mixed drink in a strip club was actually pretty cheap, I thought – I pushed the ten back to him.

"Thanks," I said. His nametag said Patrick.

"Oh, thanks very much," he said, disappearing the bill so quickly and effectively on his person that I didn't even see where it went. "Want to see a menu?"

"No, thanks. Actually, I live in the neighborhood. I had time to kill, and I heard an old family friend was working here. Thought I'd check it out." I took a sip of my drink. It was good. "This place is most definitely not what I was expecting."

He laughed like he'd heard that one before. "I know," he said. "But is that a good thing or a bad thing?"

"A good thing," I said. "I think." I took another swig of my drink, hoping he'd ask.

"So who's your friend?" he said. Good.

"Zuzi," I said. "Not so much my friend, but my brother's friend."

He snorted and wiped the bar in front of him. "Zuzi," he said. "She's the only dancer here who doesn't use a stage name. I mean, where are you going to go from Zuzi?"

"Well, she could've gone in the opposite direction," I said. "Rosemary. Susan."

He laughed. "Marjorie."

I was smiling, but I was impatient for him to tell me if she was working. Get this party started, as it were. Just then, a group of young guys came in, several in rugby shirts, all looking like they lived in a frat house. Fan-fucking-tastic. And to top it off, instead of heading to the tables, they made a beeline for the bar.

Judging by the decibel level they brought in with them, they had obviously started the party several hours earlier.

If I'd been the bouncer, I'd have given serious thought before letting them in. But the dude at the door still had his head in his puzzle book. The tip of his tongue was poking out between his lips as he tried to erase an answer. I watched as he realized he was writing with a pen. I doubted his Mensa membership was going to be in the mail anytime soon.

My new bartender friend Patrick was busy checking IDs – good for him – so I sighed and stood up, grabbing my drink off the bar. I was going to find a table, see if I couldn't get one of the dancers talking. I was sliding my bag across my body, glass in tow, when I felt a hand on my ass.

"You off-duty, baby? Wanna give us a lap dance?" I could feel his breath on my neck.

Oh, how I wanted to tear that hand off his arm. I wanted it so badly I could taste it. But I was there to find Zuzi, or any of the other dancers that might know Fred. I was not there to get eighty-sixed for crippling frat boys. Not that they didn't deserve it.

I reached back and very deliberately removed the kid's hand from my ass.

"I don't work here," I said, without turning around. "But I'm sure you'll have no problem finding lots of nice girls here who will dance for you, if you pay them enough. Ones who don't mind your breath."

There were eight of them, and I was surrounded by three. Size-wise, two of them were no taller than I was – maybe five-ten, five-eleven – but as the one who grabbed my ass was now pressed into me, I had a good idea that he was a lot bigger.

Because, of course, that's the kind of luck I have.

The two who'd heard what I said were cracking up, which I knew didn't bode well for me. Nobody likes being made a fool of in front of their friends, but when you're talking about a pack of frat boys, it escalates the chances of something stupid happening by a few orders of magnitude.

"Just kidding, honey," I said. "Hey," I called to the bartender, "get this guy a drink on my tab." I hoped he wouldn't say, "No way, you don't have a tab." I was hoping he'd signal to the bouncer that maybe, perhaps, he should look up from his remedial reading and do his job. He nodded, and continued making drinks, his attention on the sudden influx of orders. That, or he just didn't want to get involved.

I slid away from the bar, threw a smile over my shoulder to make them think I was a good sport – hardly – and started to thread myself through the guys standing around. They had all moved over closer to us. They sensed there was going to be a show.

Can a woman not go into a strip club to question strippers about her brother-in-law's disappearance anymore? I was becoming giddy. I could feel the laughter bubbling up from my belly. It was so ludicrous. I'd spent most of my summer in bars all across the city, and on some of those nights – nights when I couldn't get Dave out of my head, or chase the demons out of my soul – I would have been more than happy to fight anybody who looked at me wrong. The first time I want to actually keep a low profile, I get groped by Neanderthals. I knew a couple of people might look at me – an unaccompanied woman in a strip club is a natural curiosity – but I was really hoping I could go in, get info, and get out before Belliveau got to the bakery.

I was nearly past them, and busy patting myself on the back for the self-control I had just exhibited, when three things happened.

A strong hand grabbed me around the neck and pulled me back.

Someone else grabbed one of my breasts. Hard.

And I saw a young woman in a neon-pink negligee staring at me with her hand over her mouth, before she went skittering away in the other direction.

Zuzi? I thought. And then I fought.

TEN

I'd underestimated the potential hazards of being swarmed by drunk frat boys. I was too busy worrying about Fred and Michael Vernon Smith to take a few college kids on a bender seriously.

We all live trapped in our skin, and even when we look in the mirror we rarely see what others see. Because of my years of fighting – though they were a long time ago now – and my more recent history of doing physical harm to some bad people, I sometimes forgot that despite it all, and despite being in pretty good shape, I am, in fact, a woman. And with that fact comes less muscle mass and less sheer size than a lot of men. Not to mention the fact that, to a certain breed of man, a woman is an easy target for violence.

I'm usually prepared for the potential of regular street violence, and when I'm on high alert for danger, I feel confident enough. But in a situation like this, being inside a bar where staff are present, where most humans generally observe social niceties and don't randomly attack each other? Well, color me embarrassed. I didn't see it coming.

The one who had pulled me back by my neck had managed to get me into something of a chokehold, though I could tell he tried to make it look like he simply had his arm playfully around his girlfriend's neck. And even the bartender wouldn't really be able to see what was fully happening; the boys had gathered around and effectively blocked me from view.

The one who'd grabbed my breast was directly in front of me, and red-faced from booze and excitement. He grabbed his crotch and said something I couldn't hear, because the blood was pounding in my ears with adrenaline and rage. But his intent was clear enough.

I am one of the small percentage of women who have never been sexually assaulted in any way. Sheer luck; I'd put myself in enough compromising positions over the years. But as the arm of the guy behind me tightened around my neck, I imagined what these guys could, and would, do to a drunk young woman their own age at a party. I thought about what had happened to my sister.

I wanted blood.

I reared my head back as hard as I could, to connect with the face of the one holding me. I could tell he wasn't the big one; he was only a little taller than I was, so while I wasn't able to get enough leverage to inflict maximum damage, the back of my skull connected handily with his nose.

With one hand I reached behind before he could back up, grabbed his crotch as hard as I could, and twisted. I'd noticed that they were all wearing shorts when they walked in, because it made me wonder about the lack of dress code here. The move wouldn't have worked as well if he'd been wearing jeans, but with the preppy, light cotton shorts he was wearing, I was able to get a good grip.

I was not kind to that kid's scrotum. I used a lot of my strength on wrenching his balls as hard as I could. If there is a God, I did enough damage to ensure that he'll never be able to procreate.

The one behind me collapsed onto the floor. My body was free. The guy who'd grabbed his crotch pulled his arm back to punch me in the face, which I easily ducked and shouldered his abdomen, squatting quickly and using his momentum to flip him over my shoulder. It looks impressive, that move, but it's a lot easier than throwing a punch. From the sounds behind me, he landed on twisted-nuts guy. I hoped he'd broken his neck, but I wasn't that lucky. The other one would have broken his fall, and he'd be back on his feet swinging in seconds.

A few of the kids looked petrified and immediately backed away from me. Later when they told the story, they'd probably say they didn't believe in attacking a woman, but I know fear when I see it.

The last one in my sightline, a short, muscular guy who looked like a wrestler, was charging at me. For one wild second he reminded me of The Rhino in the old *Spider-Man* animated show. I couldn't have moved out of his way even if I'd had time. There was no room. So in a pure – and very stupid – Hail Mary move, I chucked the contents of my vodka lemonade in his face, then brought the empty glass down on the kid's head. Which did manage to stop him just before he would have tackled me. I understood my mistake when I realized that there was much more blood coming from my hand than from his skull.

Rhino hadn't fallen over, just appeared dazed. But when he caught a look at the blood pumping out of the vein I'd managed to open on my palm, his face went gray, and he keeled over in a dead faint.

Vasovagal syncope at the sight of blood. Tough guy. He was

a fainter, like me. For a minute, I nearly felt sorry for him.

The other two boys had backed further away, and I quickly turned to check on the condition of Twisted Nuts and Mad Dog behind me. They were both still on the floor. Mad Dog had stayed down after all, and was nursing what looked like a possible broken finger from his tumble over my shoulder.

But I'd forgotten one. The big guy, the one who'd groped my ass in the first place. He was leaning on the bar, behind his two friends on the floor. He glanced at Twisted Nuts, who was curled up in a ball and seemed to be finished puking. The whole thing had taken probably two minutes, maybe three. Tall Guy was smiling at me meanly, and looked about to say something.

But my buddy Patrick the bartender got there first.

"Move from that spot," he said softly to Tall Guy. "Go on. I dare you." Patrick had a baseball bat slung over his shoulder. It was an old wooden one with what looked like long cast-iron nails hammered into it every few inches.

It was definitely not for Little League, that bat.

I took a breath and looked behind me. The bouncer had finally abandoned his sudoku and was standing about ten feet away blocking the door. His arms were crossed. He might not have been the smartest card in the deck, but he was built like a Buick. And when he wasn't trying to erase his answers in pen, the expression on his ugly mug was enough to make my knees feel a little wobbly, and I wasn't even on the receiving end.

Though when I looked back at my hand, I thought maybe my wobbliness had more to do with that.

"Bar towel, please? A clean one, if you've got it," I called to Patrick.

Without taking his eyes away from Tall Guy, Patrick tossed me a white towel from under the bar, and I quickly wrapped my hand with it.

I tried not to think about how fast it soaked with blood. I didn't want to ruin my new macho image by fainting next to Rhino.

"Sheldon?" Patrick called out.

"Yep," the bouncer said, still standing with his arms crossed, looking like The Mountain from *Game of Thrones*. Sheldon? I doubted I had ever heard a less appropriate name. Snake, maybe, or Tank. Big Lou. Anything but Sheldon.

"Keep an eye on these patrons for me, would you? Make sure they're comfortable, don't slip on any blood or vomit, anything like that."

"Yep," Sheldon said. He looked at Tall Guy. "You comfortable, sir?"

I nearly – nearly – felt sorry for the kid. "Absolutely," Tall Guy said. "Very comfortable." He took a swig of beer and looked anywhere but at Sheldon, who hadn't budged, or even blinked, as far as I could tell.

Patrick stashed his bat, and motioned me to the other end of the bar. I stepped over Rhino, who was coming to. On my way past the bar, I looked out at the rest of the club. A few dancers and wait staff were standing watching, but as far as I could see, the only patrons who had even noticed were the two businessmen at the bar eating calamari. It happened quickly, and the bar was situated on the opposite side of the club from the stage.

"Good for you, miss," one of the businessmen said. "I'm sorry we didn't step in. It was pretty much over before we'd even noticed."

"Very impressive," the other one said. "I'd shake your hand, but…" He looked at the blood-soaked towel wrapped around it. "You should teach a class," he said, after I'd half-smiled and moved off. "I'd like my daughter to learn how to take care of herself."

"Tell your daughter not to hang out at strip clubs," the other one said to his friend. He sounded serious, not snarky, but I stopped dead in my tracks and turned back around.

"That, sir, is horseshit," I said. I came closer. "His daughter should be able to go anywhere she likes, without abusive rapey assholes like them," I nodded at the frat boys, "harassing her, or touching her, or saying any fucking thing they like about her body or her beauty or whatever else they feel is their right to say. If your daughter had a job here, like these girls," I said, pointing my chin at the dancers who were standing a few feet away, watching us, "maybe even just a job bartending to get through school. Or dancing – whatever. But if your daughter had a job here and was sitting at the bar after her shift waiting for a friend, say, and a bunch of drunken idiots decide she's fair game, she must be a slut, for sale or for free, less than human, because she's sitting in a place like this? Would you blame her, or would you blame the fucking sociopathic dickwads who targeted her?"

My voice had gotten louder. My hand was starting to hurt, really hurt, and I was having a post-adrenaline comedown. Plus, my chances of being inconspicuous here and getting any info had just been flushed down the toilet by a bunch of walking penises.

Not that I was angry or anything.

The dancers watching had been joined by two of the waitresses, and they all clapped and cheered when I was finished.

"Preach, honey," one of them said, and I flashed her a grin.

"I'm sorry," one of the men said. "But please, miss – you have to get to the hospital."

I held my hand up, above heart level. I remembered that from first aid. "Thanks. And I'm sorry. My blood is up, you know?" I looked at my hand. With the bloody towel, I looked like I had just walked off a horror film set. "Literally. Ha. Enjoy your evening." I walked toward Patrick.

"I'd ask to see your hand, but I can tell it's worse than I thought it was," he said. "You probably want to get to the hospital. Do you want me to get you a cab? Or phone the police? I'm sure the manager will want to talk to you, make sure you're okay, but you might want to get that looked at first."

"I'll do it," a woman said, appearing beside me. She was one of the women who'd been watching, though I'm not sure how much she'd seen. "I'll take her downstairs to the kitchen and see how bad it is, see if I can't sort it out." She looked at me. "I'm Kelly. I'm in med school, second year. Before that I was a vet." She was wearing a leopard-print teddy and, even in her towering heels, she was a good three or four inches shorter than I was. And compared to some of the girls, she was dressed like a nun.

"What would you like to do?" Patrick said to me. "Hey – what's your name?"

"Danny," I said. "I don't want to sit in Emerg for six hours. I trust Kelly. Even though she's obviously not old enough to be in second-year med school after having been a vet. Are you a crazy person, or just some kind of savant?" I said to her. I wanted to get away from the mess I'd left at the door, and get my hand looked at. I couldn't afford an injury, not now. Not with Smith close by.

"Neither," she said. "It's just dark in here. I'm older than I look." She looked at the bartender. "Patrick, get her a shot of something," she said. She looked at my face, at how white I'd probably become – I was feeling a bit faint again – and stopped him. "Make that a bottle."

Patrick grabbed something from the top shelf, a half-full bottle of Grey Goose, and handed it to Kelly. I looked over at the other end of the bar, where Tall Guy was pretending to study his phone nonchalantly, as though he was too cool to be fazed by what had just happened.

"Listen, do whatever you want about the police," I said. "But maybe just kick them out, bar them, whatever." I looked at Rhino, who was being helped off the floor by the two young guys who had stayed out of it.

"I know that's what management would prefer," Patrick said. "Having a bunch of cops in the place isn't exactly good for business. But it's totally your call," he added quickly.

"No, that's fine," I said. "Maybe they've learned a lesson."

"I doubt it," Kelly said. "But never mind. Types like that wouldn't learn a lesson even if they were arrested, so it'd be a wash anyway. And then we'd all be here making statements until the wee small hours." She gently took my arm and led me to a door at the back, past the washrooms. We descended a steep set of stairs.

"How do you do that in those shoes?" I wanted to know, as she clacked briskly down the stairs ahead of me.

"Same way you get to Carnegie Hall," she said. "Practice, practice, practice." She led me through what was obviously the bar storage, and then into a large, brightly lit kitchen. I was relieved to see that it was meticulously clean. It even smelled like lemons.

"Brittany," Kelly said. She pulled a large first-aid kit out of one of the cupboards. "She's OCD. Our dressing room would be like this, but we're not supposed to touch each other's things. So when she can't hack being on the floor, she comes down here for a while and works off her demons."

"Wish mine were so easily gotten rid of," I said.

"Right? Still, I wouldn't want to suffer from a mental disorder like that. Very little peace." I sat at the table next to the wall, while Kelly washed her hands. She kicked her shoes off as she did, and she was so petite without them, she immediately looked even younger than I had thought. I watched as she grabbed a stainless steel bowl and a bottle of what looked like rubbing alcohol from another cupboard.

"How old are you?" I blurted, then said, "Sorry."

Kelly laughed, pulling on latex gloves. "I'm thirty-three."

"Your Jesus Year," I said.

"And Hamlet," Kelly said. "Or was that thirty-two?"

"You've got me there."

Kelly put a tea towel down on the table and grabbed my hand. "Let's have a look," she said, unwrapping the gory cloth. There seemed to be one pretty major cut near the webbing between my thumb and index finger, and another smaller one in the middle of my palm. Kelly pulled a bottle of sterile saline from the first-aid kit and washed the blood from my hand with it.

"These will close without stitches," she said. "I think. Well, anyway, I wouldn't attempt to stitch this outside of a hospital setting, and there are so many nerves in the hand, I doubt I'd attempt it anyway. I'd want a neurologist to do it."

"I won't sue you, I promise," I said. "If you think it should be stitched, I'll trust you to do it." I'd rather have pain now and get it over with. And there was something so calming about Kelly's presence that I did trust her. Even in leopard-print lingerie.

She shook her head. "Nope," she said. "I'm going to clean it and do my best with it. Then we're going to sit down here for half an hour while you hold your hand above your heart, like you were doing upstairs. Good call, by the way."

"I got certified in first aid, a million years ago," I said.

"It's not spurting, so you didn't hit an artery. But if I don't like how it looks in half an hour, you are going to have to go in and have it seen to."

I just nodded. "How long have you worked here?" I asked her. She was applying pressure with gauze but I knew the alcohol would be her next step, and that was going to hurt. A lot. It was time to distract myself, and maybe I'd even get some info.

"Not long," she said. "Four months, I guess. I did this before, though, when I was an undergrad in Montreal. Some nights, like tonight, you don't make any money. It's pretty dead, and people aren't spending money. But on a good night, it can be worth it." She steadied my hand. "This is going to hurt," she said, at the same time as she poured the alcohol over my hand, into the bowl she'd placed under it.

I took a swig of the Grey Goose, and closed my eyes to the pain. It was quick enough. I would have rubbing alcohol poured over open wounds once an hour for the rest of my life if I could only find Smith, and get him out of our lives for good.

"So what brought you in here?" Kelly said. She was bent over my hand, and I decided to stop looking at it. I studied her face instead. "Sometimes groups of girls come in for bachelorette parties or whatever, naughty girls night out kinds of things. Rarely a woman alone."

"Oh, I live close by, and I wanted to get out for a couple of hours. My brother knows one of the dancers, so I was kind of curious about the place." More and more I was dubious about Zuzi's story of forced prostitution. Kelly, for one, did not seem like she could be threatened into much. And both she and Patrick at the bar seemed pretty relaxed, not nervous, jumpy, or acting as though they were operating under any kind of duress. "Zuzi," I said. "Do you know her?"

"Of course," Kelly said. She didn't glance up at me, look worried, or pause. "She's a cutie. There aren't that many of us here, really. It's a small club. Kind of a family atmosphere, weird as it is to say. And we're only open at night, though the new management is talking about opening in the afternoons, but we'll see. But yeah, we may work different evenings and so on, but mostly we all know each other."

So there was new management. That part of Zuzi's story, at least, was true.

My bag was still slung over my body and I could hear my phone going crazy with texts. I had to get home. Darren was probably having a fit. And Rosen would be so mad he might actually raise his voice. I sighed.

"Is that your man, wondering where you are?" Kelly said. "Want me to reach it for you? Can you text with your left hand?"

"Family waiting for me," I said. "We're supposed to be watching a movie."

"Well, I'm almost finished here," she said. "Do you promise that you'll keep your hand elevated, and if it keeps on bleeding in a couple of hours you'll get yourself to the hospital?"

"I promise," I said, lying. "Hey – thank you so much for doing this. I'm keeping you from making money."

"No worries," she said. "Like I said, no money to be made tonight anyway. Besides, I wanted a chance to meet the woman who busted those ninja moves up there." I laughed. "Hey," she said. "I've only lived here for a few months. Like I said, I'm from Montreal. You want to grab a coffee sometime? I don't really have any, uh, non-stripper friends."

"I don't have many friends, period," I said. "That sounds bad, doesn't it? I'm a bit of a pain in the ass, to be honest. But if that doesn't bother you, sure, let's grab a coffee one of these days."

"Excellent," she said. "I'll write my phone number down for you. My phone's up in the dressing room and you're ignoring yours." I looked at my hand, which was clear of blood, the edges of the larger cut held together by butterfly tape. She found a large gauze pad and placed it over the entire palm, and wrapped my hand with some kind of self-adhesive gauze tape.

"That's quite the first-aid kit," I said. "You'd think you worked at some kind of mountain rescue facility or something."

"Same thing," she said, smiling. "Some girls need some pharmaceutical help to get up onstage and swing their bits around. Then, of course, champagne."

"Let me guess. You get girls falling from great heights a lot," I said.

"Six-inch heels aren't kind." She nodded. "All done."

My hand felt immensely better. It hurt, but I could tell it was going to be fine. Certainly better than other injuries I'd sustained over the years.

"Awesome," I said. "Thanks so much. I mean it. Now give me your number, and I'm going to get myself home before they start the movie without me."

Kelly found a pen and a Post-it note in a drawer and was writing, when one of the calamari guys walked in. His shoes hadn't made a sound, and both Kelly and I jumped.

"Jesus," she said. "You just took ten years off my life."

The man walked over to us, smiling. Kelly didn't seem alarmed that he was down here, but my face must have shown my confusion.

"Sorry! I'm Garrett," the man said. He had an open face, and looked younger than he'd seemed at the bar. "I'm the manager. I just wanted to pop down and see if Kelly's taken care of you. I am so, so sorry for what happened to you upstairs. Sheldon… well, Sheldon is a great guy, but sometimes he focuses on the wrong things."

"Don't blame him," I said. Sheldon didn't seem like the type who would have an easy time finding another job. "He probably wouldn't have been able to catch much from where he was anyway." Kelly slipped the Post-it into my good hand, and started repacking the first-aid kit.

"Leave that, Kel," Garrett said. "I'll do it. They're going to be calling you onstage in a few minutes. You should probably get ready."

"Ah, my moment to shine under the spotlight," she said. With her back to him, she glanced at my hand and shook her head slightly, looking into my eyes. "Gotta go. Hope your hand feels better, and remember to go to hospital if it keeps bleeding."

I nodded and smiled, and when Garrett turned to watch her slip into her shoes, I crumpled the note in my hand in a little ball.

Either Kelly didn't want her manager to know she'd given me her number, or there was something on the note she didn't want him to see. I stood and moved my bag and reached for my phone with my good hand, dropping the yellow Post-it into the bag at the same time.

"Thanks for coming down to check on me," I said, smiling at the guy. "She did a great job." I started to move past him, but he grabbed my arm. Gently, but he grabbed my arm.

"Can you give me five minutes? I'd really like to have a chat," Garrett said.

"Sure," I said. I rooted around in my bag, still pretending to look for my phone. I sat back down and pulled my stiletto-hairbrush out of my bag and laid it on the table, as though it was in the way of me finding the phone. Garrett sat down, and I pulled my phone out and set it on the table as well. I sat back down in my chair, and my phone obligingly dinged with another text.

"My family. They're driving me crazy," I said ruefully. "What did you want to chat about?"

Garrett smiled at me. We were alone in the basement now. I picked up my hairbrush and twirled it in my hand as though I was just fidgeting. I kept the thumb of my good left hand close to the button that would release the dagger inside.

My heart was beating quickly. I really hoped I wouldn't have to use it.

ELEVEN

"That was impressive, what you did upstairs," Garrett said.

"From what you saw," I said quickly, then wanted to bite my tongue. I knew that it was highly unlikely that the two men at the bar hadn't caught at least some of what was going on; they had the best vantage point to witness the gang coming at me.

"From what I saw," he agreed. He started packing up the first-aid kit, and once he'd packed the bottle of isopropyl alcohol away, I relaxed a bit. I'd been half expecting to have it tossed into my face. It's what I would have done, if I had wanted to subdue someone and it was at hand.

I had no real reason to think he wanted to do me any harm, of course. Other than Fred being driven away from this establishment by a serial killer and all-around nutjob earlier in the evening. Oh, and the reports that the new management – of which he was obviously a member – was forcing the dancers into some sort of prostitution.

And the fact that Kelly definitely hadn't wanted Garrett to know that she was giving me her number. Why would he care? Why would she be nervous about that?

"I really do have to hit the road," I said. "Don't worry, you won't be hearing from my lawyer or anything. I'm not the litigious type."

"I hope not," he said slowly. "May I ask you, what do you do for a living?"

"I'm unemployed," I said. True, and the simplest answer. I wanted to tell him it was none of his business, but I was very uncertain about the nature of the situation I'd found myself in, and I was keen to make it out of Helen of Troy unscathed.

Well. Relatively unscathed.

"Good. Because I'd like to offer you a job here."

"Come again?" I said. That, I was not expecting. "I'm flattered," I started to say, but he cut me off.

"Not dancing," he said. "Not that you couldn't," he added quickly, as though afraid of insulting me. "I'm sure you'd be great. Honestly."

"I'll stop you there," I said, holding my bandaged hand up. "I'd be the least likely exotic dancer on the planet, and you don't have to flatter me." He blushed, which made me relax another ten percent. I was pretty sure I'd read somewhere that psychopaths can't blush. Could be junk science, but in my experience, evil people are too narcissistic to feel embarrassment.

Then again, I'd proven myself to be an utterly shitty judge of character on more than one occasion, so that hairbrush was staying close.

"Security," he said. He put his hands flat on the table. "I've been wanting to hire a woman to do security, and someone with half a brain. You seem to more than fit the bill."

"Well, I'm a woman," I said slowly, "but I'm not sure about the brain part."

"Yeah," he said. "I wasn't going to mention it, but 'rapey' is not, strictly speaking, a word." He smiled again, and this time it didn't look so threatening.

"Never let it be said that I let silly things like proper language use get in my way when my dander is up," I said. I couldn't help smiling.

"And, by the way, I should apologize for my friend up there," Garrett said. "He's part of the company that bought Helen of Troy, the company I work for. He's up from the States for the weekend and wanted to check how I'm running things up here." I caught a slight roll of the eyes. He didn't like the man. Well, neither did I.

"How old is your daughter?" I said. He looked blankly at me. "You mentioned having a daughter, up there."

"She's ten," he said. His face lit up, and I found my tense muscles relaxing. He pulled his phone from his breast pocket and showed me the picture on the home screen of a freckle-faced redhead with her front teeth missing. "That's two years old, that picture, but it's my favorite."

"She could be Anne of Green Gables," I said.

"Those are her favorite books!" he said. "She was so excited to move to Canada. I think she was pretty disappointed when we got to Toronto and it wasn't like Avonlea."

I handed Garrett his phone. Shitty judge of character or not, I had a hard time believing that this man was an evil pimp.

"You're a lucky guy," I said.

"Yes," he said, but with a pause first. He put the phone away, and took out his business card and slid it across the table. "So will you think about it? Please give me a call. The offer will be on the table while you decide."

"You haven't really made me an offer yet," I said. "I didn't hear anything about money. Not that I want to be so crass as to bring it up."

Garrett stood and took the bowl Kelly had been using to the sink. He looked over his shoulder at me. "First rule of business, Danny. Once we start talking money, it's a negotiation." He ushered me back upstairs, chatting about Canada's Wonderland and other places he'd taken his daughter since they'd come to town at the beginning of the summer.

"Is there a back door?" I asked him once we were back on the main floor. We were by the washrooms. "I'm parked around back, and frankly I don't want to walk through the bar again tonight." Plus, I wanted to check out what was back there.

"Of course," he said. "I don't blame you. What a bunch of douchebags. Most Canadians are great, but in this business, we do sometimes see the worst." He led me the other way to the end of the hall, then left into the bar's kitchen. I'd been inside the kitchens of a few restaurants in my day, but this was by far the cleanest. A couple of the workers greeted Garrett without any obvious nervousness, no "oh shit, the boss just walked in". One was flipping burgers, and two were plating. A skinny dark-skinned guy washing dishes nodded at me without smiling. I wouldn't smile either, standing over that steam all night.

"Garrett, table four wants to see the manager," a waitress standing on the other side of the pass yelled. "A hair in their soup."

"Are you kidding? Literally, a hair in their soup?"

"No imagination," she called back, and deftly piled more plates on her arm than looked humanly possible. "Oh, and it was a blonde hair," she said over her shoulder. She was brunette, and there were no blondes in the kitchen. I laughed. Garrett rolled his eyes. He reminded me a bit of my brother Laurence for a second.

"Go," I said. I nodded at the open door, outside of which two kitchen workers in stained whites were playing hacky sack. "I've got it from here."

"Thanks," he said. "So much for the quiet weekend. Jeffrey," he called to one of the guys outside the door, "can you make sure this lady gets to her car safely?"

"You've got to be kidding," I said. "I thought you wanted to hire *me* as security."

"Hey," he said. "You just got swarmed by a bunch of testosterone cases, and you've got a busted paw. Let's just make sure you make it off the property in one piece, shall we?" He handed me another card. "In case you lose the first one. I want you to call me," he said, smiling, before rushing off to deal with his wannabe freeloaders.

The evening was beautiful, and after my experience in the bar and my tension in the basement, I was glad to be outside. Jeffrey smiled and walked about fifteen feet away from me all the way to my car, kicking the dirt as he went. If anything untoward were to happen, I doubted Jeffrey would be of much help.

Then again, I'd thought that about Dave when I first met him.

"Thanks," I said, feeling a little stupid. I didn't have a lot of experience being ushered to my vehicle. I wondered for half a second if I was supposed to tip him. I unlocked it remotely and got in, checking the back seat by rote. After I reversed out – awkwardly; my right hand wasn't good for much – I stopped and rolled down the window.

"Hey, Jeffrey," I said. He and his buddy were back to the hacky sack. "You like working here?"

He looked at his friend, who shrugged at him.

"No English," he said, with no accent I could hear, and they both went back into the kitchen and shut the door behind them.

I wondered at how Jeffrey had forgotten his English in the two minutes after Garrett had asked him to walk me to my car.

TWELVE

I parked at the bakery and looked down at my hand. It hurt. Times like this, I almost wished I could still rely on crack cocaine as a painkiller. I sighed, and made my way to the back entrance. My phone's battery had died in the car before I could read my texts. Darren was probably apoplectic by now.

I'd been gone for nearly two hours. Time flies, et cetera. I was going to be reamed out for leaving, and even more for ignoring my phone and not having it charged. I hoped my busted hand would garner me some sympathy, but that would probably only work on Marta. Mama Estela would likely look at the wound and sniff, and tell everyone in her rapid-fire Spanish that she had done worse to herself slicing onions. More than anything, I wanted ten minutes to myself, to process what had happened before facing the fray. But, I reminded myself that I was an adult, not a teenager, and further, I was, more than anyone else under this roof, responsible for the reason why we had to live under such tight security.

I let myself into the back door and was very surprised that Rosen was not standing sentry. And that from upstairs, I could hear laughter. Uproarious laughter. And there I'd been, picturing them apoplectic with worry over me. I started up the stairs.

"Danny, get up here," Darren called down. Of course, they'd all seen me come in on the monitors. "You're not going to believe this."

Eighties movie night. Molly Ringwald probably just got asked to the prom, or something. "Just a second," I yelled up.

Something didn't feel right. There were too many voices up there. Even from the ground floor, I could hear all the laughing. More than a John Hughes movie would warrant, that's for damn sure.

I took the first set of stairs two at a time, and met Marta, who was coming out of her kitchen with two big bowls of popcorn, heading up to the boys' floor herself.

"I made popcorn!" she said, beaming. God bless Marta. I've always loved people who state the obvious. Then, looking at my hand, "What happened to you?"

I waved my bandaged right hand in the air. "Nothing to worry about."

"That's what you always say, and usually I worry anyway," she said. "Usually I have a good reason with you."

"That about sums it up," I said. I took one of the bowls from her and followed her up to the floor Fred shared with the boys, and where most of the movie nights happened. They had the sixty-inch TV and all the tech gear. On the one occasion I tried to zone out in front of their TV on my own, I fiddled with a universal remote until I'd managed to turn on the sound system full blast but nothing else, and I had to get one of the boys in to get everything going for me. This, supposedly, was progress.

We walked down the hall, and I was both relieved and

puzzled at how festive they all sounded. Then I thought that Michael Vernon Smith must have been caught, and everybody was celebrating.

That, or this was what the atmosphere was always like when I wasn't around.

"Look what the mouse dragged in," Marta said. She was picking up English idioms, but she usually got them a little muddled.

"I come bearing popcorn," I said, but stopped short in the doorway.

Darren, Rosen, Matty, Luke, and Eddie. Check. Mama Estela with a beer in her hand, sitting on a hard wooden chair from her own kitchen: one of her quirks. Check. Paul Belliveau, looking very jolly.

And Fred.

I shoved the bowl I was holding at Rosen, who was closest, and ran over and hugged my brother-in-law.

"You're alive," I said. "What did he want? Did he give a statement?" I said to Belliveau.

"I don't know what you think you saw, Danny," Fred said. He grabbed my good hand, raising his eyebrows at the bandages on the right.

"Tell you later," I said. "What the fuck, Fred?" Mama Estela shook her head and muttered to herself, and I shot her a look. I was sure she said much worse in Spanish, but she never failed to express her disapproval of my language.

"It wasn't him, Danny," Belliveau said kindly.

"No. What? It was him," I said. I looked at Fred.

"Danny, I ran into my old friend Cliff King from when I was trading," he said. "Remember we used to teach courses together, back in Boston?" Before his ship had come in, and he'd packed them all off to southern California. "He's got a condo here now. He wanted to show me what he's working on. He was really excited to run into me – he might want me to come on board! It's – well, you must have seen me get into his car."

"Cliff," I said. "Not..."

"No, Danny," Fred said gently. "I would never have gotten into a car with him. I would— No."

"You said you only saw him for a couple of seconds," Darren said. "And, Danny, we only just found out that Smith flew into Toronto. He was in your head."

"I told Rosen Cliff could look like Smith, I guess, from certain angles. Age is about right, and the nose." I looked at Rosen, who nodded.

"It's good news, Auntie," Luke said. He put one arm around me, and helped himself to a handful of popcorn with the other hand. "Fred's not dead."

"Hey, that'd be a name for a band," Darren said. "Fred's Not Dead." He and Matty started playing air guitar, while I stood in the middle of the room. I looked at Belliveau.

"Did you already make all those calls?" I asked. "To the FBI and so on?"

"I did, but I corrected it. Don't worry, they were glad to know he flew into Toronto. It's the first lead they've had on him since – well, since what happened to you all in Maine."

"So let me get this straight," I said, to no one in particular. "It wasn't Michael Vernon Smith I saw in that car, but Fred's old friend Cliff."

"King," Fred added.

"Thank you, Fred. Cliff King." I sat down next to Rosen. "I dragged Paul down from his cottage early and had him alert law enforcement all over North America that one of the FBI's Ten Most Wanted had taken my brother-in-law. I worried everyone to death and made a total ass of myself."

"That's one way to look at it, Beanpole, yes," Darren said, grinning, enjoying himself immensely. Luke kicked his uncle's foot.

"That's not nice," Luke said, and Darren looked at me quickly.

"Ginger," he said quietly, and I nodded. She was the only Cleary who didn't enjoy torturing her siblings as much as the rest of us did.

"No, it's not," Belliveau said. "Danny, don't worry about bringing me down early. You got me out of going to a barbecue at our neighbors' cottage tomorrow, and for that, I'm grateful."

"He is still in town, this man," Rosen said. "Let's not become too complacent."

"No," Fred said. "Rosen is right. It was an honest mistake, and, Danny, if I had been kidnapped or whatever, taken by Smith, you might have saved my life. So thank you."

I felt like crying. Everyone else seemed happy and relieved that it wasn't Michael Vernon Smith I'd seen. And I knew I should be relieved: Fred was safe here with his family. I was glad about that. But for a few hours I'd thought that we were close to all of this being over.

"Auntie, what did you do to your hand, anyway?" Matty said.

"Ah," I said. "Somebody get me a glass of wine, and I'll tell you all about it." Marta started to get up, but I was glad to see that Fred motioned for her to stay seated, and he went. He did seem in quite a good mood. He was buoyed by seeing an old tech friend, and the prospect of having something to do, some work again. I had to remind myself that I wasn't the only one under this roof who felt like their life was in a holding pattern.

The boys went back to playing the Xbox with their headphones on. There was a strict rule that if they were playing while there was an adult in the room, they had to at least protect the rest of us from the godawful noise of alien invasions, or whatever. Belliveau stood and took his suit jacket off and draped it over the arm of the couch he was sitting on. "You put on a suit," I said. "You keep suits at the cottage?"

"This is an old one," he said. "I kept it in the closet up there for emergencies like this. It's a bit snug, though. I think the drycleaner must have shrunk it." He winked at Marta, who blushed. Mama Estela cackled, and then stopped herself. She pretended not to understand English most of the time, but none of us believed it for a minute.

"Stay here tonight," I said. "Have a drink. There's no point in driving. We have tons of room."

He paused for a minute. "I would love to," he said. "But I doubt anybody has anything I can change into, and if I don't get these trousers off soon, I'm going to cut off my circulation."

"I probably have some pajama pants you can wear," Darren said, but Marta stood up.

"No," she said. "Wait here." She bustled out of the room, her cheeks still flaming. I hoped she wasn't harboring a crush on Paul Belliveau. He had the kind of marriage that seemed unbreakable.

Marta was probably lonely, I thought. She was only a few years older than I was, definitely under forty. I knew her husband had been some kind of no-good who'd run off when Eddie was a baby. I had no idea if she'd had anyone else in her life since, down in California, but she definitely wasn't getting out much here in Toronto. Once again I was humbled by what Rosen and Marta and her family had done for us, for the boys. The sacrifices they had made. In respecting their privacy, I hadn't asked much about their lives. But I realized they might think that I just didn't care, which couldn't be further from the truth.

While the others chatted, waiting for Marta and Fred, I thought about Dave. He'd be here soon, sometime in the next day or two. My quiet life was suddenly in upheaval, but that was good, I recognized. Being surrounded by people can drive me crazy, but it also did something to soothe my soul. And I knew I owed Dave. Not just for everything he'd done helping get this place set up, but for abandoning him when he lay in a hospital bed. When I'd been in hospital in Nova Scotia, he was at my side. Then when he needed me, I'd run off like a scared rabbit.

I really wanted that wine. My hand was throbbing. I was about to get up and go searching for Fred when he returned, balancing a full goblet of wine, followed by Marta, who had a plastic bag in her hand. She handed it to Belliveau.

"These will fit you," she said. Paul pulled out a pair of Roots sweatpants and a t-shirt with an image of a moose on it. Both looked larger than anyone in our house, and in fact looked too big for Belliveau. "I send clothes home to Mexico sometimes," she said. "Canadian things. For my brother."

"Oh my goodness, I can't take these," Belliveau said. He started stuffing them back into the bag.

Mama Estela got up and pushed the bag back into his hands. "You wear," she said. "My son… too many things." She waved in whatever direction she thought was south. "You wear," she said again. I glanced at Darren, whose eyebrows were threatening to fly off his face. I took a careful sip of my wine and tried not to laugh. Seems the Garcia women were equally enamored of Paul Belliveau.

A few minutes later, Paul came back, looking infinitely more comfortable, if slightly ridiculous, clutching a plastic bag that obviously contained the clothes he'd removed.

"Very Canadian," Rosen said. He looked as though he was trying not to laugh. "Nice moose."

"I thank you, Ms. Garcia," Paul said to Marta, bowing slightly. She went pink again. "I'll replace them as soon as possible, for your brother."

"Pfft," Mama said. "Edgar," she said, referring to Marta's brother. "Too many things."

"Looks like you're staying," I said to Paul. "No excuses now."

"Appears not," he said. "So. Perhaps now you'll tell us what you got up to tonight."

I glanced at the boys, who were still playing their game. It might be hard to tell parts of the story without it being clear that the bar I'd gone to was a strip club. And Fred's strip-club secret was definitely now out.

I told the story quickly. Rosen patted my knee when I got to the part where I took on the frat boy swarm.

"Nice place you've been hanging out at, Fred," Darren said. He was leaning forward with his elbows on his knees, hands clasped together. His knuckles were white. "Jesus. That's sexual assault. Danny was assaulted."

"Did they phone the police?" Belliveau wanted to know. He

looked incensed. He was protective of me, having saved my life once upon a time.

"No. They did give me the option, but I didn't want to be stuck there all evening with statements. I thought we had bigger fish to fry." I shook my head. Not only had I mobilized half the law enforcement in town for a case of mistaken identity, but I'd also let a bunch of wannabe rapists get away without having to deal with the law.

"So you didn't get a chance to talk to Zuzi?" Fred said. Everyone was silent for a beat.

"Are you fucking kidding me?" Darren said, and then glanced at the boys. I knew he didn't want them to witness him losing his temper at their dad, but he looked pissed. "Danny was attacked by a bunch of guys at this place, who knows what kind of damage she did to her hand, and all you can think of is your little stripper friend?"

I looked at Marta, who was watching, wide-eyed. I knew she probably didn't want her son to hear this either.

"No, I didn't get a chance to talk to Zuzi, but I think I may have seen her," I said. "I reckon I'll have another shot." I told them about Garrett's job offer.

"Huh," Darren said. "You're not thinking of doing it, are you?"

"Maybe," I said. "I did get the feeling that there's something weird going on there."

"Leave it to the police," Belliveau said. "Danny. Fred. I know you've been, uh, entangled in these kinds of things before. But you're not the police, and you're not trained to deal with this."

"Danny will have a better chance of finding things out by working there, being on the inside, than the police will by rushing in," Fred said. "I don't want the police involved." My hackles had risen, and, had we not been surrounded by the entire household and Paul Belliveau, who had driven three hours on a weekend for what turned out to be nothing, I would probably have succumbed to the urge to tear a strip off him. He didn't want the police involved? Since when did he get the deciding vote on what actions I took, after I'd had my hand torn up defending myself in a situation I never would have been in, if not for him?

I took a long sip of wine, trying my best not to take my anger out on the stem of the goblet. I'd had enough breaking glasses for one evening.

"Fred, the police are already involved. I am police. I don't put that aside when I'm not on shift." Belliveau was glaring at Fred.

Marta got up and crossed the room to her son, tapping him on the shoulder.

"Time to get ready for bed," she said. She motioned for him to take off his headphones. "School is starting soon, and you will have dark eyes down to here." She tapped the end of his nose. Eddie groaned but got up. I don't know whether it was Marta's influence or his grandmother's, but the kid never argued when he was told to do something. As she and Eddie walked past Mama Estela, Marta grabbed her mother's hand and pulled her up. "You too," she said. "Come downstairs now, old woman." Mama made a show of sighing, but she stood and picked up her chair.

"I'll do that," Belliveau said, leaping up.

"Okay," Mama said, much to our surprise, and put the chair back down. Belliveau shot me a smile and followed the Garcias out of the room, carrying their dining-room chair in front of him.

We all sat silently for a minute. Luke and Matty had taken

their headphones off, and Matty actually shut off the TV. I took a deep sip of my wine and closed my eyes. I was tired, and felt like a fool. I was vaguely worried that if I did see Fuckface Smith somewhere in the next few days nobody would believe me, now that I had proven myself to be some kind of hysterical neurotic. I wondered if I'd see him everywhere now, bagging groceries when I was doing my shopping, or sitting next to me on a bar stool.

"Your hand is bleeding," Luke said. "Auntie, look." Yup. Blood had soaked through the bandages on my palm. I sighed.

"So it is," Rosen said. "Come down to my kitchen. I am better equipped for first aid." He looked at the glass of wine in my left hand. "Alcohol thins the blood, you know. Probably you shouldn't drink."

"Probably you should mind your own beeswax," I said, but I smiled at him. "Boys, do you want to help Rosen patch me up?"

"I'll pass," Luke said. Like his mother before him, he didn't share the Cleary fascination with all things bloody and disgusting. "I'm going to bed to read."

"Me too," Fred said. "I'm getting old." Getting the shit kicked out of them does tend to make a person feel their age. I should know. In another day's time, I knew my body would be protesting every time I lifted a cup to my mouth. Belliveau came back in, and Fred offered him the spare room on their floor. They shook hands, fences presumably being mended. For now, at least.

"I'll come," Matty said. I was hoping that Matt would go to medical school one day, that his lack of anything approaching squeamishness would lead him into a real profession, rather than a life like mine.

We walked the two flights down to the main floor, Rosen,

Darren, Matt, and I. Darren had his arm slung across my shoulders, and when we got to the bottom of the stairs, he pulled me in and kissed my cheek. Matty was happily chatting away to Rosen ahead of us, and Darren whispered in my ear.

"I believe you," he said.

"Believe what?" I whispered back.

"I believe that it was Michael Vernon Smith that you saw in the car," Darren said. "I think Fred is lying."

My heart skipped a beat. It skipped two. Darren walked after Rosen and Matthew. I took a deep breath and followed.

THIRTEEN

Not for the first time, I cursed the architect and builders who had designed our renovated bakery space. Having all of us on separate floors had generally worked well – it gave us the feeling of privacy and self-containment, whilst we also had the freedom to wander into each other's kitchens if someone was out of eggs or coffee filters. We all valued what little privacy we had, as we had all signed on for the "safety before privacy" edict. But the lack of proper soundproofing made having truly private conversations difficult.

Darren and I had mutually agreed months earlier that if we needed to talk without fear of anybody hearing or walking in, we could sit in the same room pretending to be watching television and text each other. Hey – it seemed to work for teenagers.

So later that night, after Rosen, assisted by Matty, had cleaned and re-bandaged my hand and I pretended to be sleepy but light-hearted enough, we said goodnight and went up to the third floor and sat in our living room. Darren put on a late-night talk show, not loud enough to keep Fred and the boys downstairs awake, and we pulled out our phones.

Why? I texted.

He's acting squirrelly. I don't buy that story about his old work friend.

So this is a hunch? Nothing concrete?

It's a hunch, based on close and careful observation of our bro-in-law, lo these many years.

Why do you think he'd lie? Do you think he's in cahoots with MVS?

Cahoots???

We both laughed.

Seriously. F hasn't been right for a long time, if you ask me. He got beat up last night. What if it had nothing to do with the stripper? What if MVS has his talons into Fred again?

I put my phone down and looked at Darren.
"Shit," I said out loud.
He nodded, and typed.

We have to keep eyes on him all the time. We have to follow him wherever he goes from now on.

We need Dave et al.

I glanced at Darren, whose eyebrows were up near his hairline.

> Shut up. Dave and I are over. Just leave it.

> That reminds me! Luke has a girlfriend.

> ????!!??

> Moira. She's going to the same school this year. She was at the gym this summer.

> Did he tell you?

> A little. But I also saw some of the texts. In the interests of making sure the boys are safe, of course.

> Dickwad. Does Matty know?

> I assume so.

"Enough," I said out loud. "My hand hurts." We both stared at the TV for a few minutes.

"I'm going to bed," Darren said. "And so should you. Help you heal."

"What, are you Dr. Singh now?"

"I meant your hand, Bean, not your psyche," Darren said. We laughed softly. I'd go stark raving mad without Darren around. I rarely forgot that fact.

"I'll get up and do, uh, morning shift," he said quietly. He gestured downstairs, to where Fred's room was. "I'll get you up at noon. Sleep in." I nodded, and patted Darren's head as I walked past him. I was going to soak in a bath, or try to without getting my bandages wet.

I'm generally a shower person, but I've been in enough fights to know that nothing beats a soak in a hot bath with Epsom salts for muscle soreness. Plus, I was hoping it would help me relax. My nerves felt frayed. I'd been ping-ponging around from thinking that Fred had been kidnapped by an evil sonofabitch who'd vowed to destroy our family in the worst ways possible, to fighting off a mob of stupid boys with too much lager and porn affecting their judgment. Then, of course, learning I'd been very, very wrong about what I'd seen, and my overreaction had caused a lot of hassle and upset to people who didn't deserve it.

And now, the person I trusted most in the world was telling me that he was sure that Fred was lying. All the security precautions in the world wouldn't help if the enemy was already inside the barricades.

I dearly wanted a solid sleep in my own bed. But, hauling myself out of the tub with some difficulty, trying to keep my hand dry, I knew that more than any other time, the boys needed protection. Especially if Darren was right. I didn't really think that Fred would do anything to hurt the twins. He might not be winning any Father of the Year awards anytime soon, but it was difficult for me to conceive of a situation in which he'd let any harm come to them.

But then again, I also would never have thought he could have cheated on my sister, and with the nanny, no less. People change, and very often for the worse. Could my brother-in-law have sold his soul for some reason? He'd always been ambitious, and after what had happened in California, his business was all but bust. What if, to quote *The Godfather*, he'd been made an offer he couldn't refuse?

I wanted oblivion. I couldn't do crack, and I found I didn't actually want to. It wasn't the kind of escape I wanted. After Fuckface Smith was dead and buried and I knew my family was safe, I could buy a rock of crack the size of my head, go to a hotel and have a party with myself until my heart and brain exploded. But until then, I owed it to Ginger to protect her boys, and to Jack, who died trying to protect them.

I put on clean pajama pants and one of Jack's old t-shirts, which read PARTY TILL YOU PUKE. He used to like to sleep in it. He found it funny, for some reason. I grabbed my phone, pillow, and the duvet from my bed, and crept downstairs to sit sentry outside Luke and Matty's room. I was used to that floor; it was like my bed away from bed.

I heard soft laughter coming from their kitchen, so I dropped my pillow and duvet outside the boys' bedroom and went down the hall.

Belliveau, Rosen, and Matty were sitting around the table, playing cards.

"Whoops," Belliveau said. "Hide the cards, boys. Here comes da fuzz."

"The fuzz?" Matty said.

"It's what they used to call the po-lice back when Paul was a kid," I said. "Like 'five-oh' or 'the po-po.'" I grabbed a bottle of orange juice from their fridge and sat down. "What's the game?"

"We are teaching Matt the finer points of poker," Rosen said.

"It is, of course, a skill all men must learn."

"Men?" I said. "Deal me in. I'll school you fools." Matthew looked so happy I almost couldn't bear it. "Watch and learn, Matty," I said to him. "Watch and learn." I looked at his smiling face, which had grown so much leaner and adult, seemingly overnight. I wanted to burn this memory into my brain.

"Fred asleep?" I said. "And Luke?"

"Luke's texting his girlfriend. Or he was. He might be asleep now. But Fred went for a run," Matt said. "He said he couldn't sleep and he wants to get in good shape like you."

"A run, huh," I said. I looked at Rosen, who was looking back at me. "Well. Whaddya know."

Belliveau was dealing. "Fred not much of an exercise nut like the rest of you?"

"Not so's you'd notice," I said. Matt was looking at me. "But then again, not everybody can be graced with the natural athleticism of young Matthew here."

"Fred falls up the stairs," Matt said to Paul. "James says we take after our mother."

Rosen nodded. "She was very graceful and athletic," he said. He cleared his throat. It occurred to me that perhaps Rosen had been carrying a torch for Ginger when he worked for her. But as she was a married woman, not to mention his employer, he never would have said anything. The phrase "man of honor" popped into my head, and I smiled at him.

"She definitely was," I said. It was the first time in probably a year that I'd heard Matty mention his mother. "She was the best person I have ever known," I said. "Ever have, or ever will." I raised my bottle of juice. "Now, I hereby dedicate this game of

Texas Hold 'Em to Ginger, who could outplay anybody at poker, and who taught me everything I know."

"To Mom," Matt said, raising his cup of hot chocolate.

Rosen and Belliveau followed suit, with water and a beer, respectively. "To Ginger."

"Alrighty," I said. "Let's get this party started, boys. I'll deal."

I looked at the clock on the wall. One a.m. I picked up the cards.

Fred was about as likely to take up running as I was to start doing embroidery. And I could see that Rosen knew it too.

FOURTEEN

For the next three days, I drove myself crazy.

I paced. On the first day, I did a run-through of our security protocols with Rosen. Then, the next day, another drill. I prayed for rain, so we could keep the boys focused on indoor activities. I thanked God that we had our own gym downstairs, so Matty, Luke, and Eddie could burn off some steam with their invented version of hoops, which involved a Byzantine set of rules that only the under-thirteen set could understand. I watched *The Godfather* again, practically forcing the rest of the household to watch it with me. And *The Godfather Part II*. Matty and Luke loved it, which surprised me – seventies films don't have the pacing that pre-teens are used to – and I felt like I had fulfilled an important part of my guardianship duties. A bit more education in classic rock, and the boys would be nearly complete. Marta, meanwhile, had let Eddie sit in with us, but she frogmarched him out of the room when Sonny gets machine-gunned at the tollbooth.

Obviously, Marta hadn't been paying much attention to the video games the boys played.

Darren talked to Dave in Jakarta (Jakarta!), who said

they would be delayed by up to a week. He'd been told of my embarrassing identification blunder vis-à-vis Fred and the town car, and so their presence, while still required as far as I was concerned, was a less pressing matter. And apparently they had a client there who had "gone off the reservation".

I thought about working with Dave's crew again, the excitement and adrenaline, and tried to tell myself I didn't miss it at all.

One afternoon, Fred brought his old friend Cliff King around to see the place and meet the boys, and, I think, to put my mind at ease that this was the man who had whisked Fred away in a town car outside of Helen of Troy that night. I shook the man's hand and wanted to ask him to come outside and get into my car while I stood ten feet away to see if he could resemble Michael Vernon Smith from that angle, but I refrained. The two of them played video games with the boys for a while – I had never seen Fred play anything with the boys, so despite everything it was heartening – and then sat in Fred's kitchen laughing and talking for hours.

"I can't believe it," Darren said to me upstairs in our kitchen. I was so antsy, I was actually washing dishes. "Fred has a friend."

"And they hung out with the boys, too. Oh look!" I gazed out the window. "Pigs flying."

"Maybe we were wrong," Darren said. "Do you suppose?"

"Maybe," I said. "I don't know. I just know that we can't stay holed up here forever, in case that dickwad is around." I peeled off my dishwashing gloves and poked at the wound on my hand, covered still by bandages.

"School starts in a couple of weeks," Darren said. "And Dave's crew will be here eventually. Either something will happen or it won't. Maybe he's just… moved on."

"Fuckface Smith? Moved on?" I splashed water on him. "Get a life."

"He could be in Canada for a million reasons," Darren said. He stuck his head in the fridge, as though it would contain something different than it had five minutes ago. Jack used to do the same thing, as did both the twins. And Fred, come to think of it. Men, I swear. "We have to go on with our lives, but stay vigilant. Otherwise we're prisoners, and even if the man never contacts any of us again, he's still ruined our lives."

"We have good lives," I said. I didn't want to say "he's already ruined my life" but I thought it. "This is a great place. The boys have fun."

"It is a great place." He pulled a package of string cheese out of the fridge and opened it with his teeth. "But are we still going to be trying to keep the boys indoors when they're fifteen, sixteen?"

"If necessary." I stuck out my tongue at him, and he opened his mouth to show me his half-masticated cheese.

Yes. In many ways, my brother and I hadn't matured much past the age of twelve.

"I know you're right. But you're a fine one to talk. You could be making music, gigging, whatever," I said.

"I'm writing some stuff," he said. "Besides, I'd been on the road since I was twenty. I needed a break." He coughed, which I had come to notice that he did whenever he talked about performing. He wouldn't say it, but I knew he was afraid of getting on stage and simply not being able to sing.

"The boys are starting a new school. That will be an adventure in itself," I said. "Hey – didn't you say that Luke's little girlfriend is going to the same school?"

He nodded. "Moira. Do you think I should have the talk with him?" he said.

"You mean the sex talk? I think they've probably already had it. Don't you think?"

"I don't know. They're going to be thirteen soon. Some kids are already screwing like rabbits at that age, and some still sleep with their teddy bears."

"Oh God." I took one of the cheese strings and looked out the window at the rain. "I think these kids are more in the stuffed animal category. Or *Archie* comics. Graphic novels, excuse me."

"They've been pretty sheltered in some ways, at least from that kind of thing. I mean, they've been away from their friends in California for, what, sixteen months?" Darren did a few jumping jacks, which he only did when he was tired. He worried about the boys at least as much as I did.

"Something like that." I didn't care about the rain. I had to get out and run, and dispel the thought of either of my nephews actually having sex. Oh God. "But anyway, that's sort of Fred's job, isn't it? To talk to them about that?"

Darren gave me a look. "Theoretically," he said. "Look, all I'm saying is that they may still be kids, but, I don't know if you've noticed, they've shot up in the last months. They're tall, and they're filling out early. Look how much bigger they are than Eddie, even though I know he's younger. And you know what that means."

"They'll be good fighters?" I said. "Please tell me that's what you mean. If you love me, Darren, you won't say what you're about to say." I gently banged my head against the window a couple of times and scared a few pigeons off the fire escape.

"Puberty, Bean. Yes. Someday you'll go through it, I promise."

"No, thanks," I said.

"I'm going to pick Luke up some condoms." He shoved another whole cheese stick in his mouth.

I put my hands over my ears and started laughing, happy to see by his face that he was joking. At least I hoped he was.

"As we are having this unfortunate and disturbing conversation, I have something to tell you." I looked at Darren and removed my hands from my ears.

"You're pregnant," he said. "Bean!"

"What? No, ass-wipe. I was going to say, I have decided that the Summer of the Prowl is over."

"Oh, *really*? Have anything to do with one security expert of our acquaintance who's coming to call soon?"

"No," I said, though in fact there was some truth to that. "But you can feel fall in the air now. I got it out of my system. And now that the boys are going to have a new start, new school, and Fuckface is apparently in the country, I need to pursue more immediate goals."

"Like letting your hair grow out so you look female again? Hopefully?"

I chucked a spoon at him, which he caught and then balanced on his nose. "I am going to take that job. I'm going to work at Helen of Troy."

"Your goal is to be a bouncer in a peeler bar?"

"Gentlemen's club, if you don't mind," I said. "And yes. There's something wrong down there. On the surface everything looks fine," I made to continue, but Darren interrupted.

"I agree. Seems pretty wholesome, for a, uh, gentlemen's club," he said. "Nobody even approached us for a lap dance. Rosen was very relieved." Darren and Rosen had gone for lunch to check the place out. They hadn't invited me. I was not insulted.

"Maybe they thought you guys were gay," I said. "I mean, there's you, with the hair and the grooming…"

"There is nothing wrong with taking pride in one's appearance, little sister. You should try it sometime."

"…and I don't know that many straight men who are as buff as Rosen," I continued, ignoring him. "But what Fred said about Zuzi, and him getting beat on, and that Kelly chick… I don't know, I can't put my finger on it."

"Seems to me that you put your whole hand on it," Darren said. "Or in it. Whatever."

I looked at my hand. "It's healing nicely. And I highly doubt I'll experience another injury like that again. This was a fluke."

"Famous last words," Darren said.

"We'll see," I said. I felt cheerful. It was good to have a plan. "But I'll tell you one thing: Sitting around waiting for someone to try and kill us is screwing with my mojo."

"Then you have my blessing. Go forth, young woman, and retrieve your mojo."

FIFTEEN

Garrett Jones, the manager at Helen of Troy, seemed relieved and nearly overjoyed when he got my call.

"I've been kicking myself that I didn't get your number," he said. "I would have phoned and harassed you. To come and talk about working here, I mean," he added. He obviously didn't want me to think he was after anything else. I assumed that working with scads of barely dressed strippers and cocktail waitresses every day had made the man overly aware of sexual harassment boundaries.

"Well, here I am, phoning you," I said, "surprising even myself." I explained again that I lived close by, and while I wasn't interested in working full-time – family commitments – I'd be happy to do a few shifts a week. He tried to get me to agree to five days, but we wound up agreeing to a few trial hours. I agreed to meet him at the club that night to go over protocols and responsibilities, and to talk money. He warned me it wasn't much, but there were, he said, great benefits – dental and a gym membership – after a three-month trial period.

When I hung up, it occurred to me with some shame that I'd never actually had a real, grown-up job with benefits. When I was a trainer, back in my early twenties, I'd been self-employed.

Then I married Jack, and since then, I'd been living off him. And as his sole beneficiary, I'd inherited a large amount of money, larger than I had ever considered. I had burned through a tidy sum buying and renovating the bakery, including all the security, and I'd given a large amount to a charity for street kids, in Jack's name. I wanted to keep a good-sized nest egg for the boys' future, the latter being particularly important because Fred was tight-lipped about the state of his finances since Smith's cult had drained him a couple of years ago.

Having a paying job would make me feel better, I decided. It wouldn't be much money, but it was, in truth, the only kind of work I could see myself doing. Even if I had any kind of office skills, I knew I'd go stark raving mad sitting at a desk all day, and at my age and with no skills other than a certain amount of physical fearlessness and an apparent craving to put myself into high-risk situations, working for Dave's crew or working security at a strip joint seemed pretty much right up my alley.

After what had happened in New York a few months earlier, my working for Dave again seemed about as likely as me developing a fondness for high heels. At Helen of Troy, I could ingratiate myself with Zuzi, and get a sense of whether she was an outright liar, a fake, milking Fred, or whether Fred was just conjuring all of this out of thin air. He hadn't made up getting beaten up, and if it had anything to do with the club, I was going to find out.

I arrived for my first shift on a Monday night, which Garrett assured me was their second-quietest night of the week, after Sunday.

"But we still have to be on our guard," he said, as we settled into his office to chat. "As you experienced yourself first-hand, you never know when a customer will decide to take liberties."

Take liberties, I thought. *Is that what you call it?* I remembered being dragged back by my neck while some guy grabbed my boobs, and wanted to tell him that maybe he'd been reading too much *Anne of Green Gables* with his daughter. But I had been given a lecture by Darren about keeping my big trap shut, that not everyone finds my, as he put it with air quotes, "wit", amusing.

I smiled and concentrated on appearing both tough (I was the new bouncer, after all) and non-threatening (I was a new employee, and at my advanced age, it was a new experience for me).

"There are always at least three of us on duty who can fulfill a security role, if necessary," Garrett was saying. "Obviously, the door staff – you, or Sheldon, who you met, and there's also Martin, who works a couple of shifts a week." I smiled. My facial muscles weren't used to smiling so much. I probably had spinach in my teeth, with my luck. "The on-duty manager, which is very often me. If not there's Glen, my assistant manager, and Jimbo, who sort of does odd jobs for us."

I wanted to ask if any of Jimbo's odd jobs included beating up customers in the alley, but I just kept smiling. Darren would have been proud. Mama Estela would have been cackling her head off.

"So between the three of us – meaning Glen, Jimbo, and me – usually there are two people on duty at any given time. Plus the door person."

"And the bartender," I said. "Patrick was really helpful last week when I had my… altercation. Once he saw what was going on, I mean."

"Oh, *Patrick*," Garrett said. He exhaled loudly, as though he simply didn't know where to begin. "I don't know how we'd get by without Patrick. He's been here since before we took over this place. He knows where all the bodies are buried."

Note to self: Get to know Patrick.

Garrett continued with a simple explanation of what was expected of me, which did not seem to involve much past checking IDs at the door if patrons looked underage, bouncing customers who seemed drunk and/or belligerent, and, when the door itself wasn't busy, keeping an eye on the girls on the floor to make sure that none of the customers were taking, as he put it again, unwanted liberties.

After we discussed my hourly rate – which shocked me by how low it was; I had to ask Darren how much we paid Rosen and Marta, and give them a raise – and the benefits, I asked about when I would get paid.

"Hey there," Garrett said. "Look who's eager!" He leaned forward and spoke quietly. "If you're a bit short at the moment, I could probably advance you a bit against your first paycheck," he said. "Don't tell anybody else, though, or it would be chaos."

"No, no, I'm fine. Sorry, just curious about whether it's a payroll check from you, or whether the company that owns Helen of Troy has a centralized payroll, or whatever. You know, how do I account for my hours, punching in and out, that type of thing." I was winging it, and embarrassed at how little I knew about how all this worked.

And I really wanted to know how big the company was that bought this place. Zuzi had told Fred that the pressure for the girls to fuck the customers came when the new management started. I had a very difficult time imagining Garrett Jones strong-arming anybody, but I knew enough to not necessarily trust my instincts these days. I hoped that if Zuzi's stories were in fact true, that it was someone higher up in the food chain who had implemented the new regime.

"Oh, I see what you mean," Garrett said. "Well, I work – and you do too, now – for a company called the Kinder Group, so your bi-weekly checks will be issued from them."

"Kinder? Like the chocolate eggs with the little toys inside?"

"First thing I thought when I interviewed with them. And no – no relation. The founder of the company is Paul Kinder. The company owns pubs and, uh, establishments like this up and down the eastern seaboard and the Midwest." He fiddled with his tie, and adjusted the photograph he had on his desk. It was of his red-haired daughter, the Anne of Green Gables lookalike. Probably no wife, then, or there would be a family picture. "It's a fast-rising company, which is pretty phenomenal in this economy. With the Internet and what have you, people don't tend to go out as much as they used to."

"Was this place independently owned before Kinder took over?" I hoped he would see my questions as the normal curiosity of a new hire, and not simply nosy poking around.

"I believe so, yes," he said. "In any event, there's no punching in and out here. If an employee is consistently late or what have you, we have a talk with them." I wanted to ask if these chats took place in the alley, but I refrained. "But for the most part we really do have a great bunch of guys and gals here at HOT."

"Hot?" I said, then I got it. "Oh! Helen of Troy. HOT. That's clever." I thought it was about as clever as a heart attack, but hey, it was my first day. This man had just used the words "guys and gals" with no discernible trace of irony, and for once I was going to heed Darren's advice about keeping my skewed sense of humor to myself. As much as possible, anyway.

"The name was already in place, but the acronym occurred to somebody at head office early on, so that's what most people tend to call it."

"Well, it's fitting," I said. "There are a lot of beautiful women working here."

"Danny, I am not legally allowed to ask you this, and let me preface what I am about to say by making clear that whatever your sexual orientation is, it won't affect—"

I cut him off. "Please don't worry," I said. I tried to blush, to show Nice Girl color in my face. "I'm not gay. I was just making an observation. I mean, I haven't frequented these kinds of places much in my life, but the girls here seem very sort of clean-cut."

Garrett beamed. "I'm so glad you noticed," he said. "That is exactly what we pride ourselves on here." I was very glad he didn't say, "here at HOT." "If a gentlemen's club can be said to have a family atmosphere, then that's what we strive for."

I was really starting to think that Zuzi was playing Fred. Maybe she got a couple of her friends to beat him up in the alley, to get him feeling sorry for her, in the hope he would perhaps set her up in an apartment somewhere so she wouldn't have to shake her can for toonies tossed onto a stage anymore.

Garrett took me around and introduced me to the DJ and to the bartender on duty, a stunning woman with curls down to her waist named Cassie, to the kitchen staff and the waitresses.

"I won't take you back to the dressing room," Garrett said.

"I have the right to go in, and once in a while I do have to. But I don't think it's appropriate. It's a very female zone back there." He cleared his throat, and I could tell he was picturing tampons and tubes of lipstick being chucked willy-nilly across the room by girls in scanty underwear. And for Garrett, that was not a pleasant image. Bless. "Perhaps one of the waitresses will take you back on your break and introduce you around." He went over a few more quick instructions, and told me he was going to leave me on my own for a bit. "I'll be around," he said. "Sometimes I'll be by the bar, sometimes on the floor, in the kitchen, or in my office. If you get in any kind of trouble – and I know you won't – signal to Cassie and she'll ring through to me." He apologized for not having working communications devices, but promised they would be coming in a few days. Before he left me at the door, he quietly praised me for my choice of outfit – simple black pants and a black shirt. Of course, that's what he had instructed me on the phone to wear, but whatever. "You don't want to be mistaken for one of the dancers," he said seriously. "We'll have a couple of Helen of Troy shirts for you tomorrow." In the meantime, he presented me with a white armband emblazoned with the word SECURITY in black letters.

When he left me at the door, feeling like a bit of a knob with my armband, I wondered what in the hell I was doing there. I was like a teenager on my first shift at McDonald's, left handling the drive-thru window on my own. I pictured myself admitting hordes of sixteen-year-olds because I couldn't compute the birthdates on their fake IDs fast enough, or being unable to control my smart mouth and scaring away all the legitimate paying customers.

But it was a quiet night. When I started my shift at five o'clock, the club was maybe a quarter full. There was a small rush around eight and then again at about eleven, but I didn't have to so much as card anyone. There was a stool to sit on, but I stood. If any action was going to be necessary, starting from a standing position would be safer.

The worst thing about those hours was the smiling. Smiling at men – some of them, not all – who walked in with, shall we say, lascivious intentions.

And as soon as I thought that phrase, I started to understand why, perhaps, Garrett's speech seemed so old-fashioned and stilted when it came to this place. If I did too many more shifts watching men with glazed eyes and suspicious bulges in their pockets look me up and down before heading into the belly of the beast to feast themselves on semi-naked women, I might wind up clutching my pearls and having fainting fits, or something.

The bartender Cassie waved at me a couple of times and I trotted over, but she was just being friendly.

"How you doing, honey?" she asked me. "Having the time of your life yet?"

"It's my first shift, everybody has been well-behaved, and I'm already starting to hate men," I said. "Otherwise, yeah, the time of my life."

"I hear you. That wears off though." She gave me a cranberry and soda in a pint glass. "I'll take a break when Garrett gives you yours," she said. "One of the waitresses will cover the bar for me for a bit. We are so fucking short-staffed, man. Anyway, then I'll take you backstage to meet some of the girls."

Excellent. This was what I was here for.

At nine-thirty on the dot, Garrett came to take my spot at the door, after assuring me that I was doing a great job. "Cameras," he said, motioning to them. "Been keeping half an eye out in case you need help. But you're a natural, Danny." I hadn't done a thing, but he seemed very pleased nonetheless.

"What a relief," I said, and hoped I didn't sound as sarcastic as I felt.

Before we went backstage, Cassie showed me the menu and made me choose something for my staff meal. I picked fish and chips, and she phoned into the kitchen and ordered for both of us.

That, I could get used to.

I followed Cassie past the DJ booth and backstage, into the dancers' dressing room.

It smelled like twenty perfume bottles had exploded. There were about ten dressing tables along one wall, and a row of lockers on the other. Some of the lockers, I noticed, were closed and locked with padlocks, while at least half seemed to be wide open, bags of clothing open and rifled through. I saw two feather boas.

"Dominique and Fifi," somebody said behind us. "They're French. Not from France though, they're from Quebec City or somewhere, I think. They do a kind of can-can number together. Sort of burlesque."

"That's Brandi," Cassie said, waving at the girl who had just spoken, who had come in behind us from her stage set. She was standing at a mirror, carefully blotting sweat from her face and obviously trying not to wreck her makeup.

"Hey, Cass," Brandi said. She looked me up and down. I was getting used to that. "Hey, new girl."

"Hey," I said. I'm no prude, but it's a bit disconcerting

trying to talk to a nearly naked stranger.

"Did Garrett tell you that you've got to escort some of us to our cars at the end of the night? I'm only bringing it up because I saw that one of my creepy stalker dudes is here and, oh man, I am so not in the mood to put up with him tonight."

"Uh, okay," I said. "Of course." I was still thrown, being back here. A couple of women were having an intense whispered conversation and sharing a spliff, and somebody in the bathroom seemed to be crying.

It was like being in a foreign land, this land of women. I'd been living with men and boys for so long. Perhaps Darren was right, and I was starting to turn into one.

Note to self: Get some female friends. Then I thought of Kelly and her note, which I had forgotten about altogether until that moment. I felt like an idiot. After the events of that night, Kelly slipping me a Post-it didn't register much past the minute it happened.

"Danny's the one who beat the crap out of those fuckers at the bar when they tried to grope her. Two of them wound up in hospital," Cassie said to Brandi.

"No way! Righteous!" She kicked her shoes off and came over to hug me. "I so wish I'd been here that night. Everybody's been talking about it. We're trying to get Garrett to let us watch the security camera tape."

I snapped my fingers. "Oh, that reminds me. Kelly was working that night. She's the one who patched up my hand. You know, the med student? Used to be a vet? Is she around tonight?"

"Kelly?" Cassie said. She looked at Brandi. "I don't think I know her."

"Really petite girl. Early thirties but she looks way younger," I said.

"Oh, her," Brandi said. "I haven't seen her in a while, and I've worked every night for the past four nights. But you know how it is – girls come and go. I don't think she was here long." She was carefully applying lipstick and tucking her boobs into a clothing item that could probably be called a bikini, if your idea of a bikini was three or four pieces of string woven together. And this was how she was going to circulate on the floor, soliciting lap dances. No wonder they kept this place so warm.

Cassie shrugged and tapped the Bluetooth in her car. "Awesome," she said. "Come on. Our meal is ready."

We started out, and Brandi called after us. "You guys are so lucky," she said. "You get to eat and not worry about cellulite."

As Cassie and I made our way to the kitchen to pick up our meals, I thought of Kelly. I had to find that note.

As we finished our meals in the downstairs staff kitchen where Kelly had attended to my hand, I realized that I hadn't thought of Fuckface Smith in hours. In the last sixteen months, I was pretty sure that was a record.

"What are you smiling about?" Cassie said as we put our plates in the sink. I hadn't realized I was smiling.

"Nothing," I said. "I just really think I'm going to like it here."

"Cool," she said. "Places like this go through staff like water. I've only been here a few months myself and I can't tell you how many staff and dancers have come and gone."

"Yikes," I said. I meant it. That wasn't a good sign, of anything. Cassie slapped my ass. "Come on," she said. "We gotta go

back on the floor and be the backdrop for the dancers. Smile!"
She pulled a fake cheesy grin.

"I don't really have to smile," I said, grinning at her. "I'm the muscle."

"That you are, girl," she said. "Let's just hope you don't have to prove it again anytime soon."

"Your lips to God's ears," I said.

I had to find Kelly. I had to find Zuzi. And then we'd see what I had to prove.

SIXTEEN

I spent half an hour the next day looking for the note that Kelly had passed to me after she'd patched me up. I remembered crumpling it up and dropping it in the bag I was wearing that night, but it wasn't there. Nor was it under my bed, or in the drawer of my nightstand, any of my pockets, or the wastebasket in my bedroom.

It had either gone out with the trash somehow, fallen out of my bag, or – and I hoped I was wrong about this – I had missed my bag in the kitchen at Helen of Troy when Garrett had come in, and it had landed on the floor for anyone to see. I resolved to ask Garrett for her number, if she wasn't working there anymore. You know, to thank her for tending to my hand.

In the meantime, I'd seen a work rota backstage when I walked a couple of the girls to their vehicles at the end of the night. Zuzi was scheduled to work tonight.

She and I were going to have a little talk.

It seemed to me that it was significantly busier that night. I carded a group of four kids – two guys and two girls – whose obviously fake IDs had them at ages ranging from thirty to thirty-eight.

None of them could have been older than seventeen. They faded back onto the street and I could hear them laughing walking back up the road into the late summer night. The weather had changed from rainy and cool to a late-August, languorous humidity that made people want to make the most of it. Autumn came quickly in this part of the world.

Garrett had presented me with my very own Helen of Troy Security t-shirt, which had the unfortunate acronym HOT on the back in huge letters. I knew immediately that I would not be wearing this t-shirt for my runs. Darren was going to have a field day with this one.

I kept more of an eye on the floor than I had the night before, looking for the girl I thought was Zuzi. At around nine-thirty or so, I saw her approach a table of young guys, two of whom I had carded and whose driver's licenses had proven them as newly nineteen, the drinking age in Ontario. All five of the kids looked like chess club nerds, but their bravado was obviously increasing with every overpriced beer. One of them bought a lap dance from Zuzi, and I watched her dance for a minute. She didn't have the athletic talent of some of the girls, but I thought maybe she had a non-threatening sexuality that would appeal to younger guys like these. Not to mention my brother-in-law, apparently. She had thick, slightly messy dark hair and a small but softly buxom body, as opposed to the lean, hard six-packs that a lot of the girls seemed to have worked very hard for.

I caught her eye unintentionally after she had finished the lap dance. She was leaning over the table, obviously trying to talk him into another dance. She smiled at me, a friendly, open smile, said something to the boys and held up a finger, obviously promising to be right back.

"I'm Zuzi," she said. She shook my hand, and noticed mine was still bandaged. "Sorry! I just wanted to say hi. I saw what you did the other night, or at least some of it. I was so scared for you I nearly peed myself."

She spoke softly, and with no guile whatsoever. She looked twenty-three, twenty-five tops.

"And then Patrick told me later that night that you'd been asking for me? We haven't met before, have we?"

"No, no," I said. "I just came in to kill an hour that night. I live close by, and my brother-in-law had been coming in here. He told me that you two had become friends so I thought that since I'd wandered in I'd introduce myself."

"What's his name?" she said loudly. The DJ had turned the music up significantly for the next dancer, who, I'd been told, needed to feel the bass through the stage or she couldn't dance.

"Fred," I said. "Sort of skinny dude, reddish hair with lots of gray?" I indicated his height, a bit shorter than me.

"Oh yeah, him," she said happily. "Nice guy. Good tipper. No touchy-feelies. My ideal customer."

"He paid you for dances?" I said.

"Well, yeah," she said. She laughed. "That's sort of what we do here, right?"

"Oh, I get it," I said. I shook my head in a sort of "stupid men" gesture. "He made it seem like you guys were friends. Like, actual friends, as opposed to…" I waved at the stage, at the tables.

"As opposed to the professional dancer–customer dynamic?" she laughed. "They all think that. No, I should say that all a girl's regulars think that, if she wants to make money." She turned around to check her table of chess club geeks. Another dancer had moved in. Zuzi sighed and turned back to me. "Haven't seen him for a bit, your brother," she said.

"Brother-in-law," I corrected her. "My sister's husband."

"Oh shit," she said. She put her hand on my arm and seemed genuinely concerned. "I'm sorry. Really, he never even touched me."

"Don't worry about it," I said. "My sister died nearly two years ago."

Zuzi looked at me with such sympathy that I could feel my eyes pricking with tears that wanted out. And that would definitely not be cool, to have the new security person crying at the door.

"Don't cry here, Danny," Zuzi said. Her voice was a bit harder, and she put a big smile on her face and turned to walk away. Garrett was walking through the club. "Walk me to my car later?" she said loudly. She didn't want management to think she was distracting the security person? We weren't supposed to fraternize on duty? Garrett hadn't said anything like that to me, but who knew. I nodded at her, and turned back to the door, where a bachelorette party was coming in. There had to be sixteen young women, maybe more, and the bride-to-be had a tiara, sash, and heels she was a bit wobbly in. Garrett came over and greeted them warmly, smiled at me, and led the girls to the center of the club, where tables had been reserved for them.

The next hour was busy enough that I could avoid thinking about anything beyond the moment. I happened to witness a man roughly grab the breasts of one of the dancers as she was bent over in front of him dancing, and I saw the girl slap his hands away. But he was also grabbing her around the waist, trying to pull her onto his lap. She looked up in my direction, and I waved at her to let her know I'd seen and was coming over. I quickly drew the velvet rope across the door, caught Garrett's eye at the bar, and pointed at the door.

He saw where I was heading, and he took my place at the door. I could tell he was watching me as I threaded my way through the tables. My brain was working overtime. There were rules about what I was and was not allowed to do, as an employee of the club. I couldn't just walk up and punch him in the side of the head, for example, which was my first instinct. The law said I could only use physical force in self-defense, and Garrett had stressed that one of the reasons he'd wanted to hire a woman is that men felt less threatened by a woman, and wouldn't feel the need to get all macho in front of their buddies and throw a punch.

That hadn't been my life experience, but I was about to find out if it would be the case here.

When I reached the table, the dancer, a small blonde who looked more strung-out than the other girls I'd seen here, was being held by the customer in a reverse bear hug, on his lap. The man was jerking his groin into her and pushing her back onto him, hard.

It was as close to out-and-out rape as you can get with your clothes on. And it was definitely sexual assault.

She had tears streaming down her face, causing her makeup to run down her face, the black mascara making inlets into the thick layer of foundation she was wearing to cover bad skin. She'd stopped struggling, and was being bounced up and down like a doll. I saw that the man's large arms were wrapped tightly around her abdomen; it would have taken a much stronger person than she looked to break that hold.

Blood was pumping to my brain and to my muscles, and I

wanted so badly to maim that man, at that moment, that I felt dizzy.

As I approached them, I reached into my pocket for my car keys, and without thinking first, I stuck one into the man's ear, far enough to hurt, but not far enough to break his eardrum. Yet.

His eyes, which had been closed, popped open, and he released his grip on the girl. She jumped off his lap and started screaming at him. I didn't register the words. In my peripheral vision I could tell that one of the other girls grabbed her and hustled her backstage.

We were the center of attention now, at least for the tables in this part of the club. I leaned forward, smiling for the benefit of anyone watching, and whispered into the man's ear. The ear that had the key lodged in it.

"You're going to get up in a moment and leave this club, and you are never going to return," I said. "If you make a sound – in fact, if you make a single movement that I don't like right now – I promise you that I will shove this knife so far into your ear that your eardrum will burst. Trust me, sir, it's very painful, even when a person is as drunk as I presume you are." He wouldn't be able to tell it wasn't a knife.

My lips were right down next to his ear; no one else could hear me, and no one could see the key. It would look as though I was having a private word in his ear. I hoped. "Blink once if you agree that you're going to be a good boy and put your dick back in your pants. Blink twice for no, and then this conversation will get a lot more interesting."

He blinked once. My eyes were about two inches from the side of his head.

"Do it now," I said. "Put your dick away. Don't say one fucking word." I didn't look at it, just cut my eyes quickly to the right to watch his hands. He tucked in, and returned his palms to his thighs. He kept wiping them on his trousers, like they were sweating. Good.

"Did your server run your credit card for a tab?" He blinked. "We will be billing you fairly for all your drinks, but we will be adding a very expensive bottle of champagne, for the girl you just assaulted, in public. Blink." He blinked. "If you dispute these charges, some very unpleasant people will come visit you at your home. I promise that you will not enjoy this visit. Blink if you understand me." He blinked. "Now, I know that when I take this knife out of your ear, you might take it into your head to put up a fight. I don't think you're quite in your right mind." He blinked hard, rapidly, trying to indicate that he wouldn't. "If you do, not only will my friends and I have to teach you a terrible lesson, but the police will be called, and there are dozens of people in the immediate vicinity who saw you sexually assault this young woman. Oh, and of course we have the security tapes. And just so you know, no one can see the knife. Everyone around us thinks that you and I are having a friendly, if one-sided, conversation." He blinked. Sweat was running down the side of his face. He stank of fried onions and fear.

"So I'll tell you what. I'm going to remove the knife. I may nick you with it as it gets removed, but if I do, please don't worry. It'll just be a superficial cut. It won't bleed long." He blinked madly. "When I remove it, stand up, turn around, and walk toward the door. I promise you, sir – I promise you on the graves of my dead parents – that you will live to regret it if you don't do exactly what I say."

I removed my hand – and the key cupped in it – from his ear. I really hoped it looked like I was cupping his ear to whisper into it. If not, well, so the fuck be it.

The man stood, and stumbled forward a couple of steps. I

grabbed his arm as if to steady him – he was drunk – and pressed very hard on a spot on his ulnar nerve. The baby finger and ring finger on that hand would be numb for a day or two, but he'd live. He jerked upright while keeping his eyes to the floor. I followed as he walked quickly, if unsteadily, toward the front door. Garrett held the door open for him, and the man walked out.

A smattering of applause started from the patrons and staff who witnessed it all, and the DJ – Rick, his name was – blasted Aretha's "Respect".

My cheeks were blazing, but the DJ wasn't finished. "There you go, ladies and gentlemen. Here at Helen of Troy, women rule the roost. Mess with one of them at your peril, gentlemen." The bachelorette party went absolutely wild and started singing along to Aretha. The waitresses were rushed off their feet and waving at me.

"I knew it!" Garrett said. He had a ridiculous smile on his face, and I could tell he was trying to restrain himself from hugging me. "That was something else, Danny. I'm going to ask you later how you managed that, but in the meantime, why don't you take your break? Order your staff meal, get a drink if you want. You probably need to chill for a minute. Take as long as you need. Glen's coming in shortly." He put his arm around my shoulders and gave me an awkward one-armed hug. I knew he couldn't restrain himself. "Oh, and there's a friend of yours at the bar, Doug he said his name was, if you want to say hello."

My heart stopped. Doug. Doug Douglas. It was an old joke.

I walked to the bar, and there was Dave, holding a blue drink with an actual mini umbrella in it. His back was to the bar, and he was smiling at me. It was an odd smile, but it was a smile.

SEVENTEEN

"The old key-in-the-ear trick, huh," Dave said, but quietly. He handed me his drink. "Thought you might need this."

"Blue curaçao, vodka and lemonade?" I said.

"The very same."

I took a sip, and welcomed the slight hit of alcohol. Then I put the drink on the bar and, without thinking, hugged him. I breathed in the scent of his neck. When he pulled back from the embrace, I kept holding on, and he half-laughed and squeezed me back. I felt him relax into it, into me. My muscles loosened.

"Yo. Danny." Cass was bartending again. She leaned across the bar and spoke quietly. "I don't want to be a buzzkill, but ixnay on the PDA on the floor, babe." She glanced over at the door, where Garrett was presumably standing. "Your ass will be grass, you keep that up." She leaned over the bar further and stuck her hand out to Dave. "I'm Cassie. You must be Superwoman's man."

Dave grinned at her and shook her hand. "I'm Dave. I used to be her man, once upon a time, but she left me high and dry a few months back."

Cassie raised her eyebrows. "Honey, whatever you did, I

think she forgives you." She winked at him and crossed the bar to take a drinks order.

"She doesn't know the story," I said to him. "This is my second shift."

"Evidently you're fitting in," he said. "Not even the entertainment and you're still getting applause."

"I'm shit on the phone," I said. I was talking quickly. My adrenaline was still up, and I wasn't expecting to see him yet. I wasn't prepared. "I mean, I'm shit anyway, I'm unforgiveable and fucked up and all that, but I'm also completely unable to talk about anything important on the phone."

"You talk to Dr. Singh about important things, I presume," he said, twirling his coaster. "She's not right in front of you."

"It's Skype," I said, "and I'm not in love with Dr. Singh."

I clapped my hand over my mouth. The words had popped out without any thought. I tried to avoid thinking about Dave. The Summer of the Prowl was mainly about not thinking about what I'd done to Dave.

"Jesus," Dave said, after the world's most painful pause. "You really have no filter, Cleary." He looked truly surprised.

"I'm so sorry," I said.

"You're on break? Let's take a walk for a few minutes." I nodded. I was going to keep my trap shut from now on. I was going to learn sign language and pretend I was mute. I was going to seal my lips shut with superglue whenever I had to go out in public.

I followed Dave out the door, tapping my watch in Garrett's direction to let him know that I was aware of the time, that I was on break and not leaving. He nodded, and waved me out, mouthing, *Take your time.*

We walked in silence for a minute, past the few people who had retreated outside to smoke. Two of the bachelorette girls were outside, laughing loudly, and I kept my head down and my arms crossed. Submissive body language. I was waiting for the emotional blow.

"I'm going to say a few things now," Dave said. "Please just let me get them out, and then we can talk later at home."

I nodded. I pretended my lips were glued shut. It was hard to do.

He'd said "at home".

"What you did in New York was," he looked at the sky, like the right words were going to appear to him, "very painful." He looked at my face. "Ned is not your biggest fan right now. But I think he'll get over it."

I opened my mouth, but shut it again.

"We slept in the same bed for months. I held you while you cried in your sleep. I know that what you've been through is… unimaginable, for most people."

I looked at the ground. I willed myself not to burst into ridiculous tears.

"Danny, there are things I haven't told you about myself. Things that you might think are unforgiveable. Well, at least the fact that I haven't told you before. I should have. I think for people like us, trust is very hard-won. I would trust you with my life without hesitation. You know that."

I nodded. I knew that.

"But the thing I've been wrestling with these last months is whether it would ever be possible to trust you with my heart again." He pulled a pack of cigarettes from his pocket. "Yeah, I'm smoking.

Shoot me." I took one from the pack, and he lit them both.

"So what I'm trying to say, I guess, is that, yeah, I love you. But it might take some time before I can trust you. That way," he added.

I kissed him. I couldn't help it. After a second, he kissed me back, but not for long.

"We'll have time to talk about all this at home," he said. He cupped my cheek for a minute, and smiled into my eyes. "I came here because – well, because I wanted to see you, but also because as soon as Darren told me where you were, that you were working here, that they had hired you for security, I knew something was wrong." I started to tell him about the manager having seen me deal with the frat boys, but he cut me off. "I know about that. But did you know that it's against the law for them to hire you? Any security personnel – bouncers, security guards, whatever – in Canada have to be licensed? There's a whole course, a test administered by the government, everything. They can't just hire someone off the street to do what you're doing. And they must know that. Jonas is doing some research right now about the company that bought this club months ago. But we do know that they have other clubs, and bars and so on. They would know the licensing requirements.

"The fact that they went out of their way to hire you – illegally – is, uh, fishy, to say the least." He flicked his cigarette into the road. "Even if you are the best man for the job."

"Maybe the manager – Garrett, the guy you spoke to at the door – maybe he just didn't know," I said. "He came from the States for this job. It's possible that he simply didn't know about this licensing thing up here."

I was trying to put my happiness about having Dave standing

inches from me to one side. I needed to separate my emotions from what he was saying. There were so many things about this place that didn't add up. On the one hand, it seemed clean and aboveboard, especially for a strip joint. The girls, for the most part, seemed healthy and happy, though of course I hadn't spent much time with any of them. And, so far, the manager wanted to talk about little more than his daughter and Canada's Wonderland.

But Kelly. She had been more than startled when Garrett walked in while she was writing out her phone number for me, and she hadn't wanted him to know that she was passing it to me. Assuming that Fred was telling the truth, he had gotten beaten up in the alley – the alley that Dave and I were standing in front of, in fact. And then there was Fred's Zuzi, and the Zuzi I had talked to tonight.

"Possible, but highly unlikely. Look, you know better than anyone that I'm not exactly a by-the-book kind of guy."

"You don't say. How many IDs are you carrying?" I said.

"Exactly." He squeezed my hand. "But I don't advertise. You know, I operate on a different… level, than this kind of thing." He nodded toward the club, and the bachelorette group on the sidewalk, which had grown in number as well as noise. "It's a risk for them, hiring an unlicensed bouncer, and it's a risk for you."

"We should talk to Belliveau," I said.

"You should," he said. "I'm going to stay out of his way. Cops make me nervous. Especially when they know too much. Or worse, when they think they do."

"He's by the book, yes, but he's also my friend," I said. "I think we can arrange a little détente." I held my hand out for another cigarette, and glanced toward the door of the club. There was a small lineup now. Garrett had said I should take a long break, and I hadn't eaten anything, but I didn't want to leave him alone at the door. Despite the fact that I knew I shouldn't trust him, he hadn't been anything but kind. "I need to find out what my risk actually is, if some cop or government official came in demanding to see my papers, or whatever."

"By the time I get back to the bakery, Jonas will know all that," Dave said. I nodded.

"One way or another, I'm going to, at the very least, finish my shift," I said. I started to tell him about Zuzi and Fred, but Darren had already filled him in. So I quickly explained what she'd said earlier. "I'm supposed to walk Zuzi to her car at the end of the night," I said. "I think she'll talk to me."

"I'd stay, but I have really got to get my head down for a couple of hours," Dave said. "I didn't get any sleep on the flight. And I want us all to sit down and talk this through tonight when you get back. The boys should be asleep by then."

"Ha," I said. "You haven't visited in a while. Those two can stay up until dawn. Inherited the Cleary body clock." I looked at him under the street lamp, and he did look tired. I wondered what had gone wrong in Jakarta. I'd hear about it eventually.

That idea made me nearly burst with happiness for a moment. He might never be able to, as he'd put it, trust me with his heart. But then again, maybe he could. Having him standing so close, feeling his presence for the first time in months, made me giddy and hopeful. And in an instant, I felt a wave of love and calm, like Jack was giving me his blessing. I hadn't felt that before. I'd wanted to feel it. I'd been waiting. But even if it was just my own mind giving myself permission to love Dave properly, it felt as real as the ground under my feet.

"Go home," I said, "back to the bakery. Get some sleep, and don't let the boys try to keep you up playing the Xbox."

"What time will you get out of here?" he wanted to know. "In other words, when do we start worrying if you're not home?"

"Worry about me? Didn't you hear? I'm Superwoman. I just stopped a drunk with his dick hanging out from dry-humping a crying stripper." It was meant to come out funny, but I felt a bit sick when I said it. For a second I felt like I was having a delayed reaction to what had happened the week before, with the frat boys grabbing me. A surge of angry sadness took me for a second. What gave anyone the right to think that another person's body was their property, to use however they wanted?

The look on my face must have said it all. Dave was right: I had no filters. At least, not with the people closest to me. He hugged me tightly. "I told you once that you were a warrior," he said into my ear. The feeling of his breath made me shiver. It had been so long. "You are, Danny, but you don't always have to be. Do what you have to do here, but then come home. Let somebody else fly the plane for a while." I nodded against his shoulder.

"Leaving aside the fact that I'm not properly trained or licensed for this work," I said, "I don't think my temperament is suited to it."

"Temperament. And temper," he said.

"It's entirely possible that I could snap one day…"

"And snap some guy's arm in half? Yeah. I came in just as you were walking down to that table. For a minute there I thought that man was going to be leaving on a stretcher."

"I'm just glad he was too drunk to fight." I looked at my

watch. "I've really got to eat something fast and get this evening over with. As to what time I'll be home? Probably two-thirty or so, three o'clock." The small queue had gone inside; I hoped we wouldn't get another rush. Garrett would close early if there were only a few people. "I'll text Darren when I'm leaving."

"Wake me up when you get home," he said. "We'll all sit and talk then."

"Will you be in my room?"

Dave smiled at me and held his arm up, hailing a passing cab. "Maybe," he said. "Is it habitable in there? Food all over the floor? Newspapers from two weeks ago under the duvet?"

"Babe, I'm living with Darren and Marta," I said. "I can't get away with much." He kissed me quickly and got in the taxi, and I watched him drive away, happier than I'd been in months. No, happier than I'd been in years, probably.

I walked back toward Helen of Troy slowly, trying to wipe the stupid grin off my face. I didn't even freak out when one of the bachelorette girls clustered outside projectile vomited as I was passing her, and a good portion of it sprayed my shoes and the bottom of my pants. I just patted her on the back, told her I'd get her friends to come out and take care of her, and sailed into Helen of Troy with a stranger's puke on my legs and a smile on my face.

EIGHTEEN

"**A**re you okay? Did you get sick?" Garrett said to me the second I walked into the club. He was staring at my vomit-splashed legs with something between concern and horror. "Was it having to deal with that man? Because you did such a good job, Danny, and Zanzibar is just fine."

"Zanzibar? That's her name?"

"Well, her real name is Ann," Garrett said quietly. "The simpler the real name, the crazier the stage name." He looked again with distaste at my legs and feet. In the lights near the bar, it really wasn't pleasant. And I could smell it.

"Oh, yuck," I said when the odor hit me. "It was bachelorettes. Let's just say at least one of them was over-served, and I happened to be in the line of fire."

"I see. Well, you can't be on the floor like that. As soon as we get the new lockers, later this week, you should bring in a change of clothes. In the meantime, you should probably go home. That's not a great advertisement at the door."

I would have loved to go home, especially now that Dave was there, and Jonas. But if this wound up being my last shift, I didn't want to miss the chance to talk to Zuzi.

"I'll tell you what," I said. "Why don't I go backstage and see if any of the girls have a spare pair of pants or jeans or leggings or something that would fit me. Even if I'm not presentable for the door, I could still be here for backup. It's pretty busy."

"Good idea! Great initiative, Danny." He clapped my shoulder, and I embarrassed myself by actually blushing.

Hey. I didn't have the McDonald's stage in my woefully short career development. I worked at my dad's dry cleaning business in high school, and, being a Cleary, he wasn't the "great initiative" type. He was a fantastic man and a great dad, but there's a reason my siblings and I all wound up with a slightly warped sense of humor.

"But if you can't find anything, just head on home, and I'll see you for your next shift. And don't worry, you'll get paid for the full night tonight regardless." His attention got pulled away by one of the waitresses. I was dismissed.

I walked along the side of the floor, avoiding the tables by as wide a berth as I could. The smell of vomit is not appetizing when one is trying to eat a burger, or enjoy a lap dance. I grinned at the DJ when I passed his booth, and he gave me a thumbs up. I was glad there was a girl onstage doing her thing, in case he got it into his head to segue into Aretha again.

Backstage, Ann, aka Zanzibar, was perched on a stool in front of one of the mirrors, taking off what makeup she hadn't cried away. She was in her street clothes – simple jeans, a plain t-shirt and Nikes – and as I slowly approached her, I realized that this girl could not have been older than sixteen.

"Hi," I said. I grabbed the stool next to hers. "How you doing?"

"Fine, thank you," she said. She grabbed another cotton ball and attacked the makeup still lurking around her left eye. Her voice was childlike, high, but had a self-assurance about it that surprised me. She turned to look at me. "What happened to him?" she asked me. "Did they hurt him?" She turned back to the mirror. "I hope they hurt him."

"I stuck my car key deep into his ear and told him it was a knife, that I was going to burst his eardrum," I said. The only other girls in the room were chattering loudly to each other by the bathroom, paying no attention. I leaned toward her a bit so I didn't have to speak loudly. "I told him that we were putting the price of an expensive bottle of champagne on his bill for you, and that if he didn't leave quietly, if he complained, some nasty people would visit him at home."

She stopped waging war on her face for a minute and looked at me in the mirror. "You did?"

"Yes," I said. "It's only my second shift, though. I don't know how they work that out, I mean with the waitress or whatever."

"Don't worry about it," she said. "I'll make sure I get it."

"I hope that kind of thing doesn't happen very often," I said. I was speaking calmly, quietly, as though to a frightened puppy.

"Not that kind of thing, no," she said. "He seemed to think paying for one table dance gave him the right to nearly anally rape me. I can confidently say that that doesn't happen every day."

I took a breath and let it out slowly. "I wish I had cut his dick off," I said.

"So do I," she said. "But you did pretty well, I'd say."

"Do you mind if I ask," I started to say, but she put her hand up.

"Please don't ask me how old I am," she said. She closed her eyes with the world-weariness of a woman three or four times her age. Whatever that was.

"I was going to ask if you knew if anybody keeps spare leggings or something in here. Some chick outside puked on me." I showed her my pants and my boots. Of course, I had been about to ask her age, but with this one I was walking on eggshells. And I wanted to know who she meant when she asked me if "they" had hurt him.

"Angie," Ann called out.

One of the dancers near the door yelled back. "Yeah?"

"You have any spare leggings for this girl? She got vomit on her."

"Not my own vomit," I said. I stood up and showed the girls who came trotting over. "One of those bachelorettes when I was outside having a smoke."

"Oh God, those girls," the one called Angie said. "I'm glad they're out having fun and all, but they tip for shit." She looked at me. "So you're the new door guy," she said. "I heard about you, busting up those college kids."

"Yeah, well, they swarmed me and grabbed my tits," I said. "What's a girl to do?"

"Story of our lives," the other one said. She went back into the bathroom and shut the door, singing an aria from an opera my mother used to listen to. It made me homesick for Maine, suddenly, and made me want to go back to the bakery and see my family.

"Wow, she's got an amazing voice," I said to the other two.

"She does. She's auditioning at the moment. Does this to pay for her singing lessons." Angie looked me up and down. "I don't have leggings, but you can borrow a pair of my basketball shorts." Ann looked at her dubiously. "What? I play with a league a couple of days a week before I come in here. They're clean," she said to me, "just really wrinkled."

"As long as they don't smell like puke, that would be great. I'll bring them back on Friday. Or I can drop them off tomorrow, if you need them."

"Friday's fine," she said. "I'm not here again until Saturday anyway." She pulled a mammoth gym bag out of an open locker and rummaged around, then tossed me a baggy, shiny pair of long shorts. "I don't imagine you'll want to be out in the club in those, but it's better than driving home and getting the smell of puke in your car."

"They're perfect. Thanks. I'm Danny, by the way."

"I know," she said. She smiled at me expectantly. "Well, try them on. And shove those pants you're wearing in a plastic bag or something."

Ann and Angie were both looking at me. I'm not used to undressing in front of people so casually. Especially other women. Especially strippers with perfect bodies.

"You want we should turn around, doll?" Angie said. She was grinning at me. I liked her. "Protect your modesty?" She had been completely topless during our entire exchange, so it seemed a bit silly to feel shy.

"Never mind. But remember, I'm not used to having people stare at my body."

"Unlike some people in this room, she wanted to say," Angie said to Ann.

I took off my boots gingerly, trying not to get the drying vomit on my hands.

"You can borrow flip-flops too," Angie said, "but they might be too small." I pulled off my socks and shoved them in the boots. I felt like the world's least sexy stripper. I unzipped my pants and stepped out of them.

"Muscles," Angie said with approval. "Shave and get some self-tanner on those, and you could do alright."

I laughed and pulled on her shorts. They were a bit snug around the waist – like most of the girls, Angie had a waifish frame – but otherwise they fit fine. I looked ridiculous, but they fit fine. And I was very glad to get out of those pants. Angie tossed me a baggie with flip-flops in them and I slid them on. They actually fit perfectly.

"You're a lifesaver," I said to her. She was balling up my pants and putting them in an empty plastic shopping bag that someone had left on the floor, and then she tossed my boots in after them, and tied them up tight.

"There," she said. "Have fun unwrapping that."

"Something to look forward to." My wallet was in the pocket of my pants in the bag, but I'd had my keys in my hand when I came in. I wanted to leave, but I didn't. I wanted to talk to Zuzi. The whole point of this had been to talk to Zuzi.

"Shit," I said. "I was supposed to walk Zuzi to her car at the end of the night. Is she out on the floor?"

"Nah, she booked an hour or so ago," Angie said. She grabbed a stool and her makeup bag. "Said she had cramps, wasn't up to it tonight." She filled in her over-plucked eyebrows with feathery strokes of a pencil. "Sometimes, you just can't make the magic happen."

For a minute I debated cornering Garrett and getting Zuzi's number as well as Kelly's, but nixed the idea when I imagined walking through the club in the basketball shorts.

Ann cleared her throat. "I'm taking off," she said. "You want to walk me to my car?" Her tone said that she felt like she was doing me a favor, making me feel useful, but at her age and after what she'd been through tonight, I doubted that was the case.

"Sure," I said. "Let's get gone." I was hungry, regretting missing my staff meal. Damn drunk bachelorettes.

There was a side door directly from the dressing room into the alley.

"I hope you don't use this exit by yourself," I said to Ann. I picked my way over a broken bottle in Angie's flip-flops. "Perfect place for some creep to wait for his favorite dancer to leave for the night."

"Usually I go through the kitchen," Ann said. "But a couple of those guys are nearly as bad as the customers."

"Really?" I said. "I'll mention that to Garrett. That's fucked up." I kept my eyes on the ground. The alley wasn't lit, other than ambient light from the street and the parking lot behind, and it looked like some of the neighborhood junkies used the alley to shoot up sometimes. I walked carefully. I wasn't keen on getting broken glass or, worse, a hypodermic needle in the toe. I was used to wearing boots, not flip-flops.

Something caught my eye as I watched the ground. A pair of glasses in the weeds next to the edge of the building. I knelt and picked them up.

They were Batman reading glasses, white plastic with blue and black bat ears. The boys had given them to Fred for his birthday, and he always kept them in his pocket. He loved those glasses.

Fred had definitely been in this alley.

I heard a small squeal behind me, and from the corner of my eye I saw Ann's legs kicking. Someone had picked her up, someone in black. I started to stand, but something hit me hard, across my lower back. Something both heavy and sharp. I felt my skin break even through the heavy t-shirt I was wearing, and I fell forward. I tried to turn my body, to meet the ground with my arms instead of my face, but I was only partially successful. Something sharp cut my cheek.

"Stay down," a voice hissed behind me.

The unmistakable sound of a round being chambered. A gun.

No fucking way was I going to die face-down in an alley.

I tried to move, to get my legs under me, and I couldn't. Whatever had hit my lower back had done something to me, damaged a nerve. I didn't know why I couldn't move. I desperately tried to move but I simply could not.

I was immobilized.

"Don't hurt her," I said. I couldn't even twist my head properly. Why couldn't I move? "She's just a kid." I needed to see who these men were. I couldn't. I wanted to shout, but I feared a bullet in the base of my brain if I did.

I saw feet, two sets of feet, men's, and I saw Ann's limp body draped over the shoulder of the bigger one. The other one – I was pretty sure there were only two; I willed my mind to stay calm and take it all in, in case I lived – came behind me and shoved something in my mouth, a rag or something, and quickly wrapped duct tape around my head. My whole head, leaving only my nose free so I could breathe.

Thanks, guys.

There was a pause, and then my lower legs and ankles were taped together, and my arms pulled behind my back and taped together from the elbows down to my fingers.

And while this was happening, I couldn't move. Whatever nerve had been hit in my lower back seemed to radiate something – something way past pain – down my leg and up one side.

I was blinded. I heard the two men moving away quickly, and I heard them whispering as they did.

They had Ann, and had left me trussed up in the alley like a mummy.

Some bodyguard.

NINETEEN

I'd had my mouth duct-taped shut once before, when I was chained to a pier while the fastest tide in the world was rushing in to drown me. That time – through luck, salt water and the fact that my would-be killers had used an off-brand tape with crappy adhesive – I'd been able to work the tape free to scream for help.

No such luck this time.

I had to stay calm, because if I panicked or started to cry and my nose got plugged, I'd be dead, and quickly.

I'm no stranger to pain. Maybe it was a genetic quirk or perhaps just my own pig-headedness that I have usually been able to think past physical pain. Pain is your brain sending a message that something is wrong, but usually I've been able to take a Scarlett O'Hara attitude when it comes to injury: I'll think about that tomorrow.

But despite my predilection for running headfirst into potentially dangerous situations, I've got just as many phobias as the average person. Probably more. Climbing down ladders, for example. Falling from a great height. Even watching someone bungee jump on television has been known to make the carbonation in my brain start, the precursor to my fainting spells.

Suffocation is high up there on the list.

And even though it wasn't one I'd ever told anybody – a girl has to have some secrets – I have a fear of rats. Specifically, being bitten by rats while I'm helpless to do anything about it.

The tape that had been wound around my head covered only one of my ears. Whoever had done it was obviously mostly concerned about covering my mouth and my eyes. At the moment he'd done it, I'd almost been – almost – relieved that he'd covered my eyes. It meant that they probably weren't planning on killing me; they just didn't want me to be able to identify them. He'd taped my arms and legs to keep me from moving, from raising the alarm, obviously. He hadn't known that whatever I'd been hit with had already effectively disabled me. I hoped it was temporary.

I would think about that later.

But with my one uncovered ear, I could hear the unmistakable chirping and scurrying of rats in the alley.

It was the perfect home for families of rats, that alley. Only about twenty feet from where the club kept its garbage until city pick-up days, and it was dark and usually, I guessed, fairly quiet. Except, of course, when people were getting beaten up and/ or abducted. I was the interloper. And the fact that I was lying absolutely still, unable to make any noise, probably made me seem like dinner.

Suddenly, the presence of broken glass, used condoms, and hypodermic needles seemed like the least of my worries.

I had to turn over. Lying face-down as I was, there was more of a chance that my nose could get plugged. And I hoped that by moving, by showing that I was not an immobile slab of lunchmeat, the rats would decide that there were more interesting morsels to be had. I'd heard a statistic once that in North America, there is at least one rat for every human. And that their favorite meal of choice is blood – it's the only thing that rats will over-ingest. Like me and crack, once upon a time.

I flexed my feet. I was able to flex my feet, though the tape started at my ankles and went to my knees. But it didn't seem to hurt to flex my feet. I tried to arch my back, bringing my face as far as possible from the ground. I could move my shoulders, but when my lower back was flexed, the most excruciating pain radiated down my legs. I thought I could move past the pain, just ignore it. But I was also trying to be calm, mummified in duct tape, and I was afraid the pain would make me vomit. Vomiting while your head is encased in duct tape sounded like a very bad idea, and I have a long history of vomiting at inopportune times.

I resolved that staying in my current position was going to have to do. I could wiggle my feet around periodically to show the rats that I was alive. I would thank my lucky stars that I only had one ear free, because I didn't want to hear the rats in stereo. I would stay calm, and not let myself cry or throw up. And I would hope like hell that somebody from the club came into the alley to have a cigarette or smoke some weed. And eventually, when I didn't come home, Dave or Darren or Rosen would come looking for me.

I estimated that, worst-case scenario, somebody would find me in maybe four and a half or five hours. I tried to relax. I thought about Dave, and the fact that he was lying in my bed asleep. I thought about how much fun the boys were probably having with Jonas, who was undoubtedly hacking some cheats for their computer games for them.

I thought about the possibility that I could allow myself to be happy, to have a new life.

But, because I'm me, the positive thoughts led into others.

Who had taken Ann, and why? It could, I supposed, be the pervert who had molested her earlier, come back with some buddy so he could finish what he started with her, but that seemed highly unlikely. That dude was probably sleeping off his drink somewhere.

Had Kelly been taken too? Zuzi?

Zuzi had seemed genuinely surprised when I'd told her that Fred thought they were friends. Unless she was a brilliant actress, as far as she was concerned, Fred was nothing but a good, paying customer. So why was he beaten up? I believed him; I'd seen his face, and found his glasses in the alley. Had he gone too far with another girl, and Sheldon or Glen or one of the other guys gave him a beating to teach him a lesson? But no. Fred was many things, but even Zuzi had said he wasn't grabby. And he wasn't a drinker, so it's not like he could have undergone some personality metamorphosis under the influence.

And while it was a minor point compared to the others, why had Garrett wanted so badly to hire me, particularly when he must have known that I'd have to be licensed to do this job? He hadn't even alluded to it, and I hadn't known to check.

On the one hand, most of the staff seemed normal. Cheerful, even. On the other hand... well, things were definitely not adding up.

If Fred had found out about some kind of illegal forced prostitution operating out of the club, that could certainly be enough to get him beaten up. It was possible he had found out some other way, other than Zuzi, something he hadn't wanted to tell Darren and me. And I had, after all, just witnessed Ann being subdued somehow – she was limp, probably unconscious, when I caught a glimpse of her being carried away over the bigger guy's shoulder – and I doubted anybody was doing that to her to take her home for tea and cake.

And on top of everything else, Michael Vernon Smith was in the country. For once, he seemed like the least of my problems.

I'm not sure how much time passed. I heard a couple of the kitchen guys, way at the other end of the alley and around the corner, putting garbage out and laughing about something. I willed them to turn the corner into the alley. I kept wiggling my fingers to keep the circulation going, and to show the rats that I was alive. I tried not to think about stories I'd heard about rats biting people while they slept. I tried not to wonder if I was going to suffer some sort of paralysis or nerve damage from the blow to my lower back.

Then I heard something behind me, something bigger than a rat. Then something licked my foot.

"Oh my God," a voice said. Someone was there. A man was there with a dog. My savior was not Dave or a member of my household, or a patron of the club, but a guy taking his dog for his bedtime stroll. Thankfully, the man had let the dog off the leash to go into the alley to do his business, and when he came to see what his dog was licking, he found a woman trussed up with duct tape. A very thankful woman, who would cheerfully have adopted the man and the dog. I heard him talking to an emergency operator on his phone, and then the man was crouching down next to me, telling me everything would be fine.

I've heard that before, I wanted to say.

But soon, I heard sirens.

TWENTY

"Well, you're not going back there again." Darren was pacing around my hospital bed, which was a feat, as it was closely surrounded by curtains. "That place is a curse. Worse."

"Darren, please," I said. I was trying to concentrate on not throwing up from the pain in what turned out to be my sciatic nerve. "I just want to get out of here. We can talk at home."

I had refused narcotic painkillers, as I'd clearly been experiencing an insane moment when I was asked. The endorphins from not being eaten by rats in the alley had worn off. Now, I wanted whatever they would give me. I tried to reach the call bell attached to my bed, but the twisting motion sent a nauseating shot of pain across my lower back and down my leg. I snapped my fingers for Darren to hand it to me. He did, but he was acting so put out, it was as though he was the one who'd gotten strung up like a Christmas turkey in a rat-infested alley.

I was still in Emergency, in a room with two other patients, any privacy provided by curtains around the bed. Dave was in the hallway talking to the neurologist, who wanted to do a nerve conduction study and get me on the list for an MRI, but he said he was "relatively sure" that the damage was temporary. It was my sciatic nerve, as I'd feared, and the CT scan had shown some damage to the root of the nerve. Or something. I'd been in too much pain to pay much attention.

Since being taken by ambulance to a downtown hospital, I'd had X-rays, a CT scan, stitches in my cheek, refused a tetanus shot as I'd just had one in Nova Scotia the previous year when I got impaled by a very rusty ladder, talked to three different cops, fielded a very worried call from Garrett, had Darren and Dave arrive looking panicked, and for the last two hours I'd been examined, on and off, by the on-call neurologist. I was glad that Darren was writing down what the doctor said, because all I really wanted to know was whether I was going to be able to walk properly again.

Whatever the guy in the alley had hit me with, it had something sharp on it. It had broken the skin in a few places, but nothing too deep, apparently. And I had been protected somewhat by my Helen of Troy Security shirt, which the police had taken in for forensic testing. Whoever had hit me was looking to incapacitate me, not kill me.

I kept thinking about Ann. I had next to nothing to tell the police in terms of descriptions of the two men, and I felt like a fool. I also explained that I was only on my second shift, and told them, truthfully, that as I had never pursued this kind of work before, I had no idea that I required a license. The employer, I stressed, did not tell me this, but a friend mentioned it. I had been planning on making tonight's shift my last.

I had a moment's guilt about landing Garrett in trouble, but a moment was all. There was something very bad going on at that club. As the manager, if Garrett knew about it, he was obviously some brand of criminal sleazebag. If he didn't know about it, he was simply a blind idiot. Either way, I wasn't going to lie to the police any more than I had to. And certainly not for him.

The nurse came and injected some kind of opiate into my IV, and within seconds, I was a very happy camper.

"Don't get too used to that," Darren said, watching my face relax. His was set in a scowl. Still.

"What is your fucking problem, D?" I moved my leg. I moved it, and while I could tell it was painful, it was as though the pain was a thousand miles away. "I haven't done anything wrong. And may I remind you, this nerve thing could be debilitating. I could be fighting with this thing for the rest of my life. I would have thought that might garner me a little sympathy."

Dave came back in and moved around to the other side of my bed. He grabbed my hand, and Darren's eyebrows nearly flew off his face.

"I'm going to ignore that for the moment," he said. "Though I'm happy to see it."

"He's going to work on forgiving me," I said. Happy, happy, high and happy.

"You're a brave man, sir," Darren said. He smiled. Sort of.

"What is it, Darren? Seriously." I knew my brother. He should be cracking wise and trying to cheer me up, not being cranky. That was my job.

"Oh, it's probably nothing," he said. "Cliff is at the bakery hanging out."

"Fair enough. Fred's allowed a friend."

"Indeed," Darren said. "But I couldn't help but overhear them talking."

"Acoustics again," I said to Dave. "It's a nightmare." Dave nodded.

"They were talking as though they're both moving to the States. Back to California, to work for Cliff's new start-up, whatever it is. Tech company. I don't know, and I don't care."

"He's not taking the boys," I said, and I realized my voice was too loud by many decibels.

"They're his kids," Darren said.

"No fucking way, Darren. No."

"I know, Danny. I know."

"Back to California. Away from all of us, the people who love them. They've just settled in. They love it here. California is where Ginger was killed. They can't go back there. He'll never see them. He'll be working all the time and he'll hire somebody else to take care of them and who knows who it'll be this time."

Someone in the bed next to me cleared her throat deliberately.

"Pardon me," I called over. "Very sorry." I flipped the bird at the curtain.

No answer. I lowered my voice. "We need to get a lawyer. Now. Tonight."

"It's past four in the morning," Dave said. "We'll get someone tomorrow. I'll make some calls."

"Thank you." I squeezed his hand. I was very glad I had morphine. If Darren had told me this before I'd gotten the shot, I think my head might have exploded. This could not be happening. We had put our hearts and souls into setting the bakery up for all of us, as a safe and fun and loving place for the boys to finish growing up. Marta's family and Rosen had relocated to another country for them. Were they supposed to turn around and go back now?

And Matty and Luke needed us. I could barely stand thinking about having them torn away. They would be on their own.

No. I would have to relocate down there somehow. I would figure it out. Darren too.

"Maybe Fred wouldn't want to take them," Dave said quietly. "You've got a good setup. He could fly up every other weekend or something. People do it. He has to see that it would be in the boys' best interests to stay here, to not be uprooted again."

"You're right," Darren said. He looked relieved, as though it hadn't occurred to him that Fred wouldn't take the boys. He looked shattered. Actually they both did.

"Look, why don't you guys go back to the bakery," I said. "I might be here for another day, who knows, and if they let me go it means that I can at least walk."

"One of us needs to stay," Darren said. He looked at Dave. "To be honest, I should get back. Luke's girlfriend is staying over, and as I'm the one that allowed it, I should really be there."

"Uh. What now?" I said. "Am I high, or did you just say that you allowed our twelve-year-old nephew a conjugal with his girlfriend?" Dave was grinning. He looked exhausted, but he was grinning.

"She's in Marta's spare room," he said. "I talked to her dad. She arrived at the bakery in tears, had a big fight with her mom, and her dad said it's okay as long as…"

"As long as she's not in Luke's room," I finished. "Did you talk to Fred?"

"Nope," Darren said. "He and good old Cliff were elbows-deep in papers in Fred's study. Lots of macho posturing, from what I could tell." He imitated what he called Fred's businessman laugh, a sound that was completely unlike any sound we heard him make when it was just family around.

My eyes were starting to close. Strong painkillers. Eventful day. Scary news. My body wanted to go into hibernation mode.

I let myself drift. I heard Darren and Dave whispering, and that was all.

When I woke up, I had been moved to a different room. A private room. According to the nurse who was standing over me when I came to, my life was "too interesting" to share a room with another sick person. She winked. I wasn't sure what she was winking about, but I may have been a bit cranky. I was in pain, and had no adrenaline or morphine to dull it.

I'd always associated sciatic problems with old age. I was thirty-four: hardly a candidate for the nursing home yet. But then again, most people with sciatic pain came by it naturally, not because they got clocked in an alley by potential human traffickers.

Dave was asleep in a chair next to my bed. Someone had tucked a blanket right up to his chin.

"Wouldn't leave your side," the nurse said, and winked again. I was starting to think she had a tic. "Aren't you the lucky one." She said the neurologist would be in within the hour to talk to me, and I'd probably be released. She asked about my pain level, and I hesitated.

"I need something," I answered honestly, "but maybe not as strong as what I was given last night." She said something about Percocet, and started to leave the room.

"Nurse," I said, "can I ask you a quick favor please?" I pushed the blankets off me. "I need to see the pattern of the wounds on my lower back." She hesitated. "Can you take a picture for me?" I looked around for my phone, then remembered that it was in my trouser pockets. The vomit-stained trousers that Angie the stripper had bagged up with my boots. My wallet and phone had been in the pocket, and I know I didn't think to look for it when the paramedics picked me up.

And my keys. My keys had been in my hand when I walked into the alley. Because of the security at the bakery, nobody could get in there with just keys, but I wondered if my Honda was still behind the club. I sighed.

The nurse pulled a phone out of her uniform pocket, and helped me turn over. A lightning bolt of pain shot down my leg, and I hissed through my teeth.

"Hang in there," she said. She took a couple of shots, then pocketed the phone before I could see the pictures. She readjusted my hospital gown, and left me on my side when I indicated I didn't want to move again. "I'm going to see about getting you some meds, and when I come back, give me his number," she nodded to the sleeping Dave, "and I'll text them." She lowered her voice. "We're not supposed to have our phones on the ward," she said. "I can't let you hang onto it, but I'll send them."

"Do you remember the number?" Dave said, his eyes still closed. I nearly jumped out of my skin, which sent another bolt of pain down my leg.

"Fuck. Me." I was not going to be good at this chronic pain thing if that's what I was going to experience. I've had far more than my fair share of injuries, some of them pretty major. But I healed. This nerve pain already seemed like a very different beast.

"I don't think you're in any shape for that right now, darling," Dave said. He pushed his blanket down and leaned forward, stroked my hair. I rattled off his phone number, which was burned into my brain, like his emergency number I had tattooed into a mandala on my inner thigh more than a year and a half earlier.

Twenty minutes later, the pain meds the nurse had brought me had started to kick in, and Dave and I were looking at the picture of my lower back that she had texted to him.

"I am a wreck," I said. My lower back and butt were starting to develop a lovely shade of black, punctuated by what looked, on Dave's phone at least, like deep red welts. Two of them were covered in bandages.

"Wow," he said. "You sure are accident-prone, Cleary."

"Fuck off," I said happily. Pain medication. Happy days. "I just seem to get under people's skin a lot."

"You say tomato."

I wanted to talk to the boys, but it was too early in the morning. Those kids were going to have a rude awakening when school started. That's unless Fred was planning on spiriting them away to southern California again.

Why couldn't life just be simple? I no sooner had Dave back – at least, I hoped I had him back and he wasn't just being kind to the crippled lady in the hospital – when Fred decides to turn into an asshole. I hoped Darren had misheard, or it had just been idle pie-in-the-sky talk.

"I want to go home," I said.

"Soon," Dave said.

"I want to soak in a hot tub."

"That can be arranged."

"I may need help with the getting in and out part," I said.

"I'm very amenable to that," he said.

"Then I want to hug the boys, following which I plan to punch Fred in his stupid head."

"Fair enough."

"And we need to get a good lawyer if this crap is all true."

"We will."

"And I need to talk to Belliveau," I said. "I need to tell him everything, from soup to nuts. I'm leaving this Helen of Troy crap to him now." I thought of Ann, draped over some man's shoulder in an alley, and shook my head to get rid of the image. I couldn't do all of this. I couldn't.

"Sounds like a very wise plan."

"I'm not a cop, you know," I said.

"And thank God for that."

"Belliveau, the Toronto police, they can find Ann and Kelly and Zuzi and figure out what's going on there. It was a distraction, and sort of a favor for Fred. A way to feel useful."

"I know."

"Between Fuckface Smith and now Fuckface Fred, we've got our hands full."

"Agreed."

"I keep saying 'we.'"

"I noticed that," he said.

"Does it bother you?"

"I think I kinda like it," he said.

"I won't walk out on you again," I said. I looked at his face, his eyes. "I promise."

"Okay, Danny," he said. His eyes were shiny. He kissed my

forehead. "Promise me again in a week," he said. "When you're not high. And then maybe a week after that."

"I'm amenable to that," I said.

"Knock, knock," somebody said. A new doctor walked in, big smile on his face, wheeling in some equipment, followed by two nurses. "I'm Dr. Janovic, and I'll be your neurologist today. Howzabout we get this party started," he said.

It was a very good thing that I was happy, because there's nothing I hate worse than a perky neurologist.

TWENTY-ONE

One corticosteroid injection later, my herniated disc, pinched sciatic nerve, and I made our way home, aided by Dave, crutches, and a fistful of pain pills.

Most of the household was downstairs in the gym waiting for me when I came in. There were balloons. There was music. Music I actually liked, as opposed to the boys' top forty shit. I really hoped there was cake.

And I really regretted letting Rosen talk me out of having an elevator installed when we were planning the layout of the space.

"You will be sleeping in my room, Danny." The boys, of course, hooted, and Rosen went red. "And I will sleep upstairs."

Jonas came over and had a bear-hug look in his eye but Dave stopped him. "Give her a mental hug, man," Dave said. "In her current state, she's liable to fall over, and we'll have to go back to the hospital all over again."

"I hear you," Jonas said. "Danny, I used to be a massage therapist in a different life. After you get some rest I'm going to give you a treatment." God, it was good to see him.

"First a vegan chef, and now a massage therapist. You're a renaissance man, Jonas." I wasn't sure how I felt about Jonas – who was the best-looking man I'd ever seen in person – massaging my naked, bruised, and battered body. But Dr. Janovic, or Dr. Jay, as he insisted on being called, had said that massage would be a good thing. As long as it was from a licensed professional.

"I've missed you," I said. "Why don't you just move in here with us? It's ridiculous that we have to do without you."

"You may miss him, but I need him," Dave said. "But maybe he'll be visiting more often." I could see the boys giving each other a look and the fist bump thing they'd started doing. So the fact that Dave and I were back together – *were we back together?* – was becoming clear to everybody.

Dave settled me into Rosen's room, which had been equipped with fresh flowers and a tray next to the bed with a carafe of ice water and a glass, and, the pièce de résistance, an actual bell on it.

"Oh, this was a very bad idea," I said. Marta was laughing and kissing the top of my head over and over and saying something in Spanish. She tended to forget to speak English when she was emotional. "I will be summoning all of you night and day to attend to my every need."

Mama Estela was standing at the foot of the bed. She exhaled loudly and impatiently – her sighs were more expressive than most people's vocabulary – but actually patted my foot.

"Stupid girl," she said, but nicely. Everybody was silent for a minute, as it was among the first English words we'd ever heard from her, and definitely the first time she'd been anything approaching nice to me.

"I love you too, Mama," I said. She rolled her eyes heavenward, said what I presumed were a few choice words in her rapid-fire Spanish, and left the room.

Yup. She was definitely cut from the same cloth as the Clearys.

Half the household was crowded into Rosen's room. Everybody was talking and laughing, and somebody had actually opened a bottle of champagne. I should get duct-taped in alleys more often. Come to think of it, this kind of thing was not unknown to happen to me, but I didn't usually get this kind of reception afterward.

Matty was sitting on the edge of the bed and looking at the abrasions on my cheek and forehead. The couple of stitches I'd received on my cheek were bandaged, but I had what looked like road rash covering most of my forehead from lying face-first in the alley.

"Cool," he said. "But, Auntie, I don't think you should have a job anymore."

"I second that emotion," Darren said. "Your aunt is a wonderful person, the cream of the crop, but I'm starting to think that she shouldn't be allowed out on her own without a minder." I flipped him the bird, which of course made the boys laugh like idiots. Especially Eddie, who was still getting used to our Cleary humor, as his mother was giving him more leeway to spend time around the grown-ups without her present. She'd even given him an inch of champagne in a flute.

Luke's phone tinged. He looked at it and grinned, and slipped out of the room.

"Moira?" I said.

"You'll meet her later," Matty said. "She's okay. She's nice."

"High praise," I said to Matty. "So you approve?"

"I think he's too young to be tied down," Matt said seriously. Dave and Darren both looked at the floor, trying to hide smiles. "But he really likes her. She's an older woman."

"She is?" I said. I looked at my brother. "How much older?"

"She's going to be fourteen in December," Darren said. Luke and Matty would be thirteen in October. I didn't suppose ten months was going to corrupt him, but parental permission or not, I wasn't keen on any more sleepovers, even with this Moira girl sleeping on Marta's floor.

"Where's Fred?" I said to Matt.

"Dunno," he said. He had gently taken hold of my right hand, which the nurse had lightly re-bandaged from my first night at Helen of Troy. I could tell he wanted to take the bandage off to see how it was healing, so I nodded at him to go ahead. "He's gone somewhere with Cliff."

"Wow, they're spending a lot of time together," I said. "Do you guys like him?"

"He's alright." Matt was much more interested in looking at my injuries.

"Tell you what," Darren said. "I'm going to order in a bunch of food for everybody, and then those of us who didn't get much sleep last night can have a nice long nap. Especially you," he said to me. "You need to heal."

"Pizza, please," I said. "With anchovies," Matty and I said at the same time, then licked our thumbs and touched them together. "Then, yeah, I could use some sleep. And you too," I said to Dave.

"We'll sit and talk tonight," he said. Darren nodded, and rubbed his hand over his face. He looked so tired. I did forget, sometimes, how much I'd put him through. I needed to find a balance between doing what I needed to do to feel useful, and putting myself in situations where I wound up in hospital beds.

"Okay, everybody," I said. I tried to shift my weight on the bed. I thought maybe the pain was lessening somewhat, but that could have been the opiates. "I've got to close my eyes for a few minutes. Wake me when the pizza comes." Marta started shooing the boys out, and I got my head down. Dave stayed where he was, and stretched out next to me. "I mean it, Darren. I'm starving."

After a few minutes of fidgeting, I found a spot with my head resting on Dave's shoulder. I breathed deeply, and slept.

When I woke up, it was dark out. I'd slept all day, well into the evening.

Dave was gone, and Darren was sitting in the easy chair in the corner of Rosen's room, staring into space.

"If you didn't save me any pizza, you're a dead man," I said. I looked around the room for a clock.

"Paul Belliveau was here," he said. He squeezed his hands together. He wasn't looking at me. "This morning, they found the body of Kelly Pankhurst washed up by the Humber River. Her mother reported her missing a few days ago. She hadn't answered her phone or turned up for her volunteer shift at The Humane Society. Her cause of death is unknown until the post-mortem." He cleared his throat. "This afternoon, the body of Garrett Jones was found by his ten-year-old daughter when the sitter brought her back from the movies. He'd hanged himself."

There was a pounding in my ears. "His daughter," I think I

said. Anne of Green Gables girl, who was so happy to come to Canada. And Kelly, who'd wanted to be my friend.

I tried to sit up, but the room was twirling, and there was carbonation in my brain. I shouted something, maybe the word "no", and then I tried to lean my head over the side so I wouldn't throw up on Rosen's bed.

Then Dave was there, and Darren was cleaning me up, but I screamed at them to go, to get away from me, to leave. I kept screaming and screaming, but I don't think there were any words after that. I think Darren was telling me that I was scaring the boys, and Dave was trying to hold me, to hold my body still, but something in me had broken.

After a time, Mama Estela came in, moved Dave out of the way, and sat down on the bed next to me. She shoved a pill in my mouth and, with surprising strength, held my mouth and nose shut until I swallowed it.

I remember moving onto my side facing the wall and welcoming the pain from my back and leg. I think I started to try to hurt myself then, to tear at my hair, but they all held me – Dave, Darren and Mama E. – and eventually the pill I'd swallowed started licking at my brain.

Eventually, mercifully, I faded to black.

TWENTY-TWO

I'd lived through the murder of my twin sister and held my husband as he died, bloody, in my arms. I'd killed people. I'd chopped off the hand of a psychopathic cop who was bleeding to death after I'd stabbed her in both femoral arteries, because in that moment I believed she deserved it.

I'd been left for dead, and I'd tried to die.

But it took the deaths of two relative strangers to completely break me.

The days after I'd learned of the deaths of Kelly Pankhurst and Garrett Jones dragged by in some hellish blur. I was afraid to open my mouth, afraid to say anything to anyone, because I didn't want to start screaming again. And I can't even say that it was because I was worried about my nephews, about scaring them. I knew they were being looked after. It was because I was sure that if I couldn't stop screaming, my loved ones would have been forced, eventually, to take me into hospital. And somewhere in my very sick and broken brain, I had decided that once I got taken to a hospital, I'd never get out. I'd be strapped down. Doctors would try to fix me. And at some point some well-meaning medical professional would ask me to try to talk rationally about everything I'd been through, try to make me face who I was.

I knew who I was. I was a killer. I had killed, and I had caused others to be killed, just by my very existence.

I had two choices: escape by drugs, or escape by death.

I thought that the people under my roof would be safe for a little while, because there were so many of them, and they were armed and ready. Staying right where I was until I was strong enough to leave – alone – was my only option, unless I wanted to eventually cause more mayhem and death.

So I opened my mouth and swallowed the pain pills and whatever sedatives they were giving me. That was one escape. I didn't fight Dave when he held me, but I didn't hear whatever soothing words he whispered to me. I just let myself drift into nothingness. If anyone asked me anything or tried to engage me, I put my hands over my ears and turned away. I allowed myself to be helped to the bathroom, and let Mama Estela help me bathe.

Oddly, she was the person whose presence I minded least in that time. She would sit next to the bed on one of her hard dining-room chairs and speak to me in Spanish, or read to me from one of her magazines. Sometimes she'd poke me to look at one of the pictures – she was a big fan of *People* magazine in Spanish – and I would dutifully obey. She made me drink some kind of ginger tea, as though I had a stomach upset, and held the cup while I sipped. She fed me from a spoon; bland, invalid food, and I ate like a good child. She guarded my room like a warden, allowing only two people in at a time, and not allowing the twins in at all. Jonas came in and gave me a massage, and he didn't talk to me. It hurt, but felt better after. Dave and Jonas stretched my hip and manipulated my body into positions that were supposed to help me heal, and I let them.

But when someone said something light-hearted, or tried to act normal in my presence, it was like a slight buzzing would start in my brain, and I'd have to hide my head under the duvet.

I'd blocked all feelings of love, for anyone. For the first time in my life, I felt nothing for my little brother. He was just another person in the house. Dave might as well have been a stranger. Take my pills, sleep, feel nothing, say nothing, and perhaps I would eventually just disappear.

Darren brought in his laptop. I heard him mention Dr. Singh, and I shook my head.

After a number of days, I don't know how many, Paul Belliveau came in, followed closely by my bodyguard Mama E. I was sitting up in bed, waiting for my tea and pills. He was talking, asking questions. I heard their names, the names of the people who'd died.

I'd stopped covering my ears at that point. I'd found that I could just drift, thoughtless, somewhere inside my head. I could live there for a little while.

Belliveau talked, and I looked at Mama Estela. She had my pills in her hand and a cup of tea.

This time she shook her head, and put the pills firmly into the pocket of the dress she wore. "No," she said. "Talk first." She nodded at Belliveau.

I moved my head toward the wall, and sunk my body into the bed.

* * *

I didn't leave Rosen's room for two weeks.

I'd been starting to see through the fog for a couple of days before. I woke up clinging to Dave, actually glad he was there. I was asking for water and cutting back on the Percocet. I could hear the boys, and I missed them. But I didn't want them to see me like this, in this room.

I didn't want to talk about Helen of Troy yet, or Garrett, or Kelly. I couldn't bear to think about them. I especially avoided thinking about Garrett's daughter. I didn't want anyone to ask me anything. But I wanted to see the boys, and try to walk up the stairs, have a coffee in my kitchen, a shower in my own bathroom.

"I'm going to put clothes on today," I said to Mama E. one morning, "not pajamas." Mama picked up the little bell that still sat on the tray next to the bed and rang it. Dave came in within seconds.

"Jeans," she said. "Shirt." She pointed at me.

Dave smiled, and for the first time in two weeks, I smiled back. But not for long. It felt weird.

Mama helped me get dressed, though I didn't strictly need her to. The corticosteroid was doing its work; I was much less helpless. At least physically. But Mama made me feel calmer than anyone else did. She didn't ask questions, and seemed to understand what I needed.

"Skinny," she said, frowning, once I was dressed. My jeans were too loose. I felt like a ghost of myself.

"Ha! Skinny," I said, pointing at her. She was smaller than Eddie.

"Pfft," she said. I stood in the room for a minute looking at her. It felt like a big step, opening that door. This room was safe. That world was not safe for anyone, as long as I was in it.

Mama picked up the bell again and shoved it in her pocket. She loved that bell. I pitied Marta. Then she picked up her chair and headed to the door with it. Without a backwards glance at me, she carried her chair out of my room for the first time since I'd gone crazy.

I felt like a kid whose mom has left her at the gates on the first day of school. But Dave was there, waiting outside the door, and we went upstairs together.

TWENTY-THREE

A couple of days later I had a Skype session with Dr. Singh. She explained to me that she'd been talking to Dave and Darren every day while I was in bed. She'd prescribed a couple of things for me – or had a colleague in Toronto do it for her. She said what I'd probably experienced was catatonic depression. I'd been taking benzodiazepines – I'd expected that, I'd had benzos before and knew what they felt like – and, to my surprise, I'd been taking an SSRI for nearly two weeks. An antidepressant, in other words.

"Oh, that's nice," I said to her. "I've been given brain-altering medication without my consent? Outside of a clinical setting?"

"First of all, Darren assured me that he'd told you."

He might have. I hadn't heard a word.

"And secondly, as you well know, it's my medical opinion that you should have been on an SSRI long before now." I didn't say anything. "And I also talked to..." She checked her notes. "Estela Garcia. She's a retired psychiatric nurse, Danny. I checked her credentials. I felt quite safe leaving you in her hands."

"You talked to Mama Estela?" I said. "She spoke to you in English? She was a nurse?"

Dr. Singh laughed. "I speak Spanish. But I think she can get along in English if the situation calls for it."

I knew it.

"And how are you feeling? You're obviously up and around. Your affect isn't flat. You seem… well, I wouldn't quite say your fighting self, but you seem okay." She paused. "SSRIs can take six weeks, sometimes more, to really kick in. Some people get positive effects after as little as a week. From the reports I've been getting, I'd say you started to come around after eleven or twelve days."

I nodded. "So am I supposed to keep taking them?" I wasn't sure how I felt about that. I didn't want to depend on a drug for my mental state. But I couldn't go back to what I'd just been through.

"Yes," she said. "I would like it if you did. You're on a very low dose, Danny. At some point we may need to raise it, but we'll cross that bridge when we come to it. But please remember, if you really make the decision for yourself that you don't want to take them anymore, wean yourself off them slowly. There can be some very unpleasant side effects if you don't." We talked some more, and I agreed to Skype sessions three times a week for a while.

I wasn't sure what to feel. On the one hand, I was grateful that I was being cared for. On the other hand, I felt like I had moved from being a fucked-up addict to being a fucked-up crazy person.

Fred had missed the whole thing. He was on what he called a "fishing trip". He and Cliff were in California meeting with venture capitalists. He'd called the boys a few times, and Darren had talked to him once, but Fred had cut the call short, saying he was going to be late for a meeting.

I knew that Darren, Dave, and Jonas were working up plans and strategies involving the boys and custodial rights, but they had wisely left me out of it.

I was learning to let other people fly the plane. At that moment, it was what I had to do.

It was Labor Day, and the boys were starting their new school in a few days. I was spending as much time as possible with them. I couldn't work out with them, or take them anywhere yet – I was doing much better physically, but I was still under advice to rest in the times between exercises supervised by my physio that Rosen and Dr. Janovic had encouraged me to see. But we watched movies and played trivia games, and once a day I let them see the progression of the bruising and wounds on my lower back. Luke's girlfriend had gone up north with her parents for the week before school started, so we had him to ourselves. Rosen came up and we watched *Say Anything...* – Luke cried – and I actually sat through *The Breakfast Club*. It was just as bad as I remembered, but I kept my mouth shut about it. Well, as much as possible.

I concentrated on them, on the domestic, and on being healthy. I didn't watch the news or read it online. I kept a loaded gun next to my bed, and Dave slept beside me.

It was the first time since my sister's death, since I'd met Michael Vernon Smith and experienced true evil, that I didn't let worry about my loved ones' safety consume me, didn't let it be the first and last thing I thought about every day. I'd done my job. I'd set this place up. Everyone knew their roles.

I took my pills, but took the benzos – the sedatives – only at night, for sleep. The corticosteroid injection I'd been given – only one a year of this kind of steroid allowed, I'd been told, and it would take a while to really kick in – was doing its magic. I did my stretches, and I went on short walks with Dave, Rosen, or Darren.

And when I was ready, Paul Belliveau came to take my statement about the events at Helen of Troy.

He brought video recording equipment. I'd been expecting that. I'd been given a pass from going into the station, due to my injuries and mental state. I could have gone in, but I was grateful that I didn't have to.

Before we began recording, Belliveau and I sat in my living room with Dave and Darren.

"Ann Saulnier is still missing," Belliveau told us. "The home address on record for her at the club doesn't exist, and the cell phone number they had for her was a pre-paid mobile that hasn't been turned on since that night."

"So you don't even know if that's her real name," I said. "So she's not missing, per se."

Belliveau shook his head. "Yours wasn't the only hire that was done without following even the most basic legal guidelines. They didn't seem to have anybody's social insurance numbers recorded. Staff said they were paid by a check from the Kinder Group, but that Jones cut the checks himself, in his office at the club, and there were no taxes withheld. They were told they were all independent contractors, responsible for declaring and paying their own taxes." He took a sip of water. "The club is shut down, of course. The company is claiming that Garrett Jones was responsible for all of these things, and advised us that he had a meeting upcoming with the company's lawyers to hand over the first quarter's payroll and so forth. It's their first venture in Canada, and their spokesperson said that Jones was a long-term valued employee; they trusted him to follow all proper protocols. They assume he was either overwhelmed by the job, had gone off the rails somehow, or was simply stealing from them."

"Jesus," Darren said.

"I wondered about the social insurance number thing. I mean, the fact that I didn't have to fill out any but the most basic paperwork. But Garrett said that as soon as I'd done a few trial shifts we'd sit down and go through all that." And I'm not exactly knowledgeable about these things, I didn't add, but everyone in the room knew that well enough.

"Originally the working theory was that Garrett Jones killed Kelly Pankhurst, and then himself," he said. "Lover's quarrel type of thing."

I stared at him. "Impossible," I said. I told him about Garrett, about his aw-shucks personality, about his careful awareness of boundaries.

I caught Darren and Dave looking at each other. "Danny, you have a history of not seeing what's right in front of you when it comes to the dark side of people," Darren said. "You only met the man a handful of times. And every day you hear about these kinds of crimes, men killing the women they supposedly love."

I nodded. "I know. But they were not an item. I mean, I would be truly shocked." I told them about Kelly writing me the note, and trying to keep it hidden from Garrett.

"Well, that would actually fit into this theory," Dave said. "A woman who was afraid of her lover, reaching out for help." I could see him wince. He didn't want to remind me that if Kelly was reaching out for help, she certainly didn't get any from me.

I opened my mouth to argue, but then shut it. They were

right. Women in abusive relationships could be skittish and easily startled, and perhaps Kelly was reaching out to me in friendship because she really didn't have anyone to talk to. If she was afraid and needed protection – well, she had just seen me make short work of a crowd of young guys in the bar. And really, what did I know about Garrett? Other than the man had genuinely loved his daughter? That wasn't faked. But lots of very bad men loved their wives and children.

"I can't disprove that theory," Belliveau was saying. "Nobody can, at least not yet. But we can't prove it, either."

"I take everyone's point about my occasional bad judgment about people," I said. "But I cannot see that man committing suicide at a time and place when he knew his daughter would find him. I just can't."

Belliveau nodded. "The condo they were renting certainly doesn't show anything other than a father and daughter who were very close. There was no sign that an adult female spent any time there; no toiletries or clothing, nothing of that sort. They had one of those dry-erase schedules on their fridge, and it was all carefully filled in with his work schedule and his daughter's day camp and their planned outings. It had three names on it: his, the girl's, and the nanny." Belliveau saw the look Darren and I gave each other – our nephews had been abducted by their nanny, back in California – and shook his head. "She's clean. She's been thoroughly checked."

"Does she have the girl?" I asked. "Who's taking care of his daughter?"

Belliveau looked at the floor and shook his head. "Children's Aid have custody. She's a ward of the Crown now. There's no family anywhere. The girl says her mother died a few years

212

ago, and both of her parents were only children. There's a grandmother surviving, but she's got Alzheimer's."

"We can take her," I said. I blurted it out without thinking. "We've got room. We've got other kids here." I looked at Darren, who was shaking his head, but half grinning.

"Danny, it doesn't work like that," Belliveau said. "You're not a relative, and you're not a foster parent in the system already. You don't even know the girl, and she doesn't know you."

"And please don't forget our mutual friend, who may or may not be lurking somewhere in the city as we speak," Dave said. "Fuckface Smith," he said to Belliveau.

Belliveau nodded. "He's right. I understand how you feel. I do. But for the time being, let's just concentrate on what's in front of us, shall we?"

Darren and Dave cleared out, and when Belliveau switched the recording on, I answered all his questions. I told him how I got hired at Helen of Troy, and everything I could remember about Kelly Pankhurst and Garrett Jones. I told him about the man who had been molesting Ann, and about her abduction in the alley. I told him that while most of the dancers I'd met and seen seemed on the up-and-up and certainly experienced, Ann had looked like a kid. Although when I'd talked to her backstage, she'd seemed well-spoken and mature.

I was reminded, after I finished my statement, that I'd only been in the place three times. And on two of those occasions, I'd been injured.

"I don't think I've ever been involved in a case where we knew so little," Belliveau told me after we were finished. He was putting the camera away.

"Wait!" I said. "What about her car? Ann's car? She asked me to walk her to her car, and she took the alley exit. Her car must have been in the parking lot. It was free to park there. Surely you could get her name that way."

"There were no cars in the parking lot that weren't spoken for by staff or the patrons who were still there that night when the police went in, when they found you in the alley," he said. "Either one of the men who took her also took her car…"

"Or she never had one in the first place," I finished. "Maybe she just wanted to get me alone, to talk to me."

"We may never know, Danny. And you're going to have to let it go. There really isn't anything else you can do." He sat down and leaned across the coffee table and grabbed my hand. "I mean it, Danny. I know that my saying that is like a red flag to a bull where you're concerned. But you have to leave it. You're not the police. You're not even a private investigator. And you're not physically or – and I'm sorry for saying this, but – mentally strong enough to take a run at this thing."

"I know," I said. "But, Paul, I just feel so powerless. I can't stand it." I was trying not to cry, and I could tell my face was getting all red. And I knew that he knew I wasn't just feeling powerless about Kelly and Garrett and Ann. I was feeling powerless about Michael Vernon Smith, and Fred's disappearing act, and the possibility of him moving the boys away.

Paul moved over and sat next to me and pulled me into him. He took his flask from his pocket and told me to take a swig. "For luck," he said. "Remember the hospital?"

The night we'd met, the night my husband Jack had been killed, he'd sat and listened to me and to Matty. He'd fought to let us stay together in the hospital, and he'd slipped his flask under my pillow. He'd said it was a good luck charm.

I took a swig and coughed, which made me laugh. And then I wasn't about to cry anymore.

"See?" he said. "That's the lucky flask for you." He put it back in his jacket pocket and patted it, satisfied.

I had a smile on my face. It felt good but weird, like using a muscle I hadn't for a while. "Stay for dinner," I said. "Call the ball and chain – get her down here too. I want as much company as possible while we wait."

"Wait for what?"

"Wait for evil to show up at the door," I said lightly. "Wait for something I can do something about."

He had his cell phone out to call his wife. "She'll come, if only to make sure the Garcias know that I'm taken," he said. "But, Danny?"

"Yes, Sergeant?"

"You need to start thinking about how to have a life if evil never does show up at your door."

I smiled, and left him to talk to his wife while I went to tell everybody to expect two more for dinner. But I knew he was wrong.

Evil would show up at my door again. I was a magnet for it.

TWENTY-FOUR

September went by in a whirlwind of happy chaos.

All three of the boys were starting school in Toronto for the first time, after being homeschooled while getting used to all the changes in their lives. I barely slept the night before class started, and wound up on the floor outside the twins' room again. I hadn't done that since what had happened outside of Helen of Troy, what with going crazy, and then Dave being an inducement to stay in my own bed. Besides, despite the pain of my damaged sciatic nerve getting steadily better, I wasn't as keen on running up and down the stairs, not to mention parking myself on the floor for hours at a time.

I was starting to see what old age might feel like, and I wasn't liking it.

Rosen was taking them to school and picking them up for the time being. Most kids their age seemed to make their own way to school, from what I could gather, but I wasn't ready for that. With Fuckface Smith at large, not to mention my sinking suspicion that the events that had taken place at Helen of Troy might not be over – Ann was still missing, and according to Belliveau, the consensus now was that Garrett Jones's suicide was faked – I hated letting them out of my sight. Darren felt the same, and nearly every day when the boys had their lunch period, Darren would take a long walk, claiming to be exploring the city. I was sure, however, that he was going by the school to check in on the boys, walk around the block the school was on and make sure there were no suspicious people lurking in vehicles. All of us – Fred, Darren, Rosen, Marta, and I – had met with the principal and her deputy months earlier and advised them of the security concerns we had, and why. We made sure the staff knew that only one of the five of us could sign any of the boys out of school, for any reason.

Fred had come back from his "fishing trip" a couple of days before school started. He was happy to see the boys; even I could see that, and I was one antidepressant away from clocking him with a cast-iron pan. The night before school started, we had a pizza party in the gym, all of us, and after some prodding he said the trip wasn't as fruitful as he had been hoping. He was going to "regroup", as he called it. He definitely wanted to start a new business, he said, but the business plan he and Cliff had put together had not, apparently, garnered much excitement from the venture capitalists.

I had capital, and Fred knew it. Not as much as I had before – buying and renovating the bakery to our specifications had cost more than I could have dreamed possible. We joked that we should have just bought our own island in the Caribbean; it would have been cheaper. I wondered if Fred would ever have the nerve to ask me for seed money for whatever it was he and Cliff wanted to do. Not in a million years would I give him any – it was my late husband's hard-earned money, and it was for the family, for the boys. But there was something changed in Fred again. Darren and I whispered about it late one night when Fred, Dave, and Jonas were all playing the Xbox with the boys. The cold and confident master of the universe that Fred had been when he was making his money had deflated after Ginger had been killed. But lately, since getting beaten up outside the strip club and then reconnecting with Cliff, Fred was getting a little of that cockiness back.

I should have been happier that he was happier. But I hadn't liked that Fred. That Fred had brought all of this evil into our lives in the first place. My rational mind knew that Fred had more than paid for his folly, but, as we all knew well, my rational mind wasn't always in full working order.

I was trying. Dr. Singh was helping. Dave was helping. Darren wasn't helping, because if anything, he was even more attached to Matty and Luke than I was, and sometimes I was worried that he would do something really crazy if Fred actually intended to take the boys away.

One afternoon, a week into the semester, Fred and I decided to pick the boys up from school and take them shopping for new shoes. While they were in a private school, it was an informal, no-uniform school, so regular sneakers were the order of the day. As the boys were both growing an inch a month – or so it seemed – they were complaining that if they didn't get new sneakers they were going to just cut holes in the fronts of the ones they were already wearing. They'd spent the summer barefoot indoors and in flip-flops the rest of the time, so even they hadn't really noticed until now.

The four of us were in Rosen's SUV, which was the safest of our vehicles. Matty was saying that he was at the point where he was curling his toes under to be able to fit his feet into his shoes.

"I saw something on the Discovery Channel about this once," he said. "In ancient China, they would bind women's feet, just fold them right over in half, when they were really young and their bones were soft. Then their feet grew all deformed and they could never walk right."

"Yes, because men decided that women should be delicate and tiny and not be able to move around properly," I said.

"Good thing you didn't live in ancient China, Auntie," Luke said. He liked to call my footwear "canoes" because my feet were so big.

"Can you imagine their disappointment when, even after folding my feet, they were still bigger than everybody else's regular feet?" I said. "And it wasn't just ancient China. It persisted well into the twentieth century. There are Chinese women alive today whose feet are deformed because they had their toes broken and folded under."

"Your aunt is a feminist, Luke," Fred said, "which is admirable. But there were lots of sociopolitical reasons why such things persisted." He glanced at my face. "Not that it was a good thing, by any stretch."

I breathed deeply, and reminded myself that Fred was driving, so therefore it would be unwise to kill him just now. I continued. "It wasn't that long ago that women had to wear corsets made of whale bones to keep their waists tiny. Then their internal organs would actually rearrange themselves, and some women couldn't breathe properly."

"Is that why women in those old books and movies are always fainting?" Luke said.

"It certainly didn't help."

"Women wear things like that now," Matty said. "Corsets and stuff."

I turned around and looked at him. "Oh, really? And how would you know that, Matthew?" Luke laughed and punched his brother in the arm. Matty kept a straight face, but it was red.

After a moment, he rolled his eyes. "Because we have this little thing called the Internet, Auntie. You should check it out one day."

"I am attempting to educate you young whippersnappers about the subjugation of women throughout history," I said, in my most annoying voice.

"That's good, Auntie, but you don't have to worry," Luke said. He reached forward and knocked me on my head, gently. "We won't subjugate any women."

"I'm very glad to hear it," I said.

"You're the toughest person we know," he continued. He was looking at his phone now, presumably reading a text from the lovely Moira. "And it's important for young guys to have strong female role models."

I was floored, and trying not to be. Fred looked at me with eyebrows raised, and I shrugged, like *don't ask me.*

"Moira's a feminist too," he continued. "She's teaching me a lot."

"I'm… thrilled to hear it," I said. "How about you, Fred?"

"Thrilled to hear it. Absolutely. Yes." Fred stole a glance over his shoulder and I saw him grin at Matty.

I was glad to see it. I was glad to see Fred interacting with his sons at all, really, other than the spate of video gaming lately.

I needed to know that Fred could see past his current obsession with business. I needed to know that on his list of priorities, his sons came first.

Matty started asking if he could watch the next time Jonas gave me a massage – he wanted to see how the muscles and ligaments all worked together, he said.

"Abso-fucking-lutely not," I said. Fred looked at me. "I'm sorry," I said to him. "Boys, have I not been curbing my use of the F-bomb lately? Have you noticed?"

"If you say so," Matty said. "It doesn't bother us."

"Thanks, honey. And no. You may not witness my massage."

"Why not?"

"Because I'll be naked, Matt. When you get a massage, they don't do it through your clothes."

"Oh! Never mind. God in heaven, never mind!" He pretended to scream in horror, and then Luke and Fred joined in. They reminded me so much of Skipper, Laurence, and Darren, and I had a moment of pure happiness, just like that. The kind of moment that you want to hang onto, and remember, and be able to come back to.

"You people are hysterical," I said, grinning. "But seriously, especially where the sciatic nerve is, it's basically lower back and butt and down my legs. You really don't need to see that."

"No, sir, I do not," Matty said, and Fred and I laughed. "But wait – doesn't Dave mind that Jonas touches your... nakedness?"

"Well, one: Dave doesn't own me," I said. "And, two: Jonas is a professional. And we're friends."

"Moira and Luke are friends," Matty replied. "So does that mean it's okay if he massages her naked?"

"Zip it, smartass," I said. We were sitting in traffic, because of course we were going halfway across town to a specific store that specialized in the shoes both boys wanted. I looked over my shoulder at Luke, who had a big grin on his face as he was typing away. "What's up, buttercup? Entertain us."

"I'm just texting Moira this conversation," he said. "She's digging it."

"I'm so glad," I said, glancing at Fred again.

"No such thing as privacy with kids around," he said quietly.

"Or with cell phones around," I said.

"Oh, guess what? We're doing a field trip to the Royal Ontario Museum," Matty said. "It's a history and art thing."

"Oh yeah. Somebody has to sign permission forms," Luke said.

"Remind me later," Fred said.

I wanted to be able to sign those forms, and for Darren to be able to. We had to get our legal rights sorted, and quickly. As things stood, despite everything, Fred was the boys' parent and legal guardian. Their sole guardian. We needed to have that conversation with Fred about our legal rights. And with his moods, we needed to pick our moment, and pick it well.

When we parked in front of the store, I got out and stretched a bit. It wasn't the best day, pain-wise, and I elected to lie down in the backseat while the boys shopped. I took half a Percocet and stretched out. Within a couple of minutes I was asleep.

I'm at Helen of Troy. The music is loud, much louder than it really is in the club. I'm walking through tables of customers, but I'm on crutches, and I can't move quickly. A dancer is being grabbed roughly by a man, but I'm far away and I can't get there quickly enough. My crutches keep getting caught on chair legs as I try to move, so I throw them down and try to walk. I get closer, but the pain in my hip is unbearable. I don't know if I can go on, but I must. She's blonde, the dancer, she's Ann, and I have to stop them from throwing her over a shoulder and making off with her. It's very important, and no one else is watching. There are no other staff on duty. But when I am nearly upon them, I see that it's not Ann. It's Ginger. I'm only vaguely surprised. She's wearing huge fake eyelashes and some kind of gold lamé tube top. She looks like something from Austin Powers, like she's playing the role of a stripper. She's crying, but she doesn't want me to get any closer. She puts her hand up to stop me, and I'm trying to see who the man is who's got her on his lap. More important than saving her, I have to see who the man is.

"It's too late for me," she's telling me, "but not for her. Then it can be over, Danny."

I reach the man and I start to put a key in his ear, but it's not a key, it's a knife. I don't hesitate. I push the knife slowly into his ear, and then I fall to the floor. I never see his face. I just see his blood.

It came back to me days later, the dream, but by then it was nearly too late.

TWENTY-FIVE

The day of the field trip was rainy and blustery, and felt like the first real day of autumn.

"It always rained on field trip days," Darren said over coffee in our kitchen. He was back from taking the boys to school with Rosen, and had witnessed them getting on the bus. "Don't you remember? And we always had to go to that experimental farm thing. That place that pretended it was an eighteenth-century working dairy farm or whatever. And we'd all be trudging around in the mud. Miserable."

"Oh God, yes," I said. "They made me use a butter churn."

"I would have paid good money to see that." Dave came into the kitchen and messed up my messy hair.

"I think it's where I learned to swear," I said. "Anyway, the boys will be inside all day. But God, think of it. Hordes of teenagers tramping through the antiquities. Some docent will have a coronary."

I was trying to be cheery, but Dave was leaving that evening for a job in Florida. Jonas had flown ahead, and Dave promised it would be a week, max, and nothing dangerous. I'd gotten used to him being here, sleeping with me every night, being able to curl up to him when I woke from nightmares I couldn't remember. We'd avoided talking about the future, i.e. whether or not I would ever want to work with him again, or how – if – we could make whatever it was between us work. But his presence was a balm to my damaged soul.

Fred came up to our kitchen and sat down, rubbing sleep out of his eyes. I liked him best in the morning. He reminded me most of the boy I'd met back in Maine, who worked at McDonald's with my twin sister and ate most of his meals at our house.

"I said I'd go for the after-lunch part of the field trip today," Fred said. "There's some kind of lecture about ancient pottery? Or glazing? I don't know. But they needed another parent chaperone to fill in for someone who has to leave early."

"Better you than me," I said. "I'd probably start snoring. Bad example for the young 'uns."

"I stayed up reading about antiquities online and I actually drank Scotch," he said. "Why did I do that?"

"Because reading about antiquities made you feel like a grown-up, and you associate drinking Scotch with being a grown-up," Dave said. "Ipso facto."

"You're right. And I fell asleep with my head on the keyboard." He showed us the position he'd woken up in, and for Fred, it was funny. He wasn't much of a laugh-riot lately. But then again, which of us were?

"I will make us all breakfast," I said, and all three of them turned to look at me. "What? I can make breakfast."

They all pretended to look at their watches and began mumbling about places they had to be until I started throwing napkins at them.

"Somebody put avocados in our fridge," I said. "I will make us smashed avocado on toast."

"Get you," Darren said. "Did you go to a vegan brunch place sometime in the last year, Beanpole?"

"Jonas made it for me. Get this: It's toast, with avocado smashed onto it."

In the end, I had to get Dave's help with how to properly take the insides out of an avocado, but I made breakfast. And a fresh pot of coffee.

"Maybe I should be a waitress," I said, once everybody was eating. "I sort of liked having a job. You know, except for…"

"People dying?" Darren said.

"Getting tackled and tied up in an alley?" Dave added. We were all silent for a minute.

"You should have asked for hazard pay," Fred said.

"Hey! I never got paid! That company owes me money."

"You're right," Fred said. "But the club is closed, right?"

"But the parent company isn't," I said. "I'm going to call them and demand my… whatever it is. Two hundred bucks."

"Leave it, Bean," Darren said. "You heard Belliveau. Don't get involved with these people any further."

"It's a phone call, Darren," I said. "I'm not exactly rushed off my feet here. I can do it from the privacy of my own bathtub."

"That was random," Dave said. "I'm going to get some things packed and maybe have a quick nap. While the job in Florida won't be dangerous, it will be both boring and involve sleep deprivation. I want to bank some shut-eye."

"I'll help you," I said. I wanted to be horizontal with Dave as much as possible before he had to leave for the airport.

"I'm going to shower and get ready to be scintillated," Fred said.

"And I guess I will clean up," Darren said, and called after us all, "It's fine. You all go off to your lives. I'll just take care of the grunt work."

I trotted back into the kitchen – still not in running form – and hugged him. "I love you more than avocados on toast," I said.

"Things are sort of okay, aren't they," he whispered. He was hugging me back, wearing his washing-up gloves. The boys and I had got him a pair that went nearly up to his elbows, with pink marabou trim. Sometimes he wore them down to dinner at Marta's, which made Marta giggle and Mama Estela shake her head and roll her eyes.

"Shhh. Jinx."

"I know. I shouldn't have said that. Sorry." He pushed me away. "Now go and conjugate with your boyfriend, while I do man's work." He started singing Peggy Lee, "Is That All There Is?" and I went upstairs.

Dave left for the airport while I was still napping. After the, uh, conjugating. He left me a present on his pillow: a very sweet note, and a new pair of Kevlar fighting gloves tied up with a ribbon.

Some women might prefer jewelry, but I'll take tactical armor any day of the week.

The evening started out quietly. The boys told us about their day – Matty had loved the ROM, Luke less so. Moira hadn't gone to school that day, and so he'd had to endure the field trip without her. We discussed plans for the boys' thirteenth birthday, which was coming up. Rosen took them through some defense drills when they claimed to have no homework. Darren and I watched a documentary about Scientology in the main TV room on the boys' and Fred's floor.

Fred was reading a book, lying on a couch in the room with us, but he seemed edgy.

"I'm going for a run," he said finally. "I let it kind of lapse for a while but I'm going to get out there."

"Raining out," I said, barely moving my head. I felt like a sloth. I had barely moved in weeks.

"Good for you," Darren said. "Put hair on your chest."

I debated going with him. The pain was getting better nearly every day, and I hated the idea of losing my fitness because of this injury. Plus, I presumed Fred would be pretty slow, and would probably do a lot of walking breaks.

"Mind if I come?" I said. "Just to see how I do," I said to Darren, who was glaring at me.

"No way," Fred said. "Sorry, Danny, but I'm not always in the mood to feel like the klutzy one, you know? If I run alone in the dark, nobody really notices the fact that I'm barely shuffling and I can't breathe. And I don't have to be an object of Cleary comedy over breakfast the next day."

"Oh," I said. "Okay." I sat up and looked at him.

"Fred," Darren started to say, but Fred held his hand up.

"Sometimes a guy's self-esteem just can't take another hit." He left the room, and Darren and I looked at each other but said nothing. We watched the documentary, and Fred waved on his way back down the hall after changing for his run. I kept my eye on our security monitor, watched Fred leave through the front door.

"Are we shits?" I said. I paused the TV.

"It's possible," Darren said.

"Not everybody grew up like we did. We all have pretty thick skins."

"And the same sense of humor."

"Which Fred does not," I said. "It's easy to forget, sometimes. He is outnumbered, really."

"Things obviously didn't go well for him in California, and we weren't exactly sympathetic."

"No." We sat in silence for a minute. "When's his birthday?" I said suddenly. "Fred's."

Darren looked at me. "I don't have any idea."

"So we've probably been here with him on his birthday and didn't even acknowledge it."

"Well. Shit." Darren ran downstairs to ask the boys when their father's birthday was, and I sent Fred a text:

> We are awful humans, and we're sorry you have to put up with us. We're just sorry.

I thought for a second, then added:

I waited for him to text back, and glanced through the newsfeed on my phone. I had no idea what was going on in the world. I was afraid to see my name somewhere, or even something about Helen of Troy. After the time that had passed, though, I was sure there were newer atrocities.

My phone rang, and I jumped. I usually had my phone off, and not many people called me. It was Belliveau.

"Do you think that Darren and I would be difficult to live with?" I said by way of greeting.

"What? Danny, listen to me. I have to tell you something, and I have to tell you right away," he said. I heard the sounds of traffic and rain in the background.

"What is it?" I said. I was standing. I didn't remember standing.

"A body was found on Cherry Beach late this afternoon. It matches the description you gave for Ann Saulnier."

"Oh no," I said. My eyes welled up. That poor girl. That poor kid.

"Danny, there's something else." He yelled something at someone and then came back on the line. It sounded like he was getting into a car. "There were words carved on her abdomen." There was silence, during which I dug my fingers so hard into my palm that I opened the wound there.

"Just tell me, Paul. Spit it out."

"Hi, Danny," he said. "That's what was carved there. 'Hi, Danny.'"

The same words that had been written in blood on the mirror nearly two years ago, when I woke up in a motel room in California with a dead man in the next bed.

"It's him," I said. "Michael Vernon Smith." I looked around frantically for my Percocet. I couldn't afford pain.

"It looks that way," Belliveau said. "You guys do what you do. Your security protocols. I'm sending people to sit out back and in front, and I'll be there when I can. He's showing his hand, Danny. Whatever he's playing at, there has to be a reason he chose her, and a reason he chose now."

"Yes," I said.

"Or it could be just to drive you crazy," he said. "Make you prisoners in your own home."

"Yes."

I heard somebody talking over his cop radio. "Danny, I'll be there when I can."

"Fred's not here," I said. "He's gone for a run. He's out there on his own. And Dave's gone; he had to fly to Florida today." I was babbling. What was taking Darren so long? Why was it so quiet in here? It was never quiet in here.

Belliveau swore. "I'll get it on the radio for patrol to look for him. You call him. And, Danny, stay calm. You know what to do."

He hung up. I walked to the wall and pushed our "Code Orange" alarm – two short rings. Everyone in the house could see which room it was coming from, and we could – kids included – broadcast from the video monitors to all the other rooms in the house.

I made a mental note of the time. It was ten p.m. on the dot.

"Everybody come up to the TV room, please. Now," I said. I tried to sound calm, and found that I actually was. "Urgent news about Smith, but don't panic. Rosen, outdoor protocol and armed, please. Darren, bring all the boys. Marta and Mama, this means you too."

Within ten seconds, floodlights lit up every side of the bakery. There would be no skulking in darkness for anybody who might be looking for a way into this building. I heard movement downstairs, and Darren's voice. Then I breathed. I quickly moved the lamp in the corner and grabbed the loaded pistol that was secured behind it.

Only the adults knew the location of most of the firearms in the bakery, but all three of our kids had been drilled in firearm safety so often and thoroughly, they'd never touch a gun unless they had to. I dialed Fred's number, but it went right to voicemail.

I tucked the gun into the back of my jeans and pulled my t-shirt down over it.

I was about to dial Fred again, when glass shattered somewhere downstairs, and Marta screamed.

The "Code Red" alarm activated.

TWENTY-SIX

This. This was why we'd had monitors installed everywhere.

Marta's kitchen window had been broken from the outside.

Our supposedly unbreakable glass was very broken, presumably by someone on the fire escape.

I did what we were meant to do, and stayed where I was. The TV room was our equivalent of a safe room. A safe room in what was supposed to have been a very safe building. It had no windows and a large closet with food, water, emergency supplies, and weapons. The entrance to the room was a sliding steel door that would take a bomb to open without the correct biometrics.

But, then again, we'd thought our windows were unbreakable.

The boys came running in, first Eddie, then the twins. My gun had found its way into my hand in the last few seconds, and I kept my eyes on the monitors.

"Boys, into the closet, please," I yelled. The alarm was deafening. "Now."

We called it a closet, but it was really a small room, with an external ventilation system. It was a panic room within a safe room, for situations exactly like this one – the boys were safe before the rest of us were, or if the rest of us couldn't make it there. I wasn't closing the safe room door until everyone else was inside.

Marta and Mama came in next, probably twenty seconds later. For once, Mama wasn't carrying her chair. Instead, she was holding a very lethal-looking machete. Marta was shaking, but she had a baseball bat in her hand.

"Ladies, closet with the boys. Go. Lock the door until you see we're all in here." There was a monitor in the closet that showed the rest of this room, but none of the rest of the house.

Right now, I cursed that failing.

I looked back at the monitors. Rosen and Darren were in Marta's kitchen, both with guns drawn. Rosen pulled down the emergency shutter – a steel covering that could be drawn down from the ceiling, similar to the security shutters you see covering the windows of stores in bad neighborhoods after dark. He gave the monitor the thumbs up, and a few seconds later he and Darren were in the TV room. Darren slid the steel door shut.

We were locked in.

And if the rest of the windows in the bakery had been installed with the same glass – obviously not the space-age unbreakable, bullet-proof glass that we had paid for – then this was the only safe room.

Fred was still out there somewhere, but the rest of us were safe.

Darren deactivated the alarm, and there was blessed quiet for a moment.

The closet opened, and the Garcias and the twins came out.

"Where's Fred?" Matty said. He was in his pajama bottoms, a t-shirt, and bare feet. All the boys were.

"Gone for a run," I said. "The police should be here in moments, and Belliveau is having people look for him. His phone was off, but try him again, Matt." I tossed Matty my phone.

"I walk into the kitchen, and it exploded," Marta was saying.

"Marta, sit down," Rosen said. He moved the two women gently into chairs, and Darren grabbed a few bottles of water from the closet and handed them out. Rosen pulled a throw from the couch and wrapped it around Marta, who had started to rock back and forth.

"There's no signal," Matty said. His voice sounded higher than usual. "I can't get a signal."

Darren and Rosen both pulled their phones from their pockets, and the looks on their faces said the same. Mama stood and slid her hand deep into a pocket that she'd obviously sewn inside her skirt, and pulled out what looked like the newest model iPhone.

I was beginning to wonder if the next surprise I'd discover about Mama Estela was that she'd been a CIA operative.

She poked at it a few times, and shook her head.

"My phone worked in here five minutes ago," I said.

"Someone is jamming cell transmissions," Rosen said. "But I cleared the second floor. No one came in."

"No one there," Marta said, nodding.

"No one was there two or three minutes ago," Darren said. He looked past me at the wall, and his face changed.

Fear touched my spine, like a cold finger running down my back. I turned, and looked at the monitors.

They were blank. Black. Well, two of them were black, and the rest were just static.

"Fuck me," I whispered. If somebody was somehow messing with our systems, they could be disabling the biometric sensors at the doors – everything.

Including the door to the room we were in. I could see Rosen and Darren figuring that out just as I did.

"Closet, everyone. Now," Rosen said. He scooped Eddie up and threw him over his shoulder, like it was a game. He tickled Eddie, who giggled uncontrollably. That sound made me feel fifty percent better. Rosen knew what he was doing.

The door to the closet was the only door in the building that didn't have a biometric override attached. Once inside, it was like the door to a walk-in freezer, with a steel core and an enormous deadbolt, with smaller ones at top and bottom.

This small room was not built for comfort. Darren and I pulled out blankets from shelving we'd put up, and tried to make the Garcias comfortable, while Rosen picked up the landline phone. When we were planning the space, Dave had stressed that while landlines might seem archaic, they were a necessity in an emergency – if, for example, a crazy person had managed to break past your defenses and jam your cell signals, and you found yourself crammed into a closet with four adults and three adolescent boys.

Rosen replaced the phone in its cradle and shook his head slightly. I knew he didn't want to overly worry the kids. I wasn't surprised it was cut. Our security systems were shot and our cells weren't working. This had taken planning, and it was too much to hope that a landline would be overlooked.

Luke and Matty sat down on the floor cross-legged. They were quiet for the time being, though I could feel the fear coming off them, mixed with perhaps some small excitement. They had Darren and me and Rosen, not to mention the Garcias. They had a very impressive steel door protecting them from whatever was out there, and plenty of food and water. Plus, they'd heard me say I'd talked to Belliveau. This could, to a nearly thirteen-year-old, seem in some small way like an adventure. Mama Estela was curled up in the corner watching us with great interest. She looked perfectly comfortable, and very alert. Marta had taken the machete from her mother, and was licking her thumb and testing it against the blade. She had a determined frown on her face. She was sitting on her haunches, with Eddie crammed behind her against the wall. She was the very picture of mama bear protectiveness, and I almost wanted to smile.

The room was twelve feet by ten feet, and it had been added very much as an afterthought. With the security we'd constructed the place with, not to mention the large comfortable room just beyond the door, it seemed beyond the realm of possibility, back then, that we'd find ourselves in this situation. For one thing, there was no plumbing into this little room. No running water, no toilet. I crouched down by the farthest shelf and pulled out a five-gallon bucket that contained an assortment of emergency foods that didn't need heating or water to prepare – pouches of tuna, protein bars, jerky – and dumped it all out on the floor. I set the bucket in the corner, empty, and put the lid back on loosely.

"Welcome to our luxurious en suite facilities, ladies and gentlemen." Rosen half smiled, Darren wasn't paying attention, and everybody else looked at me like I was speaking Dutch. "If you have to go to the bathroom…" I waved my arm at the bucket. "One at a time, please. The rest of us will turn our backs and hum a tune."

Mama cackled, and Marta put the water bottle she had just picked up back on the floor. Eddie looked like he was going to cry.

I just love making children cry.

I sat down on the floor beside him, squeezing in between his grandmother and him with my back to the wall. "Don't worry, Eduardo," I said quietly. "Remember, I talked to Sergeant Belliveau on the phone just a little while ago. He said he was coming over as soon as he could, and that he was sending other police too. So, really, it's just a matter of waiting until Paul gets here. He knows about this room, remember?" Eddie had actually conducted part of the tour for Paul and Joanne Belliveau. He'd been very proud of his new home.

"Oh yeah," Eddie said. His little face relaxed. "Okay."

"So why don't you close your eyes and pretend you're on a camping trip."

"Danny," Eddie said, as though that was about the stupidest thing he'd ever heard.

"Hmm. You're right. This isn't much like the woods."

"I liked the woods," Eddie said. He'd gone up to the Belliveaus' cottage with us. It was Eddie's first time in any kind of landscape like that. He'd come to California from Mexico when he was a baby, and his only trip since then had been to Toronto.

"Me too," I said. "We'll go up there again soon, I promise. Maybe at Thanksgiving." I sat and wished we'd bought a big property up north somewhere after all. Though this would just have happened there, and we'd be further away from help.

I played with Eddie's hair for a few minutes, and soon he shut his eyes. I'd noticed that he always calmed down when someone touched his head. He was at that age where he could be a little boy one minute, and a brave warrior the next.

Mama, curled up on the floor on my other side, poked my hip. "Have one, girl," she said. "Baby." She nodded significantly at my lap, in the vicinity, I presumed she meant, of my ovaries. "Old."

I barked a laugh, and she cackled.

Who knew Mama Estela would turn into the member of my household who always knew what to say?

Eddie turned over and faced the wall. He was sleeping, or nearly.

I got up and rummaged through the small bin of entertainment things I'd put in here, and found what I was looking for. An old iPod of mine, and I found the "Sleepy Time" playlist I'd made for myself years ago, before Jack and I split, before crack. I put the headphones gently over Eddie's ears and turned the music on low. Marta turned and smiled at me, machete in hand.

I needed to tell the others what Belliveau had said on the phone, and Eddie didn't need to hear about words being carved into dead girls.

Rosen and Darren were perched next to the boys. I got up and moved a few feet, with my back against the door. I wanted to be able to see everyone.

"Boys, what I'm going to say is scary and very gross," I said quietly. "You don't really need to hear it, and I'd rather you didn't. But you've both been through a lot, and you know why we're in the situation we're in." I waved my hand, indicating the building as a whole, rather than the fact that we were all shoved in a closet. "If you'd rather not hear it, I can find headphones for you. I know there are a bunch in here. But I'm leaving it up to you." I looked at Darren. He looked at Matt and Luke with such sadness, I felt like my heart would break.

I knew Matt would want to hear it, and I was pretty sure Luke would not. They looked at each other and communicated silently.

"We can handle it," Luke said. Darren put his hand on Luke's shoulder.

Quickly and quietly, I told them about Ann's body being found. And about the message carved into her abdomen. I had to stop there and close my eyes. All I could see was that young girl's face when the man in the club was assaulting her. Matty grabbed my hand.

Darren then explained, better than I could have, about the incident, nearly two years ago, when a man had been killed by the same people who had killed my sister, and how the people who did it had written the same thing – "Hi, Danny!" – in blood on the mirror.

Marta had her hand over her mouth, and Mama Estela said a bunch of stuff in Spanish and nearly hit the floor with the machete, but Marta stopped her, nodding at Eddie. Luke looked sick, but like he was trying to be brave. Matty just stared at my face. He could read me almost as well as Darren could.

"This is the reason why I wanted to get everyone up here," I said. "But then, a second later, the window was broken."

"You think Smith is about to make some sort of move, then," Rosen said.

"Well, I think he has." I nodded at where we were. "I just don't know how, or what he wants." Or whether he's right outside this door, I wanted to say, but the twins' presence stopped me.

Darren had gotten up and was looking through what entertainment and electronics we had put in the closet. He found the boys' old handheld video games they'd grown out of, and headphones.

"Guys, you know we trust you. But I want to talk to Rosen and Danny privately now, okay? Put the headphones on. The police will be here soon enough."

Once he was sure the boys were set up, Darren looked at Rosen and nodded, and then at me.

"Danny, I don't want you to freak out," he said.

"We're crammed into our last-ditch panic room with no toilet and no means of communication with the outside world," I said. "I think that, all in all, I'm doing pretty well."

"It's just – look, with the security, the windows, and the monitors – how well do you really know Dave?"

"This again?" I said. "My God, Darren."

"He provided the advice, the contractors, the workers – everything."

"And he knows all the tech," Rosen added.

"And he conveniently left this afternoon." I could tell Darren wanted to say more, but stopped himself.

"Shhh!" Mama Estela was sitting up. She was waving her hand to get us to shut up. We all looked at her, and listened.

In the next five seconds, two things happened.

The lights went out, leaving us in absolute darkness.

And someone knocked on the closet door.

It was not the kind of knock the police would use. It was not an authoritative kind of knock, or a banging. It was a deliberate, light-hearted knock: shave and a haircut, two bits.

Rosen and Matt both turned flashlights on. Rosen waved the boys into the furthest corner, near the Garcias.

Rosen indicated that we should all be quiet. He had his gun drawn. So did Darren. So did I.

We heard voices, then. Barely, but we heard them. We had, on purpose, not gone for a sound-cancelling door, against Dave's advice, and the advice of the contractor. I didn't want any of the kids to wind up alone in this room, afraid, and not able to hear our voices. We were all absolutely still.

Then another knock, a different one.

"This is Sergeant Paul Belliveau of the Toronto Police Service. Identify yourselves."

His voice was muffled by the steel door that separated us. It was Belliveau. At least, it sounded like Belliveau. But something didn't feel right.

"It's us, Paul," Darren said loudly. "All of us, except Fred."

"That's good news," Belliveau said. "We've got the building now. You can come on out."

"Wait," I said quietly. I called loudly, "What's your wife's middle name?" We'd had a long, slightly tipsy conversation one night about our middle names, and Joanne was pretending to feel hurt because she'd never been given one.

Pause from outside the door, then Belliveau's voice.

"She doesn't have one, Danny. It's safe now. Come on out."

I nodded, and indicated to Rosen and Darren that they should stow their weapons. We didn't know how many police were on the other side of that door, and we didn't want anybody getting excited by the sight of a bunch of armed civilians.

I kept mine, however, tucking it into the back of my jeans.

The weight of it comforted me, and my very flawed spidey-senses were tingling.

Rosen unlocked the door, but before he could open it I stepped in front of him. I wanted to be the first person walking into the room. I'd paid for this very expensive, insecure security, and I'd trusted Dave's Toronto contacts. I'd trusted Dave. If someone was going to get hurt because of my decision, it wasn't going to be anybody but me. Darren made a move as if to stop me, but I just gave him a look. He backed off.

"Everybody else stay back. Boys, you don't move until I tell you to."

I opened the door.

TWENTY-SEVEN

Paul Belliveau was standing six feet from the door, hand on holster. He smiled when he saw me, and dropped his head in relief.

Also in the room were three uniformed cops, crouched over the body of a man on the floor. He was lying on his back with his legs and arms splayed.

I stopped breathing. I couldn't see the man's face, but even at first glance I could tell that it wasn't Fred. Nor was it Michael Vernon Smith. Or Dave. I started toward him, but Paul stopped me.

"Not yet," he said quietly as he approached me. "Let's get the women and kids out of this area first." He squeezed my upper arm. I wanted to hug him, but I didn't want to embarrass him in front of his men.

"Women and children? What am I, chopped liver?" I said. Darren and Rosen had stepped out, and I called for the boys and the Garcias to join us.

"It's all over now," Belliveau was saying to them. "Boys, ladies, please follow this officer. Directly, please."

"Who's that?" Matty said. He stopped in his tracks.

"No one we know," I said. I looked at Belliveau and mouthed, *Where's Fred?*

He nodded. "Your dad is safe, guys," Belliveau said to Matt and Luke. "An officer picked him up while he was out for his run. He's out in my car, and he's very keen to see you. We need you to go with this officer right now, okay?" The twins trooped out.

Marta, Eddie in hand, stood in the closet doorway and spoke sharply in Spanish. A full minute later, Mama E. appeared in the doorway, a huge smile on her face.

"Good for my back," she said, gesturing back to the room. "My new bedroom." I rolled my eyes at her and she nodded, following Marta and the boys and one of the officers out of the room.

Belliveau watched them leave, and went and talked quietly to the other officer for a minute. He came back to us. "This is how I found him," Belliveau said, nodding behind him at the body. "I've never seen him before. Between forty and forty-five years of age. He's deceased, but there are no apparent signs of trauma. And he's carrying no ID."

"I'll look?" Rosen said, nodding at the dead body on our TV room floor.

"Please," Belliveau said. "I'm hoping one of you can identify him."

Rosen only had to look at the man for two seconds. "It's Mr. King," he said, emotionless. "Cliff King. Mr. Lindquist's friend."

"Holy shit," Darren said. He headed to the bathroom off the TV room.

"Whoa there, Darren," Belliveau said. "Off limits. The whole building is a crime scene. You can't touch anything. We'll be getting you out of here."

"But I have to go," Darren said. "There's no…" he pointed at the closet.

Belliveau shone his flashlight into the closet. "You can use that bucket there," he said. "You guys have been in there since the beginning, right?"

"Just us," I said. Belliveau smiled at Darren, who took the flashlight that Paul handed him with reluctance, and went back into the closet, shutting the door behind him.

The combination of Darren's face when he turned to go back into the closet and finding myself ten feet away from a dead body was starting to edge me into my usual hysteria. I started to giggle, and then snort, and soon I was bent over at the waist trying to get control of myself. At least I didn't feel faint, or puke.

The cop watched me with some confusion on his face. In most circles, busting a gut with merriment in front of a dead body is frowned upon apparently. At least Belliveau was used to me. I stood up straight, serious again.

"It's going to be a long night, isn't it?" I said.

"Oh, I believe so," he said.

"We've got to get somewhere safe," I said. "The boys need sleep, especially Eddie." I was glad we had to leave. I needed some distance before I could be in here again without being very, very angry.

"You're going to my place," he said quietly. "There's plenty of room. Well, sort of."

"We can't do that," I said.

"You can and will," Paul said. "It's safer than a hotel. And Jo's getting stuff ready for you. She'll kill me in my sleep if I don't bring you back there." He shook his head then, as if he regretted his choice of words.

I nodded. Joanne could be a little scary.

"Who did this?" I said to him. "Him? Just him?"

"I'd say him, and probably with at least – at least – one other person. Somebody had to have killed him," he added. "Not to mention, at first glance, your electronics seem to have been stolen – laptops and so on."

"I guess it wasn't natural causes, then."

"Unless he let his partner leave with whatever they wanted, and he came up here to get more, or kill you all, and what… had a heart attack?" He looked at me. "Let's go downstairs. But before we do – Danny, I'm going to need your boyfriend's phone number. And everything else you know about him."

I didn't have to ask him why. I just nodded. "He had nothing to do with it," I said. "But I want to know how our supposedly top-notch security was so easily breached."

"Gavin there used to work for a glass company," Belliveau said, indicating the officer who was squatting next to the dead Mr. King. "He had a quick look at the windows on the main floor and he thinks they're all regular glass." I looked at Gavin, who nodded.

"Fan-fucking-tastic." Aside from any other issue at the moment, I felt like such a fool. But I didn't believe that Dave knew. He'd been duped or conned by his Toronto security guy.

The alternative wasn't something I could contemplate. Not now.

"Look at it this way," Belliveau said. "Having that little safe room there could have saved all of your lives. So I wouldn't say it was all for nothing, would you?"

Darren opened the closet door, and shut it behind him quickly. He was buckling his belt, and he looked slightly traumatized.

"We're getting plumbing in there," he announced.

"Whatever you say." I hugged him, and then hugged Belliveau. I didn't care if it embarrassed him. I spent a good chunk of my life in embarrassing situations; time to spread the joy.

I was glad the next day was Saturday, and we didn't have to think about whether or not to keep the boys home from school. I doubted that I was going to be able to let them out of my sight until they were twenty-one.

Paul and Joanne Belliveau lived off the Danforth, geographically only about a few kilometers away, but a world away from our industrial neighborhood. They had an old large home on a leafy residential street, steps away from the Greek restaurants, pubs, yoga centers and health food stores along one of Toronto's main commercial drags. They'd bought the house for a song when they were married thirty years earlier, and in Toronto's ridiculous real estate market, it was worth more than fifteen times what they'd paid.

"We think of selling every once in a while," Joanne told me. We were arranging blow-up mattresses and sleeping bags on their third floor, which was an open-concept loft area with a small deck. They used it as an office, but, by the looks of it, it didn't see much use. "But as I always say, then what? We sell, but we still have to live somewhere. And I can't imagine leaving the neighborhood. They'll have to carry me out of here feet first." I thanked her again for taking us all in, and she told me to zip it.

She was a bit like a more matronly Mama Estela. She was half my size but I wouldn't want to pick a fight with her.

Darren, Rosen, and the twins were all on the third floor, with Darren and Rosen billeted at each of the two large couches, and Fred on the floor with Matt and Luke. Marta politely made it plain that wherever Eddie slept, she would be with him, and nobody argued with her. So they got one of the spare rooms. And I would be bunking in with my new bestie Mama E. in the other.

Back at the bakery, crime scene techs were dusting for fingerprints and whatever else they do. Because of the Michael Vernon Smith connection and the dead body in the TV room, I had a feeling that we were going to be guests of the Belliveaus for more than a day or two.

I'd given Belliveau Dave's full name: David Andrew Stewart, and his cell number. As I did, I realized that I had taken Dave's word on what his legal name was. I knew, of course, that he had IDs under other names. I'd seen some of them. I'd taken Dave at his word about his real name, because why wouldn't I? I hadn't found out my late husband Jack's real name – at least, the name he'd had for the first eighteen years of his life – until he told me, the day he was killed. Jack had good reasons for changing his identity. If David Stewart wasn't my boyfriend's legal name – if it was just another alias, another persona – I hoped like hell that he had as good a reason for not telling me as Jack had had.

By nearly three in the morning, he hadn't phoned me, nor I him. Belliveau asked me to wait until the morning, or at least until he was able to reach Dave himself.

I didn't give him the emergency number I had for Dave, tattooed on my inner thigh. Not yet. I was jangly and wired, and I wanted either cocaine or sleep before I thought too deeply about what had happened. My mind was spinning. The Percocet

I'd taken earlier had worn off, and perhaps because of the tension in my body, the pain was flaring up again.

Hours earlier when Fred had seen the boys emerge safe and sound from the bakery, he broke down. I tried to remember if I'd ever seen him cry before. It wasn't pretty, but I was glad to see it. Sitting at the Belliveaus' kitchen table, I listened while he told us about Cliff: how he'd blamed Fred for their failure getting seed money for their start-up in California, how Cliff had been drinking heavily on the plane on the way back, and hadn't returned Fred's calls since. No one had any idea how Cliff had gotten in – Belliveau told me the police had found Fred nearly two miles away from our place, jogging very slowly in the fluorescent yellow jacket he often wore at night, and the timing meant it would have been nearly impossible for him to have let Cliff in, in case we'd been wondering about that – but Cliff had been to our place often enough to know the layout of the place. Fred thought Cliff was probably after business details on his computer, but possibly saw a payday in taking anything that could be sold – or might have information that could be sold.

"He was making me nervous there at the end," Fred said. "Especially on that flight back to Toronto. He was really asking a lot about what had happened to Ginger, and wanted to know everything I know about Smith. Certainly more than I wanted to talk about."

Of all of us, Fred was definitely the most reluctant to talk about the past, about what had happened in California and Maine. And he certainly wouldn't be keen to talk about it to anyone who wasn't there.

"I wanted to trust him," Fred was saying. "I needed – I *need* –

a career. I need to do something other than sitting around in that factory all day." He glanced at Darren, as though he was worried he was insulting him.

"We all need that, Fred," Darren said. "But we decided to put the boys first for a while. Their safety. Their happiness."

I closed my eyes. I couldn't think anymore. I didn't want to think about the sacrifices that Darren had made to babysit not only our nephews but also to babysit me. I was still a wild card, the addict who might relapse, and now the mentally ill woman who might go nuts again at the drop of a hat.

A craving for crack hit me hard, harder than it had in months. The bliss, and the oblivion.

Say what you will about my life as an addict, but I saw very few corpses when I was sitting on my couch getting high.

I excused myself, thanked our hosts again, and went up to bed.

Mama Estela was asleep on one of the twin beds, snoring more loudly than I thought possible for someone her size. The only light in the room was her phone, which she had plugged in to charge on the dresser. I took off my jeans and felt my own phone in the pocket, and looked at Mama's to see if hers was finished charging. I hadn't thought to grab my charger when we were allowed to enter our rooms, escorted, and pack a few things.

Mama had a photograph on her home screen. A picture of Marta and Eddie and the twins in their kitchen back at the bakery, with a young blonde girl. Moira, I presumed. I looked closer. I hadn't met Moira yet.

I looked again, and then turned the overhead light on in the room.

The girl in the photograph, the one whose arms were draped

around Luke's neck while Eddie made bunny ears behind her head. Moira.

It was Ann. Ann, whom I had witnessed being assaulted at Helen of Troy while she was working as a dancer. Who didn't want to tell me her age. Whom I had allowed to be abducted in the alley, and whose body had been washed ashore on Lake Ontario.

Ann was Moira, and Moira was Ann.

TWENTY-EIGHT

Darren and I went to make the identification. I confirmed that the body that had washed up on Cherry Beach was the young woman I had known as Ann, and Darren that it was the girl he'd known as Moira.

No one had reported her missing. The number Darren had on his phone for the man he'd spoken to several times who claimed to be Ann's father was no longer in service, but the police were checking on that. The home address Ann had given to the strip club didn't exist – at least, the apartment number didn't – and the address Moira was registered at with the school was inhabited by a nice family of recent Syrian refugees who seemed saddened by the death of a young girl, but confused as to why the police would be looking for information about her at their house. They had genuinely never seen her before.

Dave still hadn't called, and I could no longer leave messages. His phone was switched off. So was Jonas's. I could call his emergency contact, the number tattooed into my thigh, but something stopped me. I didn't want to think about it much. Dave had supervised the installation of our so-called security. He had left the day we were broken into. He was supposed to be on a safe, boring assignment in Florida, and he should have checked in by now. It didn't take a genius to figure out that something was very wrong.

And someone had to tell Luke that his little girlfriend Moira – who, according to the forensic pathologist, was probably fifteen or sixteen – was dead. And, oh yeah, she'd been moonlighting as a stripper. We agreed to wait a day or two to talk to him about it. Luke thought Moira was on an off-the-grid trip with her family, so he wasn't worried about her. And besides, with his home and sense of security being torn out from under him yet again, nobody wanted to face that conversation. Paul Belliveau agreed we could leave it until Monday, but that Luke would need to be questioned about Moira.

And as for me? Well, I had my own plan.

I stuffed a few things into a fanny pack, and dressed for a run. Mama Estela was in the kitchen butting heads with Joanne Belliveau over the cooking of dinner, and Rosen and Darren had taken the boys out for soccer in the park. I had no idea where Fred or Belliveau were. I poked my head into the kitchen and announced that I was going for an easy run to burn off some steam, and see where my pain level was.

"Are you sure, Danny?" Joanne said. She was washing her hands at the sink, and her cheeks were pink from the ribs she was steaming. That, or from trying not to deck Mama E. "Is this the right time to be going off by yourself?"

I tried my best to smile. This kind woman had taken in all the members of my very large household, and she had been nothing but good to all of us since we'd crashed into her life nearly two years earlier. But she hadn't gotten the memo regarding my distaste for being told what to do. Or more importantly, what not to do.

"I'll be fine," I said. "Eyes in the back of my head. And I need to let off some steam, get my body back in working order." I shot her a smile and headed for the door. I could hear Mama Estela behind me. She grabbed my wrist.

"You're leaving," she said. "Not coming back." I felt a chill up my back. It sounded like a prophecy.

"Yes, I am," I said. "Just not right away." I couldn't lie to her. There would be no point. "It's my fight, Mama. Do you understand that? It's me he wants. Or they want." I would know soon enough.

She nodded. She looked sad, which nearly broke my heart. And chilled me. Mama Estela didn't expect to see me again. "You have your pills?" she asked. I nodded, patting my fanny pack. Yes, I had my pills. I couldn't afford any possible mental side effects if I discontinued them abruptly. Mama pulled me closer and kissed me on both cheeks. She smelled like lavender. She smelled like my mother had, a little bit. Part of me wanted to melt into a puddle on the floor and let her take care of me, like she had when I'd been what Dr. Singh had called catatonic. The rest of me wanted to hit the pavement and leave any emotion behind me. It was the best way to keep the people I loved safe. I couldn't afford to forget that again.

Mama held up her hand to stop me, and pulled something from her shirt: a small canister she must have had tucked into her bra. I looked at it. Pepper spray, in a handy travel size. I grinned.

"Thanks," I said. I shoved it into my pocket, and walked out the front door.

* * *

I didn't run for long. My body wasn't ready for it, and even if it had been, I didn't want to waste the energy. As I walked, I texted Darren, saying I was going off on my own for a bit, but that I was fine. He would think I was falling off the wagon, going on a crack bender. At least, that's what I wanted him to think. I removed the SIM card from my phone and dropped it into a grate, threw my phone into the first garbage can I saw, and flagged a taxi. I directed the driver to an intersection a few blocks from where I wanted to be.

Home. The bakery. Our supposedly safe house.

I approached the building slowly on foot. There was police tape over the front entrance, but I couldn't see any police. I walked around the block at an easy pace, wondering if I was being watched by anyone, by Michael Vernon Smith or any of his people. Because I knew, now, that he still had people. Cliff King had probably been one of them, though I might never know that for sure. Whoever had killed Kelly and Garrett and Ann had been working for him. It wasn't Smith's style to get his hands dirty.

I kept my breathing quiet and steady, listening for footsteps behind me. This wasn't an area with a lot of foot traffic; I'd notice anyone approaching me. It was late afternoon on a Saturday, and there weren't any stores or restaurants on this stretch to draw any passers-by. Our neighbors were an industrial laundry, a storage facility, and an empty low-rise office building that was waiting to be razed to make way for yet another loft condo.

My car was parked where I'd left it at the back of the bakery. I pulled my keys out, popped the trunk, and after looking around again quickly, unlocked the small gun case I had stashed under the spare tire. I loaded it as I stood there – this weapon was stored legally, unloaded – and quickly retrieved a few other things from the car. I wasn't sure if I would get a chance to return to it.

In the taxi on the way down, I had prepared myself mentally. I needed to be operating fully in the moment, with no sentiment. I couldn't afford to think about anything I was possibly leaving behind, or anyone. Dave had taught me that, to think of my brain and body as a machine working together. *Pretend you're a cyborg*, he used to say, only half joking. *You have no emotion. You only have an objective, a mission to fulfill. Only then should you return to yourself.* I had listened, but half-heartedly. There had always been so much emotion in everything I'd done. Emotion fueled my rage, and rage fueled me.

But I couldn't afford that now. Michael Vernon Smith knew my weaknesses. He knew how I'd felt about Ginger and the rest of my family. How I felt about innocent people like Dom back in California, and Ann here in Toronto, getting killed, horribly killed, because of me. He'd had my name written in blood, in flesh. He wanted me angry and flailing and impetuous. He wanted me to make mistakes.

He needed me to stick close to my tribe, to my nephews and my family. He intended to pin us down so he could hold the people I loved in front of me and torture me into doing what he wanted, into giving him what he desired. I had bested him once, and his memory was long.

Danny Cleary had to cease to exist. I could, perhaps, help to capture Smith. Perhaps I could even kill him. But I knew, now, that even then none of us would be safe. He would leave that legacy. Somehow, even if he hadn't planned it, Michael Vernon Smith had ensured that the crazies who followed him, who reveled in these sick games, would probably compete to take everything. More than money. They wouldn't stop until there was nothing good left for anyone in my family, or anyone who cared for us.

My mistake had been in thinking that state-of-the-art security would keep us safe. The only thing that could keep my loved ones safe would be for me to give everything to Smith – anything I'd inherited from Jack, and any life I'd built for myself. I doubted he'd even care about killing me, as long as I was ruined. Even more ruined than I used to be, when I'd whiled away years in a haze of crack smoke.

I was going to give him what he wanted.

There was no sign of police tape over the back door. I scanned the ground for the remains of any yellow tape to see if it had been ripped off, but there was nothing. The building seemed normal from the back, except for the steel security shutter on the second floor.

The biometric sensor wasn't on. I had no idea whether it was operational, or whether it had been left off after Friday night. I let myself in manually.

"Hello," I called out. There could be crime scene techs here, I supposed, or a cop or two. Better safe, et cetera. If anyone else was in the building, they weren't there legally, and there would be no point in trying to be quiet.

No one responded, and I heard nothing.

I climbed to the fourth floor, the floor I shared with Darren.

That I *had* shared with Darren. I wouldn't be living here again. I doubted any of us would, but if things went the way I planned, it might be safe for everyone else to come back here at some point, to get back to some normalcy for the boys. I just wouldn't be here. I very probably would never see any of them again.

But I couldn't think about that now.

I went to my room. From the back of my closet I grabbed an old duffel bag I'd had since before I'd met Jack. I felt around the bottom and found the spot where I'd ripped the lining, and pulled out the fifty grand in emergency cash I'd stashed there soon after we'd moved in. I pulled out a few fifties and stuffed them into my fanny pack, and left the rest in the bag. After throwing a random and messy assortment of underwear, t-shirts, jeans, and hoodies into the bag, I pushed the hangers in my closet to one side.

We all had fireproof safes built into the backs of our closets. Darren had thought it would be a fun idea when we were planning the layout, and would give everyone that extra padding of privacy in the middle of such a chaotic shared space. The boys each had their own, even Eddie, and we had all programmed our own codes. Darren sometimes wanted to speculate what the boys put in theirs, but I didn't. I'm a big believer in privacy. I've never enjoyed going through other people's stuff, even as a kid.

I'd made good use of mine.

Inside was a Canadian passport and an Ontario driver's license, both with a picture of me, but under the name Elizabeth Jackson. A respectable, forgettable name. The name of a WASPy lecturer in humanities, or a mommy blogger. Dave had it made for me when we were in New York by the same guys who did some of his false identities. They were expensive, and I never really thought I'd need to use them. But I felt better having them. I'd wanted to have some made for Darren and the boys, too, but I hadn't gotten around to getting their passport photos taken before Dave got shot and I left him behind.

But I wouldn't think about that now.

A copy of my will was underneath the paperwork, and after a moment's thought I took it out and put it in the drawer of my nightstand. I grabbed my Danielle Cleary passport and the new, unused burner phone, still in its box, that I'd hoped I'd never need. Finally I grabbed the tiny SIG Sauer P238, a gun so small I was actually a bit uncomfortable with how light it was, which Dave had given me for Christmas last year. I put it in my bag, along with ammo.

I was calm. I was practicing being calm. I was in my own home. I had a legal right to be there; I hadn't broken police tape to enter, and I hadn't been specifically told by a police officer not to enter. The place had already been searched, to whatever extent it was going to be.

I went back to the safe, and took out the eight-ball of powdered cocaine that I had stashed there recently, in case of emergency. The kitchen guys at Helen of Troy had been remarkably forthcoming with their connections. I obviously wasn't the first woman working there who'd asked if she could score some blow.

I hadn't touched it yet. There were moments, in these past days, where I'd almost forgotten it was there.

I sat cross-legged on my bed and activated my burner phone, and put the wrappings into my bag. I didn't want anyone to be able to trace me by any serial number on the packaging. I held the phone in one hand and the baggie of coke in the other, weighing them, clearing my mind, trying to abstain from thought. Then I scooped out a bump of coke on a key and snorted it. I tasted it at the back of my throat, the beautiful numbing.

Yes.

I dialed the number. It was burned into my brain now. I didn't have to check the tattoo on my thigh.

"Tell him I'm going to the club," I said to the voice who answered. "Just me. I'll be there."

I snorted one more little bump and checked myself in the mirror, watching my pupils dilate. Then I collected myself and left. I didn't look back.

I was pretty sure that Dave would show up. I just wondered if he'd show up alone.

TWENTY-NINE

Helen of Troy was dark. There was no sign on the front saying it was closed temporarily or anything. It was just dark and deserted.

I walked back through the alley where I'd been hogtied with duct tape, and thought of the man with the dog who'd rescued me. I wish I'd gotten his name, and made a mental note to try to track it down, if I managed to live through this. I bet he wouldn't be letting his dog off-leash anytime soon. Broken glass crunched under my feet. This time, I was wearing my steel-toed boots, and I feared no dirty needles or rat bites.

The coke might have helped with that too, the lack of fear. I hadn't had anything stronger than the occasional brandy or glass of wine since rehab. It was medicinal, a way to make my mental and physical reflexes stronger. If I didn't overdo it, the cocaine would also help me overcome my emotions. In the next hours or days, I would need to forget any softness or humanity. And after that, if I was still alive, I would be Elizabeth Jackson, and I would be gone. Elizabeth Jackson didn't have any loved ones. She could go to Bali and learn to surf, or rent a dive apartment in Amsterdam and start shooting heroin until her heart exploded or her fifty grand ran out. Elizabeth Jackson would be free. Though to quote the great Kris Kristofferson, freedom's just another word for nothing left to lose.

"Fuck Kris Kristofferson," I said out loud. When I came to the alley door, the one that Ann had led me out of that night, I pulled the handle and it opened. I stepped inside.

It was dark in the dressing room, and I lit my way with my phone. I carried the Sig lightly in my left hand, but I didn't expect to need it, at least not yet. Whoever would show up here – and someone would, most probably more than one – wouldn't kill me outright. There would be talking, especially if Michael Vernon Smith was involved. The man loved the sound of his own voice. And once he – they – heard what I had to say, it would be in no one's best interests to kill me. Not right away, at any rate.

I found the light switch, and turned it on.

Without the din of the dancers flitting around and the bass thump of the music in the bar, the room looked sad and dingy. It was obvious that most of the girls hadn't picked up their things; there were hairbands and makeup and towels strewn all over, just the way I remembered it. I looked at the lockers, wondering which one had been Ann's, but they weren't marked. Besides, I'd gotten the impression that the girls just grabbed whatever locker was empty on a given night and stuck their own lock on it. Or not. They'd been a pretty trusting group, despite the peripatetic nature of their work.

I headed into the club, past the empty DJ booth. The place hadn't been cleaned since the night Ann was taken, since the night I was left in the alley for the rats. The tables still had dirty glasses and plates on them, and the chairs were pulled out like everyone was about to come back any second. In the glow of the neon exit signs, the place looked like something from *The Shining*. I guess with the police storming in and undoubtedly interviewing everyone who was here that night, none of the staff felt much like doing a regular close-down. And that was the last night the place had seen any business.

I wanted to take a look at Garrett's office to see if I could find anything. Anything about the Kinder Group, anything to indicate that Michael Vernon Smith might have had a hand in this place. But even if such evidence existed – and I doubted it did – the police would have carted everything off by now. Whether it was purely due to Garrett Jones's mismanagement or not, this place had been every shade of wrong. And Garrett wasn't alive to shed any light on things. At the end of the day, I knew he would end up a scapegoat in some way, despite his murder. If there were any corporate malfeasance, the Kinder Group would probably sail through it unscathed, as corporations were wont to do.

As I made my way through the tables, I could see there was a light on in the bar. There was a clink of bottles. And music. Over the beating of my heart I could hear Gershwin's "Rhapsody in Blue" playing very quietly.

I tightened my grip on the Sig in my hand, and, as quietly as I could, stowed my bag, with my other gun stashed inside, under a table. For half a second I debated sneaking backstage again for a quick bump of coke, but I settled for breathing. My mind reached out for Ginger as though I was reaching for her hand, and I headed for the bar.

Patrick. Bartender Patrick, loading bottles from behind the bar into a plastic moving bin. He was smoking a cigarette and had a glass of wine in front of him. He looked fully comfortable and relaxed, until he saw me standing there. With a gun at my side.

"Hello," I said, and watched his face as he registered first surprise, and then when he saw the gun, wariness. Not fear, though, I didn't think. Interesting.

"Yeah," he said. "Hi." He looked like he didn't know what to do with his hands, so he took a swig of his wine.

"Keep your hands above the bar, please," I said. I walked over. "Actually, pour me a glass of that."

He moved slowly as he grabbed a glass, and maintained eye contact. Smart, when a semi-stranger with a gun wanders into the bar you're robbing.

"Do you remember me?" I said.

"You're the girl who busted up those frat morons," he said. "And yes, I know Garrett hired you." He looked at me. "I can't remember your name, though. Well, at least not at gunpoint. Ha."

"Danny," I said. I put the gun on the bar out of his reach, and shook his hand. The color was starting to return to his face.

"Patrick," he said, shaking my hand quickly. He looked relieved, and who could blame him. Nobody likes to be confronted while getting their booze-stealing on by a girl with a gun. "I don't mind telling you, you just scared the living shit out of me."

"You hid it pretty well," I said. "We never got a chance to work together. Of course, I only did the two shifts before somebody hogtied me and left me in the alley."

"Yeah, and took that dancer girl," Patrick said. "I don't know if I ever met her, but Jesus. It's fucked up." He gestured at the bottles and the bin he'd been loading, as if to ask if I minded if he continued.

"Go for it," I said. I settled more comfortably onto my bar stool. Patrick looked as though he'd been at it for a while, judging by the very full ashtray on the bar. "Did you ever get your last paycheck?"

"Fuck no," he said. "And I still had the keys. I can't believe they didn't change the locks." He topped up our wine. "I'm just doing a little Robin Hood thing. I'm going to give most of this out to some of the girls. We all got screwed over. A bunch of us have called down to Kinder, you know, the company that owns this place? They say that since Garrett didn't keep proper books or payroll, they don't know what we're owed. They have their legal department working on what to do with us. Or so they say."

"Poor Garrett," I said.

"He was a really good guy," Patrick said. "And how could he not have kept proper records? I mean, we all got paid for the correct hours. Well, until all this happened. Anyway, the police took all that away." He held out a bottle of rye he was about to put into the bin. "You want? Help yourself, man."

"No, I'm good," I said. "But maybe leave a couple of bottles of wine for me?" We debated the merits of the Pinot Grigio versus the Sauvignon Blanc, and I felt like I was in *The Twilight Zone*. "Listen, Patrick, you should probably get out of here. I mean, finish packing up or whatever, but you should probably speed it up a bit."

"Uh. Why?" He looked at my gun again, then back at me. I put my hand over it and drew it back to me.

"I'm supposed to be meeting one of the cops here," I said.

Top of my head. "They interviewed me in the hospital, but they wanted to talk to me again and I guess they wanted to take a look around here, probably secure the place better. I live close by, so I said I'd meet him here." I hoped he'd believe me, and take off quickly. He wouldn't want to be caught walking out of the place with bins of their booze.

"You came to meet a cop, carrying a gun?" he said. He smiled at me slowly, looking me in the eye. "Pull the other one." He had a pleasingly weathered, boyish look about him, but his face seemed different, now. Then again, I had my paranoid glasses on, not to mention cocaine making my synapses fire more quickly than usual.

"Hey, after what happened that night, I wasn't coming near this place without my little buddy here." I held it in my hand, ready to fire, to move quickly if I had to. My hand was sweating, though, and I felt a bit sick. Cocaine can do that to me, when I haven't had it in a while. Especially when I haven't eaten anything, and decide to throw a bunch of wine into my stomach quickly. "I wasn't planning on waving it around."

"Then why not put it away," he said. "Guns make me nervous."

"Really? I'm the opposite. They make me feel all warm and fuzzy." I smiled sweetly. He was probably wondering if I was murderous, or just crazy. He wouldn't be the first.

Patrick broke my gaze and said something about being sick of Gershwin. When he turned to change the music, I saw the bat at the same instant that he reached for it.

The baseball bat he kept behind the bar. The one with iron nails hammered into it. The one that he'd used to intimidate the frat boys the first night I'd walked into Helen of Troy. It was old and splintered, but still deadly for all of that.

Those spikes had torn my skin.

I didn't hesitate. I'd felt what that bat could do to a body. I didn't need a reminder.

Before Patrick could turn and swing it in my direction, my gun was in my hand, and I fired.

THIRTY

Patrick didn't scream, which surprised me. I'd have pegged him for a screamer.

I walked behind the bar, where he was lying on the floor, curled up in the fetal position, protecting what was left of his right hand. He may not have been screaming, but he was doing a good job of moaning.

"Hurts, huh," I said. I felt clear, calm and oddly happy. I'd just shot a man's hand off, effectively, and that was my reaction. I knew I'd pay for my calm later, in one way or another. But it was exactly how I needed to be to get through what I had to do now.

I squatted down next to him, making sure that he saw that I still had the gun in my hand. Not that I thought he was in any state to try anything, but better safe, etc. I patted him down and took a phone out of the back pocket of his jeans. He had nothing else on him.

"Okay now, Patrick," I said. "Upsy-daisy." I pulled him to his feet and led him out from behind the bar. He slumped – his face was white and sickly – and I let him rest for a moment with his body weight slumped over the bar. But he rallied quickly, and I led him to a bar stool.

"Well, color me embarrassed," I said to him. I took off my belt, and with it tied Patrick's wrists to the copper rail that ran along the outside of the bar. It wouldn't hold long if someone was fighting to get loose, but as one of those two hands had been about forty percent blown away by an automatic pistol at close range, I figured it would do for the moment. "I really hadn't figured you for one of the bad guys." I was talking tough, but the sight of his hand was actually making me feel the carbonation in my brain, and if there was ever a moment I couldn't afford to faint, this was it.

I walked behind the bar and washed the blood from my hands, my gun stuck in the back of my combat pants, and grabbed a stack of bar towels. I went back and wrapped Patrick's hand in a couple of the towels and told him to keep pressure on it with his other hand. He was moaning less, but he looked very much as though he was going to vomit. I started to feel sorry for him, when a twinge of pain from my sciatic nerve put that to rest pretty quickly. But I wanted him verbal, and quickly. I had no idea how long it would be before we had company.

I pulled my baggie of coke out of my front pocket and my emergency bottle of Percocet from the pack around my waist.

"You a stranger to illegal pharmaceuticals, Pat?" I said. I cut a couple of lines of coke on the bar and tightly rolled one of the fifties from my pocket stash. I did one line and looked at his face. He hadn't answered, but he was eyeing the coke like it was the last water in the desert.

I started to hand him the fifty, out of habit – the rules of polite drug sharing ran deep in my psyche – but of course he couldn't use his hands. He leaned over and looked at me to help him. I stuck one end of the fifty in his nose and guided him up the line.

"In a second, you'll feel a tiny bit better," I said. I sat a couple of bar stools down from him and took a swig of wine. Then I took one of the clean bar towels and placed two oxys in one and folded it into a neat package. I grabbed one of the unopened bottles of wine and started to crush the pills. "You'll probably know this, being a career bartender and all-around bad guy," I said to him, "but snorting a ground-up pill – well, snorting anything, really – gets it into your bloodstream faster." Patrick was nodding. He had a bit of color back. He was watching closely, his eyes not leaving the towel that had the pills inside. "I know what you're thinking, Patrick," I said. "Towels aren't the best for this. But I don't carry a pill crusher with me, and I don't see any regular paper around here. Besides, these towels are lint-free." I kept working, and then carefully brushed the now-powdered pills onto the bar.

"Thank you," he said. He cleared his throat. "Thank you."

"You're welcome," I said. I carefully and slowly made four thin lines of the powdered painkiller with the knife I'd used for the coke. "Of course, the reason I'm doing this is because I want answers from you, and in my experience people in severe enough pain will say anything to make the pain go away. Anything they think you want to hear. And I actually want the truth from you."

"I don't know much," he said.

"Yes, you do," I said. "But I know you won't know everything, so please don't make shit up. I'll know if you're lying. You know that, right?"

I looked at him with as much sincerity as I could muster. I was very rarely sure when people were lying or telling the truth, but Patrick didn't have to know that.

And besides, I was the one with the drugs. And the gun.

Patrick nodded, gazing at the white lines on the bar. I actually felt sorry for him. He had effectively crippled me and left me trussed up in a rat-infested alley, and he may have killed Ann/Moira. But I'd just maimed him for life. However long his life was going to be.

I helped him snort two of the four lines, and while I waited for them to kick in, I poured myself some more wine. I hoped Patrick didn't notice my hands shaking. My calm was starting to slip. I was suddenly very weary. My body was crashing from the couple of bumps of coke and the wine, not to mention the forty minutes of sleep I'd managed the night before and the lovely morning at the morgue identifying Ann's body. I should have checked into a hotel for a night and gotten some rest before attempting any of this. I moved over and did the line of coke that was still on the bar, snorting a couple of drops of wine as a chaser.

I looked at Patrick, whose eyes were shut tightly.

"Did you kill Ann?" I asked him. He shook his head quickly.

"I don't believe you," I sang, and tapped the barrel of the gun against the bar.

"I really didn't," he said. "I couldn't kill her. I couldn't kill anybody." He looked at me. "I didn't even hit you as hard as I could have," he said. "You must know that."

That rang true. As bad as it was, I knew even at the time that it could have been worse.

"Who did?" I said.

"I don't know," he said. His voice was hollow and slow. Pain, I supposed, and fear. "I really don't. We were just supposed to take her to this dive apartment on Sherbourne and leave her there, and that's what we did." He closed his eyes again against the pain. "I swear to God, that's all of it."

"Who was with you?"

"Garrett," Patrick said.

"Garrett Jones helped you knock Ann out and kidnap her from the alley?"

"I helped him," Patrick corrected me. "Though neither of us wanted to do it." He looked at me. "You're not really meeting a cop here, are you," he said.

"No," I said, my thoughts elsewhere. "Why did you do it? What did you think was going to happen to her?"

"I thought some… customer wanted her," Patrick said. "She never wanted to go along before, and I thought somebody must have offered a lot of money to be with her. Because she looked so young," he added.

"She *was* young," I said. "She was fifteen." I blinked and saw stars at the edges of my vision. The rage had come rushing back, taking me over. I realized I had yelled the last few words, and before I was aware of what I was doing, I clocked the back of Patrick's head with the barrel of the gun. Hard, but not as hard as I could.

So Fred had been right all along about the forced prostitution. That would explain Kelly's nerves when she'd given me the note, the night she was patching up my hand when Garrett had walked in.

"Were all the girls involved in this? Were they given any choice?"

"I don't think they were all involved," he said. "It didn't seem like it. I don't even think everybody knew about it. Look,

I don't know. It wasn't my game. I had nothing to do with it. It just started when the new company took the place over. You know, when Garrett started here." He looked at what was left of his hand and moaned. I helped him snort the rest of the oxy, thinking hard. Garrett Jones? The man who wanted me to teach his daughter self-defense, who blushed at the mention of anything inappropriate in a strip club, pimping out young women against their will?

"Patrick," I said, and squeezed his shoulder, hard. "The next question I'm going to ask you is very, very important. Do you understand?" I tapped the top of his head a few times with the barrel of my gun. "Patrick?"

"Please," he said. "Please let me go to the hospital. Call the police; I'll tell them everything. I swear to God I will. And I won't tell them you were here, I promise. But please just let me go." He was crying now. The tears made him look younger, and I felt sick. What gave me the right to do this to him? Even if he made it through this day, no doctor would be able to recreate his hand. His life was forever changed.

But no. This was not a boy. He was a man. I'd shot him in self-defense. If I hadn't, he would have brought that lethal bat down on my head within seconds. Even if – if – he was telling the truth about Ann and he had nothing to do with actually killing her, he had aided and abetted forced prostitution of young women. And for what? To keep his bartending job?

"You'll get medical attention," I said. "I promise." Though I didn't promise when.

"Thank you," he said.

"But we're not finished here, Patrick."

He moaned, and put his head down on the bar. He said something that sounded like, "My fucking hand, man."

"Who was working with Garrett? Who was his boss? Did you start seeing anyone new hanging around here in Garrett's office with him?"

He was sobbing again, his face turned away from me. "I don't know their names," he finally said.

I wished I hadn't trashed my phone. I had pictures of Dave on that phone. I had to know if Dave had anything to do with this place.

Then I remembered the contents of my bag.

"Patrick, hang on another minute for me," I said. I darted to my bag and found the little leather wallet I'd kept in the safe at home. I had pictures of nearly everyone in it, in case I had to disappear without access to phones or computers. Even Elizabeth Jackson would need to wallow in memories sometimes. I flipped to a picture of Dave I'd taken in the spring in New York. I ran back to Patrick and showed it to him.

"Have you ever seen this man?" I said. "Has he ever been in here with Garrett? Or anybody else?"

Patrick wiped his eyes and looked at the picture for a minute. "I don't think so," he said. "Not that I've seen. It's hard to tell from that picture." Dave looked like everybody. It was one of the reasons he was so good at his job; he did not have a memorable face. My heart was pounding. Patrick flipped through a couple of other pictures.

"Him," he said. He jabbed at one of the pictures. "He's here all the time. He's here with the big boss, Garrett's boss."

He looked happy, Patrick did. He looked relieved that he'd

been able to give me some information, that maybe it would stop me from hurting him any further.

I grabbed the wallet back from him. It was a picture of Fred and Ginger on their wedding day on Cape Cod.

Fred.

I opened my mouth to say something. I don't know what.

But Patrick's head flew forward, and seemed to explode. In what seemed like slow-motion, I looked down at the little wallet of pictures I was holding. My hand was covered in blood and what was either bone or brain matter. And hair. A clump of Patrick's hair.

My gun. I'd left my gun with my bag, fifteen feet away.

Before I could turn to look, however, I felt the bubbles in my brain take over, and I was down.

THIRTY-ONE

I was probably only out for seconds, maybe a minute. When I regained consciousness, I fought the bile that was rising in my throat. I kept my eyes shut tight and worked on fighting the vertigo that usually came either before or after one of my fainting spells. I heard voices, and a chuckle that made my scalp tighten.

"Hello, Michael," I said, and opened my eyes.

Michael Vernon Smith was standing about twenty feet away, next to my brother-in-law Fred Lindquist. Michael was holding my gun in his hand, and smiling his avuncular smile at me. Fred looked green, and when I met his eyes he looked away.

I was going to kill him. As much as I hated Michael Vernon Smith, my hatred for Fred was, at that moment, a hundred times worse. A thousand.

I sat up. I wasn't restrained in any way, but I also had no weapon on me.

"I know Fred doesn't have the balls to pull the trigger," I said, nodding to where Patrick's body lay. In the time I was out, it had slumped onto the floor. "And I admit, I didn't think you liked to get your hands dirty."

"It's really good to see you, Danny," Smith said. He looked

like he meant it. "And no, I hate this sort of thing. I find it repugnant." He looked like a prosperous captain of industry, in what looked like a bespoke suit and tortoiseshell glasses. He tucked my gun into his pocket.

"You should have brought a different right-hand man, in that case," I said. "Hiya, Fred."

Fred nodded at me, and crossed his arms in front of him. He was holding a Taser. I laughed. "Not allowed to handle the big-boy guns yet, Fred? Never mind. Maybe someday."

I hadn't been followed here; of that I was fairly certain. Patrick hadn't made any calls in my presence to alert anyone that I was here. I'd ditched my phone and SIM card, so I wasn't being traced.

The only person who knew I was coming here was Dave.

What I'd suspected – what everyone had suspected, though I hadn't wanted to hear it – was true. Dave was somehow working for, or with, this evil fucktard. I'd called Dave's emergency number, the one he'd mailed to me back in Maine eighteen months ago when I was recuperating from my last run-in with Smith and his crew. The one I'd relied on so much I'd had it tattooed onto my thigh, so I'd have it even if my mind was gone to the point that I couldn't remember it. Fuckface Smith wouldn't have known I was coming to the club. Dave must have let him know.

It dawned on me, in that moment, that Dave must have been the one who'd spirited Smith away that night in Maine, the night that Fred had stabbed Smith in the eye with the corkscrew and I'd killed what we had hoped was the last of his followers, and watched her body burn in the fireplace. His footprints had disappeared into the snow, and there was a blizzard. Searchers looked for his body for weeks. Nobody knew how he could have survived the night without help.

I knew that my instincts about people were often flawed. It had been proven, time and again. So perhaps my flee from Manhattan in May was the right move. For once a deeper, intuitive sense had been telling me to cut ties with Dave.

I would have to think about that later. If, of course, there was a later.

"So how long has this been going on, anyway?" I said, motioning at the two of them. "This little bromance." Then I put my hand up to stop the answer. "Actually, before we chat, since we're in a bar, would anyone like a drink? I know I would." I stood, feigning more pain than I really felt. I wanted them to think of me as helpless, or at least unable to move quickly. I did have some twinges, but my sciatic pain tended to come and go. And the bit of coke I'd done helped.

Fred looked as though he was getting ready to Tase me if I came within ten feet of him, but Smith put a gentle hand on Fred's arm. "A fine idea," he said. "I see you and Patrick already had a head start." He looked at Patrick's body. "Poor choice of words, I guess," Smith said. "Head start." He grimaced with distaste, as though Patrick was a dead mouse he'd found under the stove. As though he wasn't the one who'd shot the guy in the head.

He moved behind the bar, and I took off the light hoodie I was wearing and draped it over Patrick's shoulders and head.

"Patrick had," I said. "I was just getting started." I took a stool, further away from the side of the bar where Smith and Fred were. As I sat, I realized it was the same stool I'd occupied the first night I'd come in to Helen of Troy. The night I'd had my face-off with the frat boys. I kept focus on Smith, just keeping

Fred in my peripheral vision. I couldn't look at him directly and keep my composure.

Plus, I had to rethink my plan, and quickly. Fred being here meant the boys could be in jeopardy, depending on how the next hour or so of our lives played out.

Smith was saying something about the crappy wine selection, and I tuned him out. I rubbed my lower back tentatively, as though it was causing me pain.

"Do you mind if I indulge in one of my old habits?" I said to Smith. He had moved down the bar and put a glass of what I think he said was a Pinot Noir in front of me. I pulled the little plastic bag of coke out of my pocket before Smith could reach into his and shoot me with my own gun. I shook the white powder down. "I'm sure Fred has told you that I've been clean," I said. "But some days just call out for a bit of indulgence in one's old vices."

"Smoke 'em if you got 'em, my dear," Smith said. He appeared to be looking for clean glasses. "That's my motto."

I cut myself two generous lines and snorted them both easily. I refrained from dabbing wine into my nostrils, though. Smith looked as though he was savoring his wine so much he might actually shoot me for being so gauche.

"So why did you call this little meeting, Danny?" Smith said. "Not that I'm not happy to see you! I am, very much. I've been saying to Fred here, 'Fred, when are we going to bring Danny back into the fold?' But Fred seemed fairly sure that you wouldn't be amenable to that. Didn't you, Fred?"

"I did," Fred said. "And correct me if I'm wrong, but she was never in the fold." He was still standing to attention, holding onto the Taser as though it might save his life.

Not if I had anything to say about it, it wouldn't.

"There's a point," Smith conceded.

"Here's another one," I said, taking a dainty sip of my wine. He was right; it was very good. "I didn't really call a meeting, as such. At least not with you. I was testing my friend Dave, you see. After the events at the bakery, it seemed apparent that he might have conflicting loyalties. If you showed up, I'd know for sure."

"And now you do," Smith said joyously. "Dave's out of town on business, as I think you know, but he passed on your message to us."

I nodded, outwardly calm. It had not, however, occurred to me that if Smith were to show up Dave wouldn't be with him. If Dave had anything to do with Smith and The Family, I thought he would also be lying about the Florida trip. That they could both be true hadn't figured into my planning.

"Why are we here, Danny?" Fred said. He was trying for nonchalance, but it wasn't working. I didn't know if it was conscience or fear, but he looked as though he'd rather be anywhere else.

"Michael," I said, "if it's all the same to you, I'll address you and only you. The business I have is between us."

"Fred is not your favorite person at the moment," Smith said. "I understand that. This must be a shock to you." I nodded and even managed a small smile. I took a larger sip of wine.

I wanted my gun back. My trigger finger was actually itching, I wanted so badly to shoot Smith where he stood. Preferably starting with the ankles and working my way up. If I thought it would end all this and make the boys safe, I would have. But I knew the satisfaction would be fleeting. None of us would be safe, and I would have ruined my best play on selfish gratification.

Besides, even if I was able to take out Smith and Fred somehow, Dave was out there somewhere. I had to end it.

I was toying with the stem of my wine glass, and grabbed Patrick's corkscrew off the bar to give myself something to do with my hands.

I suddenly remembered the moment back in Maine when Fred had surprised me – and definitely Michael and his foster daughter – by plunging the business end of a corkscrew into Michael's eye. I'd never known Fred had it in him. I'd been impressed.

I looked at Michael's face, at his eyes. He was watching me, and he obligingly took off his glasses and leaned over a bit so I could see them more clearly. He winked. I tried not to vomit.

"Either that is the best ocular prosthetic known to man, or…" I started.

"Or Fred didn't really gouge out my eye with that corkscrew," Smith finished for me. He put his glasses back on. "Danny. Did you really think that Fred would have the stomach for something like that?"

I looked at Fred, who looked quite comfortable now, sitting at the other end of the bar. He shrugged and grinned. Somehow, I managed to stay seated, and not take a running leap at Fred's head.

"We had some stuff mixed up…" Fred said, and Smith interrupted him.

"Ketchup and soy sauce, with a little mayo mixed in," he said. "I was never happy with the color. Or the consistency. But you were flying high on crack. We didn't think you'd be able to get very close."

"Yeah," Fred said. "He was going to squirt some on his face and go running out. You had the broken ankle."

"And as it turned out, I was otherwise occupied," I said. I shook my head, as if impressed at their wiliness.

"Oh boy, were you ever!" Smith said. He shook his head, as though remembering great old times. "You made very short work of Jeanette. Not that I saw the whole thing, of course."

"Not short enough," I said. I remembered her falling into the gigantic fireplace after I'd plunged a titanium crack pipe into her eye and shot her with an AK-47. "And then you, what, faked that asthma attack?" I said to Fred.

He nodded. "Stopped me from having to pretend to run into the snow to look for him."

"Nice one, boys," I said. "You got me good." I felt sweat breaking out along my hairline, and it wasn't just from the cocaine. "So your alliance, then…"

"Oh my goodness. How long would it be now, Fred?" Smith leaned his elbows on the bar. He looked like a happy, relaxed man, recounting his salad days.

"Since we moved to California," Fred said. "Soon thereafter, at any rate."

They looked at each other and burst out laughing at some private joke. It didn't matter. I knew all I needed to, at least for now.

"So, Danny, you see, we really are a family. We are one already. Your brother-in-law. Your boyfriend. Someday soon, your nephews, and hopefully all the other Clearys." Smith laughed. "There are so many of you, you could franchise out!"

"Sort of like a pyramid scheme," I said. Oh, for my gun. My kingdom for my gun.

"That's actually a pretty good analogy," Fred said. He was earnest now, leaning forward, using his business voice. "Danny, you're special. You're essential to those boys. Essential," he repeated.

I opened my mouth but no words came out. For once, I was without speech.

"I know I'm not the world's best dad," Fred said. "That's one of the reasons I went along with this whole converted-bakery thing."

"It takes a village," Smith said, with no irony.

I had officially stepped into *The Twilight Zone*.

I nearly asked where Ginger had fit, or not fit, into their grand plans. She had no wealth or income other than Fred's, so there was nothing she could give to them that way. And Fred would never have been able to tell her about any of this; Ginger would have packed up the boys and taken them to the nearest police station. Easier to encourage her to get hooked on drugs and end her.

I had to put Ginger out of my head, and I had to put Dave out of my head. I had to get what I needed, change my plan on the fly, and make sure that these two crazy, evil fucks never got their hands on Matthew and Luke.

I drained my glass of wine, and pushed my glass a bit toward Smith. "Just half a glass, please," I said, as though I was a lady out for lunch. "I might as well tell you both what I was going to tell Dave. Get him to pass on to you, if he showed up."

They both looked at me with vaguely expectant looks.

"Uncle," I said out loud.

"Pardon me?" Smith swallowed the wine he'd been swishing around in his mouth.

"Uncle," I repeated. "I give up. You win. That's why I wanted to meet."

"My, my," he said. He looked surprised. "There's one for the books. I never thought I'd see the day, Danny, I truly didn't. This makes me very happy."

"Well, we aim to please." I should have done this a long time ago. Why hadn't I?

"And what, exactly, have I won?"

"What you always wanted," I said. "Money. All of Jack's money. I will freely transfer everything to you, or to whatever organization you like. Right now." I spun the corkscrew around on the bar. I needed to keep my hands busy, so I wouldn't launch myself over the bar and bite his face off. "I have a few conditions, of course."

"Of course," Smith said. He looked amused.

I looked at Fred. "You leave the rest of my family alone. And that includes the boys." Fred started to interrupt, but Smith held up his hand.

"Let her continue, Fred," he said. "I'm sure Danny has a plan."

"If the boys want to become part of your Family when they're twenty-one, well then, so be it. But I owe it to my sister to give those boys a few years of normalcy, at least. You can still be in their lives to some extent," I said to Fred. I hoped I was being convincing, because if I had my way, Fred would never get to clap eyes on his sons ever again. "We can discuss that. But you leave my family alone," I said, looking at each of them. "All of them. My brothers, my nephews, my household and my friends. Michael, you disappear to wherever it is you've been living until you flew into Canada. I will never tell any law enforcement that I've seen you."

"Go on," Smith said. "Something tells me you've got more up

your sleeve, Danny. You always were a wily one."

"You answer some questions for me," I said. I nodded at the bar. "I've got all the time in the world, and we have privacy here. We can sit and have a civilized drink, answer some questions for each other, take care of whatever banking details need to be sorted, and we can part as… well, I can't say friends."

"That's a pity," Smith said, and the batshit crazy fucker sounded sincere. I'd forgotten that about him, how oddly likeable he could be, in his murderous insanity.

"We can shake hands and go our separate ways. I concede defeat. And in turn you, as a man of honor, can humor me by filling in a few blanks for me."

"It would be the gracious thing to do," Smith said. I knew he'd like that. In some ways, he seemed to want to think of himself as fair, even generous. But I could tell that he wasn't buying it. He wanted the money, and I believed that he'd answer questions for me. He'd probably even tell me the truth. But the price of having Michael Vernon Smith out of our lives was going to be steeper than that. I could see it.

"Do we have a deal, Mr. Smith?"

"Oh, Danny, don't fall back to formalities at this stage! I much preferred you calling me Michael."

"Fair enough, Michael. What do you say?" I took a sip of wine. My hand wasn't shaking. Good.

I nodded. It was what I'd been expecting. In some ways, I even welcomed it.

"Me," I said. I looked at him, openly and honestly. "You can have my life. You can take my life, Michael. You can make me suffer, if that would please you. You can somehow try and pin all of these crimes on me. Whatever you need to do. As long as you answer my questions first, and as long as I believe that I'm buying my family's freedom. Before we leave here tonight – whoever leaves here," I added, "we'll make a conference call to Darren, telling him this. He needs to know not to trust you, Fred, and he needs to get a head start on getting the boys away. If I think you're lying to me, I won't let you take anything. And if that's the case, I'll take your life. And I'll spend the rest of mine hunting down and killing each and every one of the people who follow you."

Big words, from a woman who had no weapons on her.

Smith was pacing again, still with the thoughtful smile on his face. He was quiet.

"I should add," I said, "that in case you're debating just killing me and going after my family anyway – you know, for fun," I added, smiling, as if this would never have occurred to him, "I've changed my will. If anything happens to me now before I transfer money, the entirety of my estate will go to a few select charities. With a small stipend for my funeral costs, of course."

Fred slammed something on the bar. I wasn't looking at him, though.

"Clever girl," Smith said. He was nodding. "An unpleasant shock to your family, though, I'd think."

"No, my brothers know about this. They helped me choose the charities. You see, in *my* family, love doesn't come with dollar signs attached." I couldn't resist. This was, after all, the man who'd pimped out his foster children and let them keep ten percent of what they earned. "I have no heirs, Michael. This ends with me." I took another sip of my wine, and in a moment I was going to have to pull out my eight-ball again. "Of course, if you don't take the deal – if you decide just to kill me now, or try, not only will you not get a cent from us, but you will spend the rest of your life looking over your shoulder."

"Oh? How so?"

"My nephews have been in training to kill you since you killed their mother," I said. "They're still young, granted. But kill their mother *and* their auntie?" I shook my head. "They're already six feet tall, and they're not yet thirteen. And they have what you might call the Cleary sense of justice. Wouldn't you say, Fred?"

This was all exaggerated, of course. We'd worked hard not to instill our anger and bitterness into the boys. But from previous experience with Smith, I knew that he admired our family's dogged loyalty. It was close to what he'd tried to achieve with his own twisted version of family.

I opened my mouth to say more, but clapped it shut again. Coke can make one a bit too verbose, and Smith's silence was starting to worry me. This was a man who liked the sound of his own voice.

"Do you mind if I sit down?" Smith said. He gestured at a bar stool, not too close to mine. "These old bones," he said. "Not as young as I was."

"I don't know about that," I said. "You look like you've been drinking the blood of virgins or something." Smith settled himself in and sighed dramatically. The motherfucking bastard was loving this. "You haven't aged a day." He looked trim and fit, and more than ever like a former Eastern bloc gymnast.

What was he waiting for? My previous experience with the man had proven him to have a bigger mouth than I did.

"My other option," I said, cutting myself a couple of lines on the bar, "is to leave here and walk into traffic. Or run at you and attack you so that you have no choice but to shoot me. That way, you and yours will get nothing." I rolled up a twenty and quickly snorted both lines. I didn't want to have my head down and vulnerable for any longer than necessary. I stuck my finger in my drink and dabbed my fingers at my nostrils. I wasn't worrying about etiquette any longer.

"Oh, and one more thing," I added, smiling at Smith. "It would go a long way toward cementing trust between us if you would agree."

"I'm all ears, my dear."

"I would like the chance to hit Fred. Just once. No weapons, and I'm happy for him to hit me back if he needs to. I think that being lied to for all these years – not to mention… everything else," I added, "gives me the right." I twirled the corkscrew around on the bar. "And you have my word of honor that it will be one blow. Nothing fatal or debilitating."

Smith looked over at Fred, who was getting red with anger.

"You're not actually considering this," he said to Smith. His voice squeaked. I smiled.

"The young lady does have a point," Smith said. "You were a lousy husband to her sister." I nearly choked on my wine. Of all Fred's transgressions, that's what he was focusing on.

"You've got the Taser, Fred," I said to him. "I'm unarmed. If you're worried I'll keep hitting you or whatever, you can put me out of commission."

Smith nodded in Fred's direction, as if conceding a good point.

"Remember, if you decide you want to kill me, I won't resist you. But I won't transfer the money to you until after we all talk to Darren. And before that happens, I need a few questions answered."

Smith looked at the clock over the bar. "All right, Danny," he said. "Let's chat. And while we do, I'll decide whether I want to take your deal. Either deal."

I nodded. We had to move more quickly now. If I was going to be tortured to death, I'd rather it happened while I was on a nice coke buzz. I could focus, now, on what was in front of me, and when the ghost of Dave threatened to saunter into my brain I could punch him down.

I was edgy, but with some small sense of relief. I was ending this, once and for all. I had put my rage about Ginger and Jack behind me. I had to, if I wanted to save the boys and the rest of the people I cared about. There was no price that was too high for that.

And how much could I value my own life, when I'd been so ready to end it myself?

"Ann," I said. Smith nodded wearily. "Why?"

"Why, indeed," Smith said. "Fred? Why did we need to end the life of poor young Ann?"

"Or Moira, as your son knew her," I said. "You know. Luke's girlfriend?"

Fred looked at Smith. "Do we really need to do this?"

"It was the one thing she asked for," Smith said. "And I'm still holding out hope that Danny will change her mind about us. Join us," he said.

Fred looked disgusted. He knew me better than Smith ever would. He knew I would never come on board, but he was obviously accustomed to bowing to the boss.

"I loved her, if you must know," he said.

"Ann? That little girl? That's who you were…" I hadn't thought I could be any more disgusted. I was wrong. "You were screwing your son's girlfriend?"

"I knew her long before she met Luke," Fred said. "She was trying to make me jealous. Playing some kind of game."

Smith looked at me with raised eyebrows, in a kind of *isn't he a poor deluded fool* look. As though we were shooting the shit over beers, talking about the miserable state of our love lives.

"So let me get this straight," I said, attempting a calm tone. "You killed your fifteen-year-old girlfriend because she was two-timing you with your son?"

"To be fair," Smith said, "it was a bit more complicated than that. Ann was Cliff's daughter. You remember Cliff? Fred's friend?"

"Of course," I said. "He wound up dead in my TV room last night."

"The very one," Smith nodded. "Stupid business, that was."

"Nothing to do with me, that one," Fred said, hands in the air.

"I'm aware," Smith said. I watched their banter, and felt more and more like a fool. "Anyway, Ann's been part of The Family since… well, birth, really. She was wise beyond her years."

"An old soul," Fred said. He was playing with the Taser and looking wistful.

"But she was – well, I think – and it's just my opinion, Fred, you can take it or leave it – that she'd actually fallen for young Luke. She wasn't ever asked to meet, uh, gentlemen outside of the club. Because of her status as Fred's paramour, she was exempt."

Fred nodded.

"Nevertheless, she was making threats about going to the police. Saying things that she knew very well enough not to say."

It was my turn to nod.

"And is that why Cliff—" I started to say, and Smith cut me off.

"We think so. We think he wanted to probably kill Fred here, and take off with his computers. All The Family business. Who knows what he thought he was going to do with it all."

"So it was just a fluke that you had gone out for a run?" I said to Fred.

"I know, right? Talk about luck."

It was that which set me off. That Fred grin, the shake of his head with amazement at his own luck. I couldn't look at it, not for another minute.

I exhaled, took a sip of my wine, and then I moved.

THIRTY-TWO

I threw my wine glass, hard and precisely, at his head. I used to be a pitcher, back in my baseball days. My muscle memory didn't fail me, and the coke gave me an added burst of strength. At least I thought it did.

I launched myself off my bar stool, ran a couple of paces and jumped at Fred where he'd been pacing, while he was still stunned from taking the glass to the middle of his forehead. The glass didn't break, but it knocked his head back when it hit his forehead. He brought the Taser up just as I tackled him – he seemed to remember suddenly that he was holding it – but I knocked it out of his hand easily. Straddling Fred's chest, I grabbed the Taser from the floor and brought it to his face. I paused for a second, deciding whether it would be more painful in the eyes or the mouth.

Behind me, I heard the unmistakable click of a gun's safety being disengaged.

"That's enough, Danny," Smith said. "Get off him. Slowly. And slide that stupid weapon toward me." He sounded amused.

For a second or so, I thought about Tasing Fred anyway, and risking a bullet. Smith wouldn't kill me yet; I hadn't transferred money, and he now knew that he wouldn't be able to get it from my family if I was dead. But that wouldn't necessarily stop him from shooting me in the knee or the elbow, somewhere painful and debilitating, putting me out of commission physically. I couldn't afford that. Not yet.

I slid the Taser away, and before I stood, I paused.

"One punch," I said to Smith. "I think I deserve to be able to hit him once, don't you? I won't kill him. You have my word."

"Your word is good with me, Danny," Smith said. Weirdly, I knew it would be. "Go ahead."

"Thank you," I said, and as Fred was opening his mouth to protest, I hauled back and punched him in the mouth as hard as I could.

Of course, Smith probably hadn't noticed that I was wearing my heavy rings for just this reason, with my knuckles and fingers taped underneath. I'd done that hoping to get a chance to punch Smith, or Dave, knowing that one punch was probably all I would get away with today. It made the blow extra hard and bloody for the recipient, and protected me from breaking a knuckle or a finger. Win-win, you might say.

I stood up as soon as I'd punched him, and put my hands in the air, backing away. I smiled at Smith, and nodded thanks. Fred was on his side spitting blood onto the floor, and when he stood up, I saw that I'd knocked out two teeth. My smile got wider.

I knew that this was as good as it was going to get tonight. My brother-in-law was working with the man who had orchestrated my sister's – Fred's wife's – death. My boyfriend was somehow working with the whole bunch of them. And if I allowed myself to be killed before I got in touch with Darren, my nephews would still be in this man's care.

I sat back down at my bar stool, and Smith went behind the bar. He deftly poured us all soft drinks. "No ice, I'm afraid," he said. I raised my glass to him and drank. Punching people is thirsty work. Especially when you throw cocaine into the mix.

Fred was wrapping up the teeth he'd lost in a napkin. His mouth was cut and bloody, and I was hoping that he'd start crying any second.

"Are you happy now?" he said. It sounded like speaking hurt. Good.

I smiled. "I'll never be happy again, Fred," I said. "You know that."

"Well, you got that out of your system," Smith said. "Feel better?"

"I do," I said. "Thank you." I wanted to shake my hand out – no matter what, it hurts to punch somebody in the face – but I wasn't going to give Fred the pleasure. "So. I take it you're the Kinder Group," I said.

"It's a legitimate business," Smith said, nodding.

"Aside from the enforced prostitution," I said. Smith shrugged. "But why try to get me working here? It doesn't make sense. You had to know I'd find out eventually."

"That was my idea," Smith said. "I wasn't planning on spending much time here in person, at least at the beginning. And as I said, I wanted you with us. We thought you'd make a good doorperson," he added.

"And you were bouncing off the walls, and obsessed with finding him." Fred tilted his head at Smith, and winced. "We thought it would be a distraction for you."

"What can we say? Good help is hard to find," Smith added. "As far as I'm concerned, the best businesses are family businesses." He was being serious, and I was reminded again of his bizarre, seemingly earnest, code of conduct.

"And Garrett? Kelly? Why did they have to die?"

Smith laughed, and Fred looked a little green. I didn't know whether it was pain from losing teeth and having his mouth cut up, or from a reminder of the death he had surrounded himself with. Voluntarily. Fred was both weak and greedy, but it had never occurred to me that he could be actually evil. By aligning himself with Smith, he had signed away his humanity. Whatever else happened here tonight, I couldn't let Fred walk out of here.

Smith had my gun, and probably one of his own, and Fred had the Taser in front of him on the bar. I had nothing but coked-up energy, and my other gun in my go-bag, fifteen feet away where I'd stashed it under a table before I'd walked into the bar. I had to keep Smith talking. I had to think. I cursed myself for destroying my old phone. Darren and Rosen could have tracked me here with it. I'd wanted to protect them, but yet again I'd miscalculated.

"Garrett was my fault," Smith said. He looked at me seriously. "One thing you must know about me, Danny, is that I always admit my mistakes. Any man who won't admit when he's wrong can't call himself a man." He was polishing glasses, looking perfectly at home behind the bar.

"No argument here," I said. "I screw up daily, and I don't mind admitting it." Fred grunted his assent. I turned my head slowly and looked at him, and he looked away. Coward.

"Whether you want to believe it or not, Danny, you and I are cut from the same cloth," Smith said.

"Oh?"

"We don't let society tell us how to live our lives," he said. "We believe in family, and we're ruthless in pursuit of keeping our families together."

"Fair enough," I said. "Was Garrett a member of your Family?"

"No, no," he said. "His late wife was. I knew Amy from the time she was a teenager."

"Another foster child?" Another teenage girl you used sexually before you pimped her out, I wanted to say. But I didn't want to bring things to a head until I had a plan. Right now, the plan was simply to keep him talking, keep him occupied. Luckily, Smith loved to talk.

"As a matter of fact, she was," he said. He was removing all the wine from the fridge behind the bar and inspecting labels. "Garrett was lost when she passed. Absolutely lost. He'd worked in hospitality management, so I thought a change of scenery might do him good, him and the child." He found a bottle of Prosecco and seemed pleased. And it didn't require a corkscrew. He opened it and poured us each a glass.

"So what went wrong? Apparently he wasn't keeping proper employee records, or deducting taxes, things like that," I said. "And I was told after the fact that I should never have been hired. You need a license to work as a bouncer."

Smith looked at Fred, who was avoiding his gaze. "Well, as I said, I take responsibility for putting Garrett into a position he wasn't ready for. It was too soon after Amy's death, I suppose. And your brother-in-law here wasn't keeping a very careful eye on things."

"Maybe he was too busy keeping his eye on the strippers," I said to Smith, who laughed.

"That's exactly right!" he said. "Exactly right. Classic fox in the henhouse situation."

Fred nodded like a chastened little boy. I hated him more with each passing second.

"Do you mind if I do another line?" I said to him, wiping my face. "I haven't been doing this, but in case this was my going-away party, I wanted to enjoy it."

Smith smiled sadly at me, and refilled my Prosecco. "Go ahead, dear." Dear. Next thing you knew, he'd invite me to move in and let me choose the wallpaper for my room. But for the moment, at least, I was going with it. It was giving me the time I needed to think.

I was trying to breathe. In for four, out for four.

"I did love her, Danny," Fred was saying. "Ann. Moira. Whatever you want to call her."

Then I heard Ginger's voice, clearly, as plainly as if she'd been sitting directly behind me. *Danny, pay attention. Protect them*, she said.

I opened my eyes, and Michael Vernon Smith was looking past me.

Matthew and Luke, their hands bound in front of them, walking into the bar through the club.

And Dave behind them. Holding a gun on them. He was holding a gun on my nephews.

THIRTY-THREE

Oh God, no.

I kept my eyes on Matty and Luke. I tried to see if they were hurt anywhere. If I looked closely at Dave, I was afraid I would lose all control and get myself killed before I could get the boys out of here. Somehow.

Luke was crying, his face red with rage. He was looking at his father with all the hatred I felt but couldn't show.

"Nice one, Fred," Dave said. "Way to stay classy."

Fred looked like he wanted to die. "Luke, I am so sorry," he said. He looked like he was going to say something else, but he shut his mouth.

I got up and started to go to the boys, but Dave waved me back with the gun. "I'm sorry too, Danny," he said. His face was hard.

I was only about ten feet away from him. I could have gone for him, possibly before he could have gotten a shot off. But probably not; he was a very good shot, and his instincts – unlike mine – were nearly infallible.

I was going to kill him. Fred first, and then Dave. Smith for last. This, I would do. I had cocaine and adrenaline and pure rage coursing through my veins. I was going to get blood on my hands tonight. More blood. And I was going to enjoy it.

"Everyone, let's all relax," Smith said. He came out from around the bar, and started to move a couple of the high-top tables and chairs over. "Luke, I'm really very sorry you had to hear that," he said. "What your father did was disgusting. Inexcusable."

"What are they doing here, Michael?" I said. I looked at the boys. Matty looked like he didn't know who he should hate more – Smith, Fred, or Dave. Luke just looked broken. "You said Dave was out of town."

"A little white lie," Smith said. "I wanted to surprise you. Besides, I wasn't sure how long he'd be, and I didn't want you getting impatient." He seemed to be counting heads in the room, and dragged a couple more chairs over to the table.

"I asked Dave to bring the boys along because everything we have to say concerns them," he said. "Like it or not, we've all wound up in each other's lives. We all have grievances to air. Stories to tell. I want a clean slate, Danny. You said I could take your life in exchange for your family's safety and freedom. But first—"

"No!" Matt said. "No way. We won't let you." He was starting to cry now. They were still twelve years old. They might look fifteen, but they were twelve. They shouldn't have to hear any of this, let alone see it.

"It's okay, guys," I said. "Sometimes you have to know when to fold 'em. Remember?" Poker and Kenny Rogers.

"No, you don't," Luke said. He had snot on his face mixed with the tears. I grabbed some napkins off the bar and marched over to him. I glared at Dave as I did, daring him to shoot me. He just shook his head, and I wiped Luke's face. I hugged him. I hugged both of them, and Matt whispered something to me, so quiet I could barely hear it.

"He's with us," he said. Or at least, I was pretty sure he said. I looked at Luke, who didn't look at all okay.

"Danny, please take a seat now," Smith said. "Boys, I understand that this is a difficult evening for you. But it's time you learned to be men."

"They are twelve fucking years old," I said. Actually, I'm pretty sure I screamed it. "And thanks to you, half their childhood was stolen already."

I could feel the control slipping away. I was okay, until I saw the boys. I would have gotten through it. But having Michael Vernon Fucking Smith tell those boys they needed to be men? No. No goddamn way.

I started toward the table where Michael was standing. I took a deep breath, and kept my body language submissive and resigned, despite my outburst.

As I was close to where Fred was sitting at the bar, I moved.

I slammed Fred's head down on the bar hard with my right hand, and grabbed the Taser with my left. As Smith was reaching for one of the guns he had on him, I Tased him. It hit him mid-chest, and he went down. I kept the power surging – really, you're only supposed to use the Taser in five-second bursts, but I kept the juice flowing – while I felt his outer pocket and pulled out my gun. Before Smith could recover, I kicked him in the balls. With my steel-toed boots. Hard.

I twirled around with the gun, shouting at the boys to move away from Dave. They didn't move. Then Matty slid out of his cuffs, and so did Luke. They were waving them, and gesturing at Dave and yelling something at me, but I couldn't hear them over the pounding of blood in my ears.

My ankle shattered, and I went down, the gun skittering across the floor.

Smith had shot me. Shot me with what looked like a small cannon. It was on him, inside his jacket maybe, or tucked into a holster around his ankle. I'd missed it.

Chaos. I registered the boys running over and Dave pulling them back. Thank God. Smith was aiming again, but wildly. He was clutching his chest and curled up in the fetal position from the groin kick, but he had the gun in his other hand.

Then Fred was there, standing over Smith, and he kicked the gun out of his hand. It was the first time I'd ever seen Fred make contact with something he was trying to kick, and I had watched him try to play soccer in high school. Then Fred slid to the floor, his back to the bar.

Things went in slow motion then. I made the mistake of looking down at my leg. It seemed to end in a mess of bloody pulp and white bone. What was left of my foot was sitting at an unnatural angle, like one of those wooden marionettes on a string. And it was twitching frantically. My foot was twitching like a seizure victim, and I wasn't in control of it at all. It was mesmerizing, for about a second.

Until the pain hit. The pain didn't hit until I saw it. I closed my eyes for a couple of seconds and breathed deeply, willing myself not to faint, willing myself to let adrenaline take over, just for another few minutes.

"Keep the boys back," I yelled to Dave. "Repeat!" I'd somehow gone back to the shorthand we'd developed in the short time I was working with him.

"Keeping the boys back," he called back. "EMS?"

"Not yet."

"Waiting on your word," he called.

I looked at Fred, who was alternating between staring at my leg and at Michael Vernon Smith, who was lying on the floor, his shirt drenched in sweat. There was no color in Michael's face, and he was clutching at his chest, or trying to. His muscles still seemed locked.

"My heart," he said. His face was sweating.

I glanced back at Fred. "Don't you fucking move," I said to him. He nodded. I doubted he could if he wanted to.

"Do you need medical attention?" I said to Smith, quietly.

"Yes," he said.

Maybe he had a pre-existing heart condition. He wasn't a young man, and I had juiced him, but good.

I slid over to him and pushed him from his side onto his back, the effort sending waves of nauseating agony down my leg. He groaned, and some white froth came out of his mouth. I hoisted myself up onto him and ripped open his shirt like they taught us in First Aid. I carefully removed his glasses, and did eight chest compressions.

Leaning forward as though to clear his airway, I slid the corkscrew out of my pocket where I'd stashed it earlier. I told him to open his eyes, and while he was watching, I plunged the business end of the corkscrew into his eye. Once, twice. Pause. A third time. He tried to scream, but I was now kneeling all of my body weight on his chest, over his heart and lungs.

"That was for Ginger. That was for Jack," I said softly to him. When he stopped breathing, I slid off his chest, onto my back.

I let myself scream once, loudly, for the pain in my leg and the pain in my heart.

I looked at Fred, who was staring at me. I nodded at him, and he nodded back.

"Hey," I called out. I looked at the blood on my hands. I was pretty sure there was some on my face, too. "Kids, it's kind of messy over here. Don't look. Dave, keep them there. Don't call EMS." I had an idea, and unfortunately for me it was going to involve a delay in getting medical attention.

"Is anybody dead?" Matthew called out.

"Yup," I said.

"Who?" Luke asked.

"Michael Vernon Smith is dead," I said.

Michael Vernon Smith was dead.

"Ned," Dave yelled. He seemed very far away.

Ned was there suddenly, holstering a weapon at his side. I couldn't fight. I watched Ned rip the tie from around Fred's neck, and then he was wrapping it into a tourniquet around my thigh. He politely, wordlessly passed me napkins to clean the blood off my face and hands. When I was finished, I told Fred to take his suit jacket off and cover Smith's face with it. He obliged silently.

"What the fuck," I said to Ned.

"You didn't think I was going to leave you alone with these two fuckers, did you?" he said. He grinned at me, but I could see he was scared. "Dave would have had me drawn and quartered if anything had happened to you. This was the only way."

Too many questions, and right now I had more pressing concerns.

"I've got Percs," I said, nodding to the pack at my waist. Ned got them out for me, and I forced a couple down. I wished I had time to grind them.

I could hear Matty and Luke arguing with Dave, who seemed to be trying to hold them back.

I was gritting my teeth so hard it felt like they were going to break. "Kids, just stay where you are for the moment, okay? I mean it."

"Are you hurt?" Matty called over. I was staring at the ceiling now, and I thought my face was probably as white as Smith's was.

"Yeah, a little." As long as you don't count the bone sticking out of my leg with a floppy foot attached. "Stay the fuck back, guys, I shit you not. Love you," I added.

When Dave rounded the bar and saw me lying on the floor next to a very deceased Michael Vernon Smith, with Ned timing my pulse on his watch, the look on his face said it all. And because I'm wired wrong, his face, combined with pain unlike anything I'd experienced to date and the fact that I was lying side by side next to Dead Fuckface Smith, I started with the hysterical laughter.

"I'm calling 911," he said, holding his phone.

"Don't you dare," I said.

He hesitated for only a second. I didn't have time to question him, or worry about whether he was on the wrong side of all this. Smith's gun was too far away for me to reach. "Get him away from that," I said, nodding at Fred and the gun. He could have shot me with it already if he'd wanted, but I wasn't taking any chances.

Dave and Ned were whispering, and one of them was wrapping my leg with a t-shirt. I was trying not to puke.

"Crush me some pills," I said to them, "and bring the boys over now. They have to help."

Five minutes later, with Matty and Luke's help, my leg was elevated on a chair, Dave had made the necessary calls, and Luke had put handcuffs around his father's wrists. Tightly. Ned had crushed a couple more pills and dissolved them in something very strong that he got from behind the bar. And as the oxy began to kick in, the boys sat next to me, Luke holding onto my hand tightly, and they distracted me with a very bad rap about my general badassedness.

Believe it or not, I've had worse evenings.

THIRTY-FOUR

I had a private ambulance to hospital. Dave had arranged it. Whoever the paramedics were who took care of me, they knew not to ask questions about the dead body lying next to the bar.

While I was at the hospital being examined and then prepped for surgery, my last-minute idea took shape without me.

Dave had quickly told Belliveau about how I planned to keep us off the radar of any of Michael Vernon Smith's acolytes. While I was in an ambulance, Belliveau made some strategic calls to a few of his contacts. After what was apparently a very tense couple of hours, the FBI and the RCMP agreed.

Michael Vernon Smith's body was disposed of quietly as a John Doe. He remained on the FBI's Most Wanted list. Belliveau told me later that only sixteen people knew that Smith was actually dead, including those of us who were there that night.

Fred Lindquist had access to Smith's banking and emails – the email he used to communicate with his people. All involved were shocked at the lack of firewalls and online security he employed. After some toing and froing with the FBI, an email was composed and sent to everyone on Smith's email list, supposedly from him, saying that he was retiring and going underground, probably somewhere in the South Pacific. He told his followers to discontinue any "campaigns" – a word he'd used often in his previous correspondence with them – involving any current "income streams". He alluded to moles, dangers, the necessity to lie low. He promised to get back in touch in a couple of months to advise if he wanted them to continue any activity.

In the meantime, law enforcement agencies would be working to trace the email accounts of all of his followers. They were confident they'd get most, if not all, of them.

While all these arrangements were being made, I was otherwise occupied.

I was undergoing emergency surgery to have a below-knee amputation of my left leg.

I was only at the hospital for maybe thirty minutes when two doctors told me that there was too much traumatic damage and medical science can only do so much. They drew on my leg, several inches below my knee, to show me where they would be cutting. They called Darren for me, as I found I wasn't so good at speaking just then. They said Ned had probably saved my life with the tourniquet. They explained the dangers of not doing the surgery, but if I was listening, I certainly didn't take it in. The upshot was that this surgery was happening.

I nodded and signed something, and they gave me a nice dose of a very relaxing drug. After that, I was being wheeled through bright hallways and a bunch of people whose faces were covered were telling me everything was going to go well, and not to worry. I wasn't worried. As long as I had this drug in my veins,

I doubted I'd ever worry about anything ever again.

Fade to black.

I woke in the recovery room screaming, or trying to scream. The pain in my ankle was beyond the limits of human endurance. But when I looked, my ankle wasn't there. I was trying to remove my oxygen mask, but a nurse was putting it back on.

"The surgery went well," she said. "What you're feeling is normal. You're going to go back to sleep for a while." She adjusted something on my IV pole, and I sunk down into the dark.

The next time I woke up, Darren was there with Mama Estela. He tried to look as though he hadn't been crying.

"Everybody's here," he said. "Laurence and Skipper flew up." He saw the look on my face, I guess. "Not here, here," he said. "Back at the bakery." I squeezed his hand, and I think I slept again.

I got a private room in the hospital, and by the time I was feeling well enough to sit up, everybody was there. Skipper's wife Marie had flown in from Maine, and Laurence's boyfriend Antonio had even come up from New York. He was the first boyfriend Laurence had introduced to the family, despite having been out since high school. It was ClearyFest, hospital-style. The nurses on my floor were somewhere between charmed and tortured.

My family did what my family does. They made me laugh and indulged in a lot of dark humor regarding peg legs and my new career as a pirate. Marie brought me home-cooked food, and Darren and Laurence made sure the nurses were never a minute late with my pain meds. Matthew and Luke had put together a slideshow of famous amputees. Matt spent a lot of time talking to the surgeon, who was very kind and explained the whole procedure in more detail than I had paid attention to. Or wanted to, as a matter of fact.

Luke was trying to be upbeat, but I could see he was faking it. His first girlfriend had been murdered – not to mention she'd been working as a stripper under another identity – and his father was going to jail. And he and his brother had seen more blood and pain than anyone their age should have to. Than anyone should have to, at any age.

I noticed that he was sticking pretty close to Laurence. Those two had a special bond. I was glad Laurence was here. I was glad they were all here. For a couple of days, at least, the presence of my family was keeping me sane.

I'd told Darren, in a quiet moment, that I didn't want to see Dave. He and the boys had explained to me about Dave showing up and telling them about the message I'd left on his emergency number, and trying to convince them to come down to Helen of Troy in handcuffs – which were large and only partially closed at the loosest rung, allowing the boys to slip out of them easily. Dave had explained to Darren his role in the whole thing, including his relationship with Smith.

"He told me everything, Bean," Darren said to me quietly. "He had proof. I'll let him tell you about that. But you know I wouldn't let the boys go with him unless I knew they were going to be safe, right?"

"You didn't know that, Darren," I said. I looked at my leg. What was left of my leg. "They weren't safe. Dave might have been on the right side, but there were guns in that room. There was evil in that room. They should never have been there." I didn't add that part of that evil was me, or at least it felt like it at the time. Smith was having a heart attack, probably from the Taser, probably due to a pre-existing heart condition. The old corkscrew in the eye thing was, well, above and beyond.

Though I couldn't make myself regret it. He had it coming.

"No matter what the reason, Dave should never have brought them there," I said. "And you should never have allowed it." I wouldn't let him say anything else about it.

I needed Dave away from the hospital for the time being. I wasn't ready. I wanted to revel in the company of my family, especially Laurence and Skipper. I wanted to enjoy a world without Michael Vernon Smith in it, even from a hospital bed, even with one leg. I had a feeling that Dave's story would break my heart in some ways, and I just wasn't ready to take anything else on. I'd been living with rage and horror for nearly two years, and the man who'd set it all in motion was finally gone. I needed to sit with that for a while. And, of course, let my family bring me ice cream.

For a few days after the surgery, I was actually almost fine. I would learn to cope. I had more support than anyone could ask for. I couldn't look at my leg without a fluttery feeling of panic and horror, but, whether it was down to the meds or my family, the feeling would subside quickly.

Besides, I was riding a high. Michael Vernon Smith was out of our lives permanently, and I was nearly certain we wouldn't be dealing with any of his followers again.

Before long, though, I began retreating to a dark place

in my head. It wasn't as severe as the catatonic depression I'd experienced after hearing about Garrett and Kelly's deaths, but I wasn't myself either. I felt empty and hollow, devoid of joy or purpose. I was maimed for life. I had to deal with prosthetics and learning to walk again. And without Smith to worry about and rage against, I didn't know how to define myself. I had fulfilled my goal. Time and again over the past months, I'd promised myself that if this chapter of my life came to a close, I could live – or die – the way I chose. I wasn't necessary in the world. The phrase "surplus to requirements" kept rolling through my brain. Sometimes I found myself setting the phrase to music, in my head. It was a refrain that wouldn't stop.

I asked Mama Estela to tell the family that I needed some time alone. A couple of days, just to adjust. Their presence had been a balm to my soul for a few days, but when the darkness started to take over again, I couldn't face having to fake being okay. And the only person I could imagine having around was Mama E.

I didn't have enough energy to make the decision to kill myself. I didn't have enough energy to really eat, or listen to the news, or look at a newspaper. I didn't want to talk, and she seemed to understand that. The thought of going home and playing the Xbox filled me with dread. I would die there, with no purpose. I would wither away, a shell of a person, a one-legged freak. The people who were dead were still dead. Killing Smith hadn't brought Ginger back. And in taking his life – and his eye – I'd given my leg.

More than ever, I felt removed from anyone who hadn't been through what I had. Who hadn't committed the heinous acts that I had. I could fool myself that it was all for the goal of making my family safe, but I knew there was more to it than that. I hadn't needed to stab Smith in the eye. It hadn't been necessary for me to chop a woman's hand off, back in Nova Scotia, as she lay dying. My soul was dirty, and no amount of picking up strange men or running myself into collapse would change that.

And I couldn't imagine having the energy or the will to start living my new life as an amputee.

A hospital psychiatrist came to my room. He said he'd talked to Mrs. Garcia, and to Dr. Singh. He talked about PTSD and depression and dopamine and serotonin. I just stared at him, and nodded when he said that after consulting with Dr. Singh, he was upping my medication, changing my medication... doing something involving my medication. And he told me that Mrs. Garcia had assured him that I would be taking it. And, for a while, I was to Skype with Dr. Singh daily.

I nodded, to shut him up and make him leave the room. Didn't these doctors know that when a person is having an existential crisis like this, that adding more to the laundry list of things one can't ever imagine having energy for is actually counterproductive?

But swallowing pills, I could do. There was no fight in me. Passive acceptance was the best I could manage.

I was kept in the hospital for an extra week, and someone had wrangled it so that I got to stay on the post-op ward instead of in psychiatric. I was glad to be staying. I still wasn't allowing any visitors other than Mama E., who didn't make me engage with her other than to force me to do the basic minimum physical therapy and hygiene. I slept. I had nightmares that I was grateful not to remember. A psychiatric resident came to talk to me, and I listened. When I was forced to speak, I said that I was depressed. I was tired. And no, I was not suicidal.

On that one, I was sort of crossing my fingers. I was pretty sure I'd kill myself as soon as I felt well enough to organize it properly, but that seemed like a faraway goal.

I was letting other people fly the plane, and in a small way I started to revel in it. Everybody was fine. I didn't have to worry about anyone else. One of the nurses said that Dave had come to visit despite the no-visitor rule I had in place, and that he'd seemed very keen to see me.

I was unmoved. I would see him some day, or I wouldn't. I would hear what had happened regarding his relationship with Smith, or I wouldn't. I didn't really mistrust him. If Darren believed him, I was sure it was all valid and solid. I just really didn't care.

On the morning I was being released, I woke refreshed. I felt, if not exactly myself, then a reasonable facsimile thereof. I knew the medication must be working when I smiled at the porter who brought me my breakfast, and I found I had an appetite for it.

When I took a sip of orange juice and it tasted good, I found I had tears in my eyes. I closed them and said a silent prayer of thanks, to whoever might be listening. Although I knew I wasn't exactly better, I felt something akin to alive. I thought about what life must have been like for Jack. My depression, or whatever the clinical diagnosis was going to be, didn't hold a candle to the demons he'd fought for so many years. I thought that if I ever heard another person making fun of the mentally ill, they'd have me to answer to.

And that thought made me laugh out loud. I must be feeling

better if I was fantasizing about smacking people down.

Mama came in from her rounds – she'd slept the night again, and left unchecked she tended to trail after the nurses, presumably making sure they were up to snuff. She looked at my face, and at my nearly empty breakfast tray.

"Good girl," she said, surprising the living hell out of me. Then she kissed my forehead, and I thought I must have stepped through the looking glass. "Strong girl." I grabbed her hand and kissed it. "Harder to be sick here," she said, tapping my head, "than sick here." She tapped my leg.

I nodded, unable to speak. After a minute, I asked her which of my brothers had been tasked with coming to collect us and take us home.

"Tall one," she said, making herself comfortable on the chair next to the bed. She settled in with the latest Spanish issue of *People*.

Since my brothers are all between six-two and six-six, it was anybody's guess. I laughed, and she shushed me, pointing at her magazine. Back to normal, then.

I was ready to go home.

I must have fallen asleep then. When I woke up, Dave was standing next to my bed with flowers and a nervous expression on his face.

"Tall one!" Mama said, pointing at Dave. She cackled. Very funny. Dave was probably five-eight in shoes. I rolled my eyes at her, and she went back to her magazine.

He looked different to me now. I didn't know if it was the new medication, or the beginning of a new life.

"Do you trust me to take you home?" he said.

"I do," I said.

"Do you want to hear the whole story now?"

"God no," I said. "I don't want to hear any story that involves that man for at least six months."

"Do you trust that I'm on your side?"

"I do," I said. I did. I was calm. I wasn't exactly riotous with joy, not yet. My brain and body had a lot of healing to do. But I felt calm.

"I'm taking some time off," he said. "Ned can run the shop for a while."

"Good for you," I said.

"Maybe we can just have fun," he said. "Start fresh. Hang out with the family. Play Scrabble. Go for walks."

"Haven't you noticed?" I said, pointing at my leg. "I have a slight injury."

"You'll be like Oscar Pistorius in no time," he said. "Minus the going to jail for shooting your girlfriend thing."

We grinned at each other. Mama Estela picked up my bag and shoved it at Dave.

"You two? Six months, you'll be looking for people to shoot," she said. She looked at me. "Stay home, get better, see if he's the good one for you, then back to work."

"Doing what? You want me to take up my illustrious career as a bouncer again?"

"Stupid girl," she said. She started to pull me out of the bed by my arm. "Go save the world." She and Dave got me into the wheelchair, and we followed Mama down the corridor.

"She scares the shit out of me," Dave whispered to me. He was pushing my chair at a much slower clip than Mama was walking.

"Nah," I said. "She's a pussycat."

"Ha!" Mama Estela called over her shoulder. "Hurry up. Hospitals, too many sick people."

We followed her outside, into the sun.

EPILOGUE

Six Months Later

Some of what happened in August remained a mystery, at least to us.

The RCMP and the FBI apprehended sixteen members of Michael Vernon Smith's Family: ten in the United States and six in Canada. Some of them were forthcoming, some were not.

I opted to not learn any of their names. I told Belliveau that unless any of their activities were a continuing threat to me or mine, I didn't want details.

The Kinder Group had been set up in the States as a legitimate corporate entity, though the social insurance numbers of most of its principals were fraudulent. Fred – who was forthcoming about everything he knew, or at least he seemed to be – said that Garrett Jones was being pressured and strong-armed by Smith. He had a daughter to protect. He might have been skimming money to give to Smith. He had been forced into helping with the escorting side of things, but when he finally balked after Ann was murdered, Smith had him killed. Fred claimed not to know by whom, and as he was being forthright with law enforcement about other activities, there would be no reason for him to lie.

Fred's case hadn't gone to trial. Due to the nature of some

of the charges – criminal conspiracy, and charges that fell under the aegis of mob-related activities – he was kept in custody.

The boys hadn't visited him. Neither had Darren or I. Laurence did, once, and came back to the bakery that day silent and with a face like thunder.

Luke was doing Skype sessions a few times a week with Dr. Singh. She'd recommended several good therapists who worked with children, but Luke was insistent on seeing my doctor. He had a hard time trusting new people, and was still quiet and withdrawn, compared to the boy he'd been before that night at Helen of Troy. He stuck to Matty's side, even more than before.

Darren and I became the boys' legal guardians. Fred waived all parental rights, and our application went through without a hitch. And Laurence stayed with us for a few months, flying to Manhattan every couple of weeks to see Antonio.

Dave and I were cautious with each other for a couple of months. I switched rooms with Rosen for a while, until I became more confident on the first, and then the second prosthetic. The stairs were killer. I told Dave I wanted to sleep alone, to let things sit for a while. I wanted to get used to my new body, and I wanted to be psychologically ready to hear whatever it was that he had to tell me about his involvement with Smith.

One evening, when we'd all had a good dinner in Marta's kitchen and a few bottles of Chianti between us, I told Dave I wanted to hear it all. He seemed relieved; I'd started to realize that not coming clean was weighing on him.

Dave had grown up with a single mother, Adele Stewart, in various small towns in Pennsylvania. His dad was a Vietnam vet who had died of cancer before Dave was born. Dave and his mother moved around a lot, and his mother took a series of low-paying, under-the-radar jobs. It was, he said, where he started to learn how to live as different people; he became adept at switching personalities for each school he attended.

When Dave was in his early twenties and living life as an aimless ski bum in Colorado, his mother was diagnosed with her own cancer, and he went home to help nurse her. She told him the truth, then. She told him who his real father was.

Michael Vernon Smith.

She didn't tell him much, but said she couldn't die with the lie on her conscience. But she told him that the man was evil. That was the word she used: evil. She had been a young girl, just fifteen, when she met Smith, who was in his late twenties at the time. He was a line cook at the diner where she'd gotten an after-school job waitressing. He was tall and handsome and charismatic, and he had won her over quickly. Within weeks, Dave was conceived.

Smith insisted on marrying Adele, despite her family's wish that she either have an abortion or give the baby up for adoption. Adele was a good student, and being tied down with a husband and baby at fifteen was not what they'd had in mind for her. But Smith's charm, along with Adele's attachment to the life growing inside her, won out. For a few months, she told Dave, everything was okay.

After the baby was born, however, Michael started complaining about how hard it was to afford a wife and child. Everybody in a household, he said, should contribute.

That was the day that he brought home a stranger he'd met in a bar, to have sex with Adele. For the princely sum of seventy-five dollars, the man could do what he liked with the sixteen-year-old girl, as long as he didn't leave too many bruises.

This continued for nearly a year. Three times a week, sometimes fewer, sometimes more, Adele would be required to "contribute to the household". When she refused, Michael threatened to get one of these men to do worse to Adele's own mother. And maybe her father too. Adele complied. She believed him, the monster she had married.

It wasn't until Michael read her a story from the newspaper over breakfast one morning about a woman who had been arrested for selling her baby daughter to a group of pedophiles that Adele got the strength to escape. She was afraid that one night, the stranger who walked through their door would be there for her baby son instead of for her.

"When he was at work that day, she packed a few things for us, and took me and left," Dave told us. "She said she literally gathered change from the couch cushions, and she had managed to save something like sixty dollars from the grocery money. She purposefully left her wallet, her ID, behind." She didn't want to go to her parents or to any of her old friends. She feared what Michael would do to anyone who helped her. She walked to the bus station with the baby, and bought a ticket for Philadelphia.

Dave said his mother didn't tell him much about that time, but we could all imagine how hard that must have been. Sixteen, with an infant and no money. By the time Dave could remember anything, they were always decently, if poorly housed, sometimes sharing apartments with other single moms and their kids. Adele had gotten ID by picking names of people in obituaries and going to government offices claiming to have lost her wallet. She had gotten the idea from television, and back then it still worked.

From the time Dave learned the truth about his father until we all met him in California a dozen years later, he had not stopped looking for Michael Vernon Smith. In the meantime, he made himself something of an expert in private investigation and security, apprenticing for some of the best investigators across the country to learn all he could.

But when he finally found his father and learned about The Family, Dave realized it wouldn't be as simple as just killing the man. "I had to stop them all," he said. He looked like he wanted a cigarette. He had given them up. "Look at what Danny did, or at least her idea about what to do when she finally killed him. The people he had with him – a lot of them would just have gone on with whatever project they were working on, whatever person they were going after. With some of the psychos he had working for him, he really was just a figurehead." He looked tired. "I did stop some. A lot of what I've been doing for the last years, the jobs I've been doing, involved that man."

It was only very recently, he said, that he'd presented himself in person to Smith. They did a DNA test, and once Smith knew that it was a match, he was glad to welcome his biological son into the fold.

"The only way to stop this was to be on the inside," he said. "When he flew into Toronto, I knew I had to do it. And from everything we know about him... well, the family bond was important. More as he got older. And once I was here and spending time with you all," he looked at me, "I couldn't stand what this was doing to everybody."

Smith had been careful. Dave had never known that Fred

was a member of The Family. He presumed that was one of the reasons Smith had insisted that Dave bring the boys to Helen of Troy on that fateful night.

"I will never forgive myself for that," Dave said to us. "Never." I wasn't sure whether he meant the fact that he hadn't known about Fred, or the fact that he'd made the decision to do what Smith insisted that night by bringing the twins to the club. For the moment, it didn't really matter.

Dave had, however, had his suspicions about Cliff King. "I thought King was involved in what was going on, somehow," he said. "Of course, I didn't know that it was Fred who'd gotten Cliff involved with The Family back in the day." Fred had trusted Cliff, who knew nearly everything about our security. He really didn't know that Cliff had plans to break in that night.

"I don't know whether he was planning on stealing all the computers and getting the information on The Family to blackmail Smith, or whether Smith sent him in to scare you, or kill you, or who knows what. Maybe pit Cliff King against me to see who would be more loyal or something. We'll probably never know."

"Oh," I said. I felt very sober, suddenly. I had to remind myself that these evil people were dead.

"I killed Cliff King," Dave said. He looked around nervously. "Ned was watching this place, and I wasn't far away."

"When you were supposed to be in Florida," I said.

"When I was supposed to be in Florida," Dave said.

"What about the windows?" Laurence said. "Those were supposed to be unbreakable. You installed them."

"Yes," Dave said. "That was down to me. And let's just say that my former associate who did that job is no longer working in the security industry." I looked at Dave's face. He was even and still. I'd learned that he was at his most angry when he looked like that. "Whether it makes any difference at this point, the guy wasn't trying to fuck up your security. He did the same thing for a number of clients around that time. Money. Normal glass is cheaper, and most people don't test it."

Darren and Laurence had a few questions, but I didn't. I'd heard the story, and I knew it was true. I'd felt Jack's blessing that day on the street in front of Helen of Troy when Dave had shown up. I knew who Dave was, just like I knew who my brothers were. And I didn't need to hear any more of the story. I didn't want to even say the name Michael Vernon Smith again, and other than whatever testimony I might have to give at Fred's trial, I didn't want to think about him ever again.

The night Dave told us the story, Rosen and I switched back to our regular rooms. And Dave moved into mine.

The next day we had a family meeting, where we all voted to start the process to become a foster family. Garrett Jones's daughter was in a group home; two foster homes hadn't worked out for her, and I was having dreams about her, dreams that felt as though they'd been sent by Ginger.

We had a safe home, full of love, and she'd have three big brothers who'd look out for her. Eddie was especially keen on the idea, as he was the non-twin of the under-eighteen set in the house.

"This means that you'll have to stay in Toronto, Auntie," Matty said. "You can't commit to having a kid and then decide to go move to New York or wherever." My heart broke a little. The boys had lost both of their parents now, effectively. I couldn't up and leave them. Not again.

"I'm not going anywhere, little man," I said. "You're stuck with me like gum on a shoe."

"Crap, you've done it now," Darren said. "We're never gonna get rid of Peg-Leg." I chucked a dinner roll at him, which clocked him on the chin.

Luke was smiling, a better smile than I'd seen for a while. I had to stay. That smile was worth everything.

"You?" Mama Estela said to Dave. "Back to New York? Save the world?" She was eyeing him hard. There was a moment of silence.

"Maybe I can save the world from here," Dave said. "Maybe I can save it part-time. Besides, this one needs supervision." He gently punched my shoulder, and I scratched my face and flipped him the bird.

Laurence and Marta went to get dessert.

It was a good day.

ACKNOWLEDGEMENTS

Writing Danny Cleary has been a trip.

Each of these three books has pieces of me embedded so deeply, it's like they're printed on my skin. (Now, aren't you glad you stayed to read the acknowledgements?)

The few years during which this series has been written and published have been tumultuous and challenging for me. As I type this, it's August 14 2017, and my wonderful, funny, brave eldest sister Pam died two weeks ago. Like Ginger in *Cracked*, she lived in Orange County, California, though the resemblance between the two ends there. Pam wasn't my twin – she was fifteen years older than me – and happily, she didn't follow me down the rabbit hole of crack addiction a dozen years ago.

I'm the youngest of six living children – well, five now. We are all close, but the girls (Pam, Judy, Isobel and I) especially so. We traveled together, woke up the neighbors at my old apartment by doing runway walks on my twentieth-floor balcony singing "We Are Family" at four in the morning, kept an entire gated community in California up the night before Thanksgiving a couple of years ago because we were laughing so hard while playing Pictionary, and while we all live thousands of miles apart

(Cali, Vancouver, Toronto, Nova Scotia) and are spread widely in age, we understand each other in ways that baffle people outside the family.

I'm joined to my sisters in a way that I am so grateful for.

Pam read *Cracked* and *Rehab Run* probably ten or fifteen times each. She was a great reader, and in fact when I was a very little girl I would pick up the Agatha Christies that she'd put down when she was going out for the evening. She was so cool; I wanted to be reading what *she* was reading. Very sadly, Pam only got to read the first twenty pages or so of *Unhinged*. She became ill suddenly in June, and after she went into hospital on June 10 I promised her I'd send the manuscript to her once she was released.

She was never released.

She died on August 1 2017.

I made a huge error in not including acknowledgements in *Rehab Run*.

I want to thank my editor of that book, the lovely and brilliant Cath Trechman at Titan Books, who was so incredibly helpful and sweet, despite being more and more pregnant as the writing of the book went along – not to mention dealing with a wee one at home at the time! (Women amaze me constantly.) I also want to thank Ella Chappell, who edited this book – she took me on while Cath is on parental leave, bless her! – and her kindness and patience while I've been grieving have been a balm to my soul.

I am fortunate enough to have law enforcement and lawyers

among my friends and family. (Lawyers! I know! But believe it or not, most of them are quite nice!)

My nephew, RCMP Constable Peter Zacher, was hugely helpful, especially during the writing of *Rehab Run*. (And just to be clear, I, of course, took certain liberties. The vast majority of Royal Canadian Mounted Police officers are not psychopaths. And if there were any errors in my portrayal of the RCMP, it was artistic license, and not incorrect information given to me.)

My old friend, Detective Daniel Silver of the Kingston, Ontario police, provided some strip club info that I didn't have, but I'm not sure if that was from his position in the police or from his own personal experience. (I don't judge. Kidding, though – he's a very happily married man with two lovely daughters.)

As always, my agent extraordinaire, Sam Hiyate of The Rights Factory. Sammy and I have been friends for longer than either of us would probably care to admit. And Ali Nightingale, who was my Titan guardian angel, and signed me in the first place.

My readers, my little modern family: Christos Grivas and Lisa Grossi, for friendship and being the best idea bouncers in town. Judy for being an amazing sister AND reader.

The Leslie-Graves: Isobel, Mike, Ian and Madeleine: the love. That's all. I'd cut my own throat for any of you, any day. Yes, even you, Michael.

And as always, my lovely extended family and friends, especially Marilyn Cleary (no relation), whose love and support has gotten me through many a dark day.

ABOUT THE AUTHOR

Barbra Leslie lives and writes in Toronto. Visit her at www.barbraleslie.com, or follow her on Twitter:

@barbrajleslie

CRACKED

Barbra Leslie

Danielle Cleary is a nice middle-class girl with a bad habit. After her stormy marriage ends, the former personal trainer jumps down the rabbit hole into a world of crack cocaine. But when Danny's twin sister Ginger is murdered, Danny and her rock musician brother have to find the people who killed her, struggling both with bad guys and Danny's own demons in their quest to find the killers, in a darkly comic roller-coaster ride to redemption.

"A Quentin Tarantino-style roller-coaster ride, with wry humor, a graphic body count, and lots of drug detail."

Booklist

"Her writing style and twists can be addictive, even if they're not crack."

Kirkus

REHAB RUN

Barbra Leslie

When Danny's twin sister was murdered and her nephews kidnapped, Danny crossed North America with her brother Darren pursuing those responsible—and being pursued. Now Danny checks herself into Rose's Place, a remote drug rehabilitation facility on the east coast of Canada, where Danny starts to come to terms with her losses. After finding a human hand on the property however, Danny's rural idyll is shattered...

"An honest portrayal of a woman whose weakness could very well be what keeps her alive."

Joyous Reads on *Cracked*

"This trilogy starter is wild, violent and surprisingly emotional."

Romantic Times on *Cracked*

TITANBOOKS.COM

For more fantastic fiction, author events, competitions,
limited editions and more

VISIT OUR WEBSITE
titanbooks.com

LIKE US ON FACEBOOK
facebook.com/titanbooks

FOLLOW US ON TWITTER
@TitanBooks

EMAIL US
readerfeedback@titanemail.com